REVENGE IN PARADISE

PARADISE SERIES

BOOK 6

DEBORAH BROWN

REVENGE IN PARADISE
All Rights Reserved
Copyright © 2014 Deborah Brown

ISBN-13: 978-0-9903166-4-0

Cover: Natasha Brown

PRINTED IN THE UNITED STATES OF AMERICA

REVENGE IN PARADISE

Chapter One

The sun peeped through the rain-laden clouds as they rolled east out into the Atlantic, and a rainbow spread across the sky. Emerald-turquoise water surrounded the highway on both sides of the Keys for as far as the eye could see. Palm trees with spindly trunks and long branches lined the far edges of the beach, interspersed with colorful tropical plant life. I rolled down the window and a gentle breeze blew through my long red hair and tousled it into an unruly mess.

I sighed when we veered off the Overseas Highway into Tarpon Cove and pulled up in front of Jake's Bar; yellow crime scene tape stretched across the driveway. An assortment of law enforcement vehicles filled the street. The bomb squad had turned out, outfitted in riot gear, the local fire department and sheriffs pushed aside in favor of their more illustrative counterparts. Several K-9 dogs patrolled the property in bulletproof vests, sniffing every square inch. My employees filed out of the building in a single line, their hands in the air. Mother looked frazzled, her blond bob wind-whipped, and the ever-cool-under-pressure Fab followed right behind her. Both of them were cuffed and each had their own police escort.

I peered through the passenger-side window. "Somehow this will be my fault," I said to Creole.

He squeezed my hand. "I'll give you a written excuse. You've been with me for the last five days."

"Shh, you need to get my story straight. I've been with my childhood friend, Marcy, at her wedding in Myrtle Beach."

He shook his head. "I don't understand why you didn't just go ahead and tell your family you left town to take your cousin on a sexual test drive."

My aunt Elizabeth willed all of her colorful friends to me. It turned out she'd known Creole long before I did. He'd been neighbors with my aunt growing up and she had loved him like a son, and now, so did my mother. His real name is Luc Baptiste, but when you're an undercover detective you get a street name, so we keep his real identity a secret. He had been as close as family before we started sneaking around.

I groaned. "Some people would hear that and think, 'That's why she's so weird,' and then begin the inbreeding jokes."

"What kind of trouble have those two gotten into now?" He laughed.

"Can I get another kiss? Who knows when we'll get another chance? This looks like a long afternoon." I stuck my hand under his T-shirt and ran my nails up his chest.

It still amazed me that I'd finally agreed to have a relationship with him. The words barely left my lips before he rushed me out of town for a week on the beach in Key West. We never left the hotel room for the first two days, opening the door only to room service. My favorite part of the trip happened on the last day. He took me to a secluded spot on the beach on the pretext of a picnic and swimming and we spent the afternoon entangled in each other's arms surrounded by nature's beauty.

Creole's blue eyes sparkled with amusement as he pulled into a parking space in front of the trailer court I recently acquired. It sat back from the highway and was at the opposite end of the same block as the bar. "I don't recognize a single officer. I'll give Harder a call; he can get us a quick update."

Chief Harder of the Miami Police Department is Creole's boss. Their relationship extended outside of the office and they always had each other's back. Harder and my relationship had improved considerably from when he thought I was a criminal. He helped me on several occasions and I returned the favor whenever he asked.

I ran my fingers through Creole's shoulder-length black hair, pulling his face to mine. "I had a great time."

We both jumped at the pounding on the window.

"What in the hell?" Creole yelled.

Professor Crum glared at him. "I'm having you towed," he snarled.

I threw open the passenger door and slid off the seat of Creole's black over-sized pickup and onto the ground, managing to keep my sundress covering my butt.

"You have anyone towed off my property and I'll evict your old ass. No court hearing," I said, "just a special friend or two to tie you up and deliver you to Minnesota."

"Didn't see you there, girly. Who's he?" Professor Crum stood ramrod-stiff, with his usual good posture, dressed up in his cowboy boots and boxer shorts, his white hair sticking up on end.

"Her boyfriend," Creole growled. "If you ever look at her like that again, I'll blacken both your eyes and I won't care if you are one hundred."

"And to think, you could've had me," Crum said, and winked. "Too late, I'm taken. Got a new lady. We're going out to dinner."

Creole threw his head back and laughed.

I bit my lip. He'd clearly usurped the title of most colorful tenant. "Is that why you're dressed up? I found out your first name is Ernest—or do you prefer Ernie?"

Crum's eyes turned to dark slits and he said, "You do not have my permission to call me anything but professor or Crum."

Crum's condescension didn't bother me anymore since he looked down his nose at everyone.

"What's going on at the bar?" I asked.

"Your mother and that delicious French girl opened the back room for poker. I don't know if they couldn't keep their mouths shut or what, but word spread like a sex disease." He then pulled a condom from the back of his boxers. "I never leave home without one of these babies. I sew pockets on the back of my nice shorts." He turned, wiggling. The pocket turned out to be a piece of mismatched material, this one a piece of a red bandana hand-sewn in place with sloppy stitches.

Creole's phone rang and he stepped away to answer.

"I haven't been gone long enough for them to commit felonies."

"The cops have been there at least two hours," Crum said. "My opinion: They chased a couple of dirtballs out a few nights ago, and the guys came back to get even. Bistro, the loan shark, and his sleazy muscle, Jethro. I overheard the hot one threatening to shoot them."

Creole walked up in time to hear. "I know Jethro. I can make sure he never bothers you again."

"Let's go see how much bail money is needed."

Crum tossed his head in Creole's direction. "I think you can do better," he said.

I tugged on Creole's hand. "Can you make this go away?"

It was a short walk to the bar. Mother and Fab had been separated off to the side, away from the other employees, and were not able to communicate amongst themselves without shouting. If I'd summed up the situation correctly, no one would be going anywhere soon because, at this point, there was more standing around than action.

"I'll call in favors to make sure no one in the Westin family goes to jail—and that includes Fab. Or I'll make sure that they don't stay long." He gave me a wry smile. Creole dragged me behind the dumpster for a long, slow kiss against his six foot four frame. I stretched up his chest and, standing on my tiptoes, we fit together snugly. My body quivered at the contact, a moan escaping, begging for more.

Kevin Cory called out my name. He was almost a family member and I knew he hated that idea. He liked my brother, Brad, and approved of him dating his sister, Julie, but he thought Mother and I were crazy and unsuitable role models for his teenage nephew, Liam.

When we drove by, I'd seen him questioning Philipa, the bartender. Arms across his chest, he didn't look happy about whatever answers she was giving him. We called the bartender Phil—a second-year law student who dazzled the customers with her bubbly personality, long blond hair, and butt-cheek-baring shorts. I didn't worry about what she'd say.

I heard my name called again and turned to see Mother waving, Fab next to her sporting an angry scowl. Before I could take a step, a female sheriff stepped in front of me.

"No lookers," she said as she pointed to the street. "This is an active investigation."

I checked out her uniform. It turned out she was local. Her badge read, *Tarpon Cove*.

The Cove sat at the top of the Keys, the first small town to greet you upon entering the Overseas Highway after leaving Miami far behind. We had a small sheriff presence and I knew most of them by name.

"We haven't met—I'm Madison Westin, the owner."

Her dark brown eyes arched a bit at what I assumed was my not offering a courtesy handshake. Anyone who knew me also knew I didn't observe that nicety, but most people just assumed I was ill-mannered. I disliked the term "germaphobe," but I also hated anything slimy, murky, green, watery, and abhorred all bugs in general.

"I've heard about you." She looked me over, amusement on her face. "I'm Kevin's new partner, Officer Ivyliss Sotolongo. You can call me Ivy."

"Johnson's replacement." I smiled. "I heard he got kicked — transferred — somewhere far from the Cove."

"He had a lot to say about you before he left," she said, and laughed. "It was his dream to lock up your criminal ass which, to his disappointment, was a wish unfulfilled."

"Do you mind if I speak to my mother and make sure she's okay? Her health is fragile," I said, and managed to maintain eye contact to sell the blatant lie.

Ivy looked over at Mother, who stared back. "She might want to cut back on the cigars. You can have five minutes."

Mother loved a hand-rolled Cuban cigar; she found a family run store in Little Havana that she frequented often. She'd been to the factory and knew everyone by name.

I didn't want to hear the answer to my next question — fearing the worst — but I asked anyway. "Is she under arrest?"

"It's not my call. But evidence is missing, along with a couple of witnesses and their stories are full of potholes, and did I mention they barely agree on anything?"

Damn!

"Jake's caters to law enforcement; they have a special area in the corner of the back deck, one of the best views in the place. Hope to see you soon."

I walked over to Mother, enveloping her in a

hug. "What in the hell," I whispered in her ear. "Brad will flip when you tell him." One thing's for certain, I wasn't going to be the one to tell my brother and wanted to be out of town again when he found out.

"He doesn't need to know," she snorted. "It was a huge misunderstanding."

"Mother," I mimicked in her no-nonsense voice, "I'm sure it wasn't. Who knows you better than I do?"

I looked at my best friend and roommate, Fab, and stage-whispered, "You couldn't stay out of trouble for a few days?"

"Get your lawyer on the phone. I'm not up to a trip to the big-girl jail." Fab's dark eyes shot Mother hate-filled looks. "I'm so glad you're home. I want details."

"Mother," I continued to whisper, after noticing Ivy moving closer, "you're in frail health if anyone asks. You can have a miraculous recovery once we get you out of here."

Mother dabbed her eyes.

"Stop, you don't fool me. What the hell happened?" I shook my head. "The truth, not the cleaned up legal version."

"When Fab and I were on a recovery job, we discussed opening the back room for a friendly card game, to a select group of friends. Things didn't go as planned." She sighed.

I snapped around and glared at Fab. "You took Mother to boost a car? Were guns drawn?"

"It was an easy job for a change. Found the BMW at the girlfriend's house, I got in and drove away."

"There is no such thing as an easy recovery job. I'll bet cash there's more to your story."

"I didn't have anyone else," she hissed. "You know I need a driver. All she had to do was follow me to Brick's for the drop-off, what could go wrong?"

Brick Famosa owned a high-end car sales/rental lot, Famosa Motors. I thought he stopped renting to people without a credit and background check, especially when they paid with all cash. But apparently not; he kept Fab and I busy driving all over South Florida recovering cars that failed to be returned.

"You're asking me that with a straight face when ninety percent of our jobs end up with threats of violence?"

"You exaggerate at ninety percent," she huffed. "Have you ever tried to tell your mother her idea is a sucky one? She has voices in her head and only listens to them."

"Since when do all these different agencies show up for an illegal card game?"

"Some jackass called in a bomb scare. They burst through the doors. I wanted to run but got down on my knees, like they told me."

"Officer Ivy informed me that no evidence was found. I'm assuming she meant evidence about the card game. How did you make that disappear? Nice job, by the way."

"I texted Madeline, she took care of it; swept everything off the table into garbage bags and sent the men out the secret back door."

Fab must be mad—she called Mother by her first name.

Mother put her head on my shoulder and said, "I thought I had everything covered since I ran a couple of practice drills before we opened."

Creole walked up behind us, scooping Mother off of her feet and into a bear hug. "Since when are you in the habit of ticking off drug-dealing pond scum?" he asked.

Kevin joined Ivy, and together they glared in our direction.

I cut in. "Mother, did you give a statement to anyone?" She shook her head in the negative.

"Don't say one word until I get Cruz on the phone." Cruz Campion was a hotshot lawyer I kept on speed-dial for just such occasions.

Creole and I exchanged looks.

"Bistro needed a get-out-of-trouble card for a violation of his parole conditions," he said. "In retaliation, he concocted an elaborate story about guns, gambling, and bomb making."

Fab groaned. "I picked up Bistro's car. The BMW belonged to him."

The jail bus rumbled into the driveway. I recognized it as the one they used for special occasions like drunk-driving checkpoints. I watched as my employees filed on board.

"Break up the love feast, ladies, time to get yourselves a seat," Ivy yelled, advancing on us. She looked at me. "We're going over the bar one more time and, unless anything new turns up, you can reopen tomorrow."

"No more questions," Creole advised Ivy. "Every one of them is lawyered up."

"All of them?" she asked in astonishment.

I smiled at her. "If you ever need a criminal attorney, Cruz is the best in South Florida. He boasts the whole state."

Kevin, who had stood quietly at Ivy's side, spoke up. "It will be a while before they're released and you're not welcome to hang around."

He grabbed Mother's arm. "You might be my nephew's grandmother one day. Why can't you be a good example and bake cookies or something?"

"I don't need to bake as long as there are bakeries."

Chapter Two

Fab rudely interrupted Jazz's nap and threw herself onto the couch, the cat on her chest. "What took them so long to release us?"

My hundred-year-old cat was king of the house. When he meowed, you'd better jump or it got louder until a person's ears couldn't take it any longer.

Creole picked Mother and Fab up near dawn as they filed out of the sheriff's station; they were the last to be released. "You're lucky Brick posted all the bonds at no charge," he said, his sinister smile unnerving me.

He continued. "The officers deliberately stood around doing nothing until shift change, foisting all of you on the next crew to process. That raised the irritation level."

My patience having evaporated, I yelled at Mother and Fab. "What in the hell were you two thinking?"

I tugged on Creole's shirt and motioned for him to sit on the large footstool in front of my chair. I stopped myself from wrapping my legs around his waist.

"You were going to open it anyway!" Mother

paced around, finally smacking Fab's leg and sitting down next to her. "What's the harm in a practice run?"

"And you," I said, glaring at Fab, "can manhandle bad guys all day long and you can't control one old woman?"

"I'm not old!" Mother shrieked.

I knew that would get her attention.

"Next time," Fab said, shaking her finger at Mother, "I'm calling Spoon."

"You wouldn't dare."

Clearly, Mother never thought that would be used as a threat.

"Try me. I hate jail and I'm not going back." Fab twisted her waist-length brown hair off her neck and pulled it into a ponytail.

What Mother would soon find out was that her boyfriend, Jimmy Spoon, had a pipeline to news as it happened. So he already knew she'd been carted off to jail and he wouldn't be happy. Mother thought she had him wrapped around her finger, but she'd see his surly side now that she'd gotten herself arrested.

"I planned to open the room legally and have an appointment to talk to the county licensing board. You two need to stay out of trouble until this fiasco can be salvaged." I gave them a tight-lipped stare.

"How did your stake-out go?" Mother asked Creole, changing the subject to switch the focus off of her.

"Did you get your man?" I smiled, knowing she was referring to the time we were out of town together.

"They're all in jail. On to my next target." He looked over his shoulder at me, licking his lips.

"How was the wedding? Mary, wasn't it?" Fab's eyes flicked between me and Creole.

I turned and stuck out my tongue. "Marcy! And I had a great time."

"Maybe next time I'll go." Fab smirked.

"That's one way to make sure you stay out of jail."

The front door flew open as hurricane Brad blew in, slamming it closed behind him. "What the hell, Madeline Westin?" he roared. His brown eyes were a carbon copy of Mother's. Tall and brawny, his easygoing personality buried under his fury.

I barely noticed Julie, his girlfriend, who took cover behind his back. She peeked out and waved. Both looked as if they'd spent the day on the water, her sunburned cheeks a giveaway. He spent long hours on the ocean as a commercial fisherman, so it surprised me that he still enjoyed pleasure boating.

"Don't look at me, I just got back home. I thought you weren't due to dock your boat for a few days? Come in early to sneak around with your girlfriend? And not calling Mother. You know how she worries." I made a sad face, trying not to laugh.

"My love life is off limits," Brad said, and glared.

Julie reached for his hand, squeezing. He sat in the last remaining chair and pulled Julie onto his lap.

My living room was a large open space connecting to the kitchen, and to the patio and pool area through the French doors. I inherited the house along with a rental property from my aunt Elizabeth. I updated the house with fresh paint and throw rugs on the hardwood floors, and replaced most of the furniture with over-stuffed, slipcovered, comfortable pieces I brought with me when I moved to Florida. I kept her favorite chair that seated two and had it recovered in a tropical print.

"Oh good. Rules," I said. "Then you can extend me the same courtesy."

"Not likely." He scowled at Mother. "Would you like to explain how you got arrested?"

"It's just a misunderstanding and will soon be cleared up," Mother said. "Who the heck is making breakfast?"

"The only reason you're not sitting in jail and may skate on these charges is because Kevin forgot about the back door. He warned us that he won't overlook it again." Brad's voice brimmed with frustration.

"What?" Fab fumed. "Kevin got hot on the phone like a tattle-tell?"

Julie cleared her throat, blue eyes full of fury,

and glared at Fab. "My brother is an upstanding person, a respected sheriff who doesn't break the law. You should try it sometime."

Time to break this up. I didn't think Julie had it in her, but the young blonde looked ready to take on Fab.

I jumped up and said, "I promise Jake's will not be used as a hotbed for illegal activities."

The front door opened again and every woman's fantasy, Didier, walked through, dropping his travel bags onto the floor. Fab's model boyfriend had returned from a photo shoot in New York. His blue eyes scanned the room and, surprised to see everyone at such an early hour, a dark expression filled his face.

Fab flew across the room and flung herself in his arms. She whispered something French in his ear and he growled something back. He leaned down and kissed Mother's cheek, also whispering in her ear, which made her smile.

Creole smirked; he spoke three languages and understood every word between them. During our time away, we shared all the good memories of our childhood with one another. He told me that his mother spoke Italian, his father French/Cajun.

"Glad you're back, model boy," Brad said. "Do you know what your girlfriend has been up to?"

"Enough," Creole barked. "Fabiana has had a bad day. I'm sure she'll tell you about it—" He inclined his head toward the stairs. He turned back to Brad. "Why don't you take your mother to breakfast?"

Didier scooped Fab off her feet and carried her up the steps. Stopping half way, he turned and looked at me. "Welcome back, Cherie." Seconds later, Fab's bedroom door banged shut.

Everyone was tired and running on adrenaline. I tried to lighten the mood. "Look at the bright side, Brad. You didn't have to wait months to hear about the latest family adventure."

Brad complained incessantly about being the last to know about Mother's and my misdeeds. We used the excuse that we didn't want to upset him. When he confided that it made him feel foolish, I felt thoroughly chastised and resolved to share future information before he found out on his own.

"We'll see you later," Creole said as he stood. Pulling me up next to him, he draped his arm across my shoulders.

Mother arched her brows. "I thought you two were taking it slow."

"I don't see why you're so resistant to keeping it in the family," I said.

Creole looked at me, silently communicating: *That's the only thing you could think to say*? "I have an announcement. I'd like you to meet my new official girlfriend." He kissed my cheek. "I would hope that you'll all be happy—and if you're not, keep it to yourself."

No one said a word as they waited for Mother's reaction. She was afraid we'd date, then break-up, and Creole would divorce the family.

He pulled me toward the door, and I stopped briefly to kiss Mother and whisper, "Love you."

* * *

Traffic was non-existent in the early morning hours so Creole rocketed down the Overseas, the Atlantic on one side of the highway, the Gulf on the other. The sun slowly made its appearance shining down on the water, making it sparkle — an open invitation to come for a swim. His hideaway was located in Hibiscus Key, not far from Tarpon Cove. The exit sign gave no clue that anything existed other than a loop around to the opposite side of the highway. A wall of trees hid several homes that dotted the waterfront along the exclusive strip of roadway.

"Your brother's a bit of a drama queen," Creole said as he veered off the highway.

"If the sheriff hadn't been called out, Brad would've laughed it off," I said, defending him. "He's very protective since our father died; he takes his man-of-the-family role seriously. He would like it if Mother were more low-key. He just wants her to be safe. He'd marry her off in a second to a stable gentleman her own age if he could get away with it. I know he's come to tolerate Spoon but, let's face it, he'd like it if they broke up."

Spoon was ten years younger than mother and came with a colorful past, which he turned around through his own hard work.

The street we turned onto wound around in a semi-circle. Creole stayed to the right and pulled into the last driveway at the end where he had an unassuming beach cottage that perched over the water. Painted all white, he'd recently built a tall wooden fence that wrapped around the perimeter, the gate opening into the courtyard. He liked the added security and had installed security cameras.

The surprise came when you walked through the front door and stepped into one big room with a solid wall of sliding pocket doors that opened to a patio and pool that overlooked the beach below. He portioned off the bedroom from the living area with two large bamboo screens, which looked good but would offer zero privacy if he had overnight guests. A large kitchen and mammoth bathroom were my favorite rooms in the house. He had done all the inside remodeling himself, all first-class finishes: travertine tiles, bamboo floors, and top-of-the-line appliances.

"It seems like we just left here."

"It got way too crowded at your house." He turned me toward the massive king-sized bed and said, "Take your clothes off."

"That's so romantic," I said to his back as he

disappeared into the bathroom. Next thing I heard was the water running.

"Stay right there until I come and get you," he yelled.

I had already slipped off my flip-flops and left them by the door, always going barefoot after I got inside. I pulled off my short-sleeve T-shirt dress and tossed it over the chair, followed by lace boy shorts and matching chemise. He had about three seconds because I wasn't standing in the middle of the room au naturel, trying not to look embarrassed.

He must have tapped into my thoughts because the bathroom door opened and he threw a pose against the jamb, stark naked. He held out his arms and I walked straight into them.

He scooped me up and set me in the large claw-foot tub that was rapidly filling with warm, bubbly water. I caught the scent of my favorite bath gel, frangipani. He stepped in behind me, catching me by the shoulders. Relaxing against the back of the tub, he drew me into his arms, dipped a large sea sponge into the water, and ran it across my shoulders.

The bathtub sat in front of a large glass window and the sun shined brightly, overlooking a secluded section of the beach out across the Gulf water.

"Another new rule today," he murmured in my ear.

I leaned forward. "What?"

He pulled me possessively against his chest, the firm muscle of his thigh meeting my stomach.

"We're going to sleep together every night I'm not working, whether it's at your house or mine. I'll find you." He licked the inside of my ear, his teeth nibbling on the lobe.

"Is this where you're going to tell me you want Fab to move out?" That had been a sticking point with my last boyfriend. He asked every time he came over when she was moving. I got good at giving evasive answers.

"I like Fab and Didier and it's not like we have to share a bathroom."

I realized I'd held my breath waiting for his answer."Four adults is a lot, but I'm fine with it. I think it's going to work because we all get along."

"There will be rules," he said and cupped my chin, twisting gently so I could see that he was serious.

I rolled my eyes. "Rules? Did you know Fab has them?"

Creole grinned. "Underneath that pretty face, Didier has some good ideas. It's where I got the idea."

I reached for the soap, lathered my hands, and massaged his foot. Unwrapping his leg, I ran my soapy hands up and down his inner and outer thigh. "I don't have to write them down do I?"

He pinched my bottom. "First, you will not do anything that puts your life in danger. Second, no lying. Lastly, if I tell you not to do something, you will not just go ahead and do it anyway."

"I don't usually lie. I tend to shade the truth when needed and then there are those times I make up stories out of whole cloth."

He put his lips to my ear and chuckled. "Do you agree to the rules? A simple, 'Yes, sir,' will do."

"What if I'm naughty and forget?"

"I'll check with Didier and get back to you. I forgot to ask that part."

"No more man-bonding for the two of you." I flicked water on him.

The two of them enjoyed exhausting sports. They ran sprints on the beach, challenged each other to see who could do the most push-ups on the sand, and went for grueling bike rides that took them up and down the Keys.

He tipped my head, cradling my face in both hands, and bent his face toward mine, seeking my lips and brushing them slightly. "I thought about you all day," he whispered. His mouth fell upon mine, pressing me with a bruising kiss.

"Thank you for announcing to the family that we're together. I would've waited until we were caught naked. My favorite part was when you sealed it with that look daring them to say anything." I lifted his hand to my lips, kissing his fingers.

"Who's going to be the one to tell them there was no wedding in South Carolina, that we ran off and spent very little time out of bed?"

"No one's going to ask except maybe Mother and I'll change the subject."

"You're all mine now," he whispered.

"Yes, I am."

Chapter Three

Trying to enter unnoticed, I turned the knob to the front door slowly, peering around the corner into the kitchen.

"No one's here but me," Fab said, filling her coffee pot with water to drink her early morning cup of mud. The bag said "coffee," but I wasn't convinced. "Brad drove your mother home last night. Her car disappeared a few hours later so I assume Spoon must've had it picked up and delivered to her."

Spoon owned an auto body shop down in the seedy section of the docks. This family didn't have car problems; he picked them up, left a courtesy car, and delivered washed, waxed, and noise-free running vehicles when they were returned. He made it very clear that he'd prefer us to get rides home at night and made sure our cars were waiting in the driveway the next morning.

"You in trouble with Didier?" I asked.

Fab looked ready for work in her halter-top and white mid-thigh shorts, showing off her long legs. She reeked of sexiness. Her signature Walther lay in front of her on the counter.

"His initial anger pretty much evaporated when I launched into an excruciatingly detailed explanation instead of weaseling. He told me he was proud of me for being upfront. Then I jumped in his arms and sniffled about how happy I was that he came back early."

"What's your version of what happened? Hit the highlights and don't gloss over the unflattering details like you usually do."

She pressed her lips together but not before an exasperated sigh escaped. "I caught your mother, which is probably not an accurate description since she sat at the bar and made calls to set up her game, oblivious to anyone listening. It sounded like fun at first, so I offered to be security. I had second thoughts the night before, but telling your mother she should rethink her bad idea is a waste of breath. The game barely got under way when out of nowhere the shit hit the fan. I texted your mother. You know the rest."

"Thank goodness there wasn't any cash lying around."

"She had that angle covered." Fab gave me a wary smile. "Set it up as a pre buy-in, the money held by that CPA of yours. Once they finished, they'd cash out. In retrospect, we shouldn't have tried to hide anything and let the cops investigate. The game didn't have the appearance of anything illegal. But the doctor, lawyer, and CPA didn't want their names linked in a headline with gambling. So they hit the secret door at the first sound of trouble."

The microwave dinged and I took out the hot water and mixed myself a cup of coffee. Fab teased me that mine was nothing more than colored water as compared to hers that guaranteed to grow hair on your chest after half a cup. I slid onto a stool at the large island across from Fab. All important conversations took place in the kitchen.

"We need to talk," Fab said as she pulled her long brown hair off her neck and secured it with the clip that she held between her lips. "Now that you're becoming a real estate mogul, where does that leave our partnership?"

"Still partners is where it leaves us. While I was out of town, were you perhaps auditioning a replacement?"

Fab laughed. "I need you tonight for a Brick job, and as you pointed out, they can go south in a second. I'd like backup. I'm to show up at Miami International dressed in something skimpy, sexy and pick up three businessmen and deliver them to the Ritz-Carlton Hotel."

"Who's loading the suitcases?" I flexed my arm, tapping my bicep.

"If you'd work out more, I'd let you do it."

Jazz sauntered in, meowing. Fab scooped him up and reached into the refrigerator for some butcher-paper-wrapped treats. To my surprise, she bypassed the counter and slid down to the floor to feed him.

I watched as he gobbled up the turkey; he had trained everyone in the family to spoil him.

"In the meantime, I've got to check on my mini empire. You driving?" I tossed her the keys.

* * *

Fab rocketed around the corner using the brake sparingly in my shiny black convertible Hummer. I'd gotten an excellent deal from Brick after reminding him several times that it had a lot of mileage, which made it a used car. He finally caved when his nephew boosted it and used it as a cheap motel room.

Fab squealed into a parking space in front of the office at The Cottages, a ten-unit property of small individual houses, steps from the Gulf of Mexico. I had inherited the property from my aunt Elizabeth.

We catered primarily to European tourists, recently getting a slew of reservations from Scotland. I looked forward to the first good-looking Scot to show up in a skirt. That would have the crazy women of the neighborhood converging. I had several year-round tenants and a firm rule—that got broken with regularity—not to rent to locals. I recently removed the welcome mat for the occasional murderer, drug dealer, and just plain riff-raff.

"Who's that?" I pointed to a man, seat back,

lying down behind the wheel of a banged up Chevy Vega, gunning his engine at the curb, desperately in need of a muffler.

"Why are you asking me?" Fab grumbled. "I don't know the people in this neighborhood. That would be you. Go make friends with him and I'm sure he'll tell you his life story. I'll wait inside."

I turned up my nose. "You need to get some social skills." Fab was right. I'm not sure why, but I could be minding my own business and a random person would spill intimate details of their life into my ear.

Fab kicked the office door open. "Feet off the desk, that's not professional," she barked at Mac Lane, the manager.

Mac, a curvy middle-aged woman, had on her favorite light-up tennis shoes and was dressed in an unfashionable pair of culottes and a wife-beater shirt. Energy drink-addicted, she noisily slurped every last drop and threw the can across the room into the trash. I never regretted hiring her. She was tough, ballsy, and not afraid to use her Beretta to rid the property of undesirables.

"Just filled the refrigerator." She put a fresh piece of bubble gum into her mouth, flinging the paper wrap in the direction of the trash, though it missed by a mile. "How was the bogus wedding trip?"

"Toe-curling, excruciatingly amazing," I sighed. "And if you tell anyone, you're fired."

I plopped down onto a chair in front of the desk. Fab claimed the couch, stretching out and shoving pillows under her head. I redecorated the office tropical island style—rattan furniture covered in shades of green, with bright splashes of tangerine and cream. Office rule: A full snack bowl topped off with crackers, cookies, and mini candy bars.

Mac banged her feet against the desk, sending the running lights racing around the bottom of her shoes. The problem was that only the left one worked. "I knew Creole would be hot." She frowned, staring at her shoe. "You're a little skimpy on the details."

Fab snickered from the couch.

I changed the subject. "Who's the scurve at the curb?"

"Did you get a close-up look?" Mac crossed herself. "He's creepy looking—his face scarred up from one too many fights. The most impressive one runs from his ear to the side of his mouth. Looks like he sewed it up himself. And he has mean, narrow, beady eyes. Heard him laugh once and it sent shivers up my spine."

"Please, tell me you didn't rent to him." If she said yes, I'd need aspirin.

"Hell no!" Mac's eyebrows came together in a scowl as she said it. "He doesn't even live in the neighborhood, I checked. That's Jami's boyfriend, claims to work construction but I don't believe him. He drives her to every job and stands guard."

Jami had been the gardener since right after I took over management of the property. She rode up one day on her bicycle and insisted I didn't know anything about planting; turns out there's more to it than throwing a plant in a hole and covering it with dirt. She conducted her business from the back of her bicycle, carrying small tools around in its dual baskets. My green thumb was not a match for my father's, I should have paid more attention all those times I followed him around his garden. Now I excelled at lugging plants home from the nursery with instructions for where to plant them. Jami was always outgoing and friendly but had two distinct personalities: the responsible one that showed up to her accounts every day and the other one, a hard partier by night.

"What happened to her husband?" I had met the man a few times. He was older than she was—I suspected he provided stability. He had a good sense of humor, which sold me.

Mac stuck her pen in the large bubble she'd blown and the sticky mess covered part of her mouth, a piece sticking to her brown hair. "She traded down, apparently he wasn't exciting enough. She needs to be careful with this more sparkly model."

I glared at Mac when she brought her shoe down hard on the desk again.

"Damn. I may never find another pair like these." Mac patted her shoes.

Interrupted by a knock, Fab reached out and turned the knob, giving the door a shove.

Jami stood in the doorway in her signature, barely covering anything short-overalls, her hot pink hair pulled into a ponytail sticking out of the top of her head, wearing a T-shirt advertising her skills, and bathed in sweat. The last time I'd seen her, her hair screamed fluorescent red.

"I hate to ask," she said, shuffling from one foot to the other, "but can I get a pay advance, we're getting kicked out of our trailer?"

I raised my eyebrows. "I thought you and your husband lived in an apartment."

"I got tired of being a boring vanilla wife." She twisted a pink lock of hair around her finger. "I packed my clothes one day while he was at work and left a note."

Ouch! "I'll help any way I can," I said. I liked her, but she made terrible decisions.

Jami looked around the room and back at me. "If you'd let me stay at the Trailer Court, I wouldn't need much of an advance."

Fab burst out laughing.

The estate of Gus Ivers had just settled. We'd been business partners for a short time, and his bequest left me the owner of an entire block of commercial real estate, except the portion I already owned, Jake's. Most of it run down and in need of repair.

"The place is a dump and I haven't decided what I'm going to do with it yet," I told her. "There's only one person living there and he has a bad attitude." Becoming a slumlord was not in my future.

"I know the professor." Jami smiled. "Caught him prowling around the yard of another client, stealing apples. Now I take him a bag at least once a week."

"A professor? Why am I the last to know?" Mac smacked her gum. "What's he like?"

"He's a piece of weirdness in underwear," Fab said, and rolled her eyes.

Jami gave Fab a dirty look. "He's really large and pants are too confining."

Fab started laughing again, rolled on her side, and almost fell off the couch.

Mac looked at Jami. "How would you know?"

"One night after a few beers and chasers I asked him." Jami pulled out her phone that had just beeped, read the message, and turned it off.

I held up my hands. "Stop. You can have the advance and I'd like to meet your new boyfriend."

She pulled on my arm, walking me over to the Vega. The back seat had been removed, and suitcases were piled up. The man reclined back, his head blocked from view by the steering wheel. He looked me over and then hung his head out the window and spit a wad of chew, barely missing my foot.

"Edsel, honey, this is Madison. She owns The Cottages."

"It's Ed!" he snapped at her. "Don't forget again." His nostrils flared with anger, eyes dark pinpoints.

Oh, great! There went the hairs on the back of my neck, standing straight up. I'd bet one of his body parts he was full-on trouble. Another policy of mine: Never wager one of my own body parts. My radar was on high alert. This man didn't appear to have a single redeeming trait—I never wanted to end up anywhere alone with him.

I stepped back. "Ed…"

"Ed Winer." Jami ran her fingers down his cheek, an adoring look on her face. "She's going to let us stay at the Trailer Court."

Ed smacked his lips together, hanging on to his anger, and stuck out his long tunnel tongue, running it slowly around his lips. He never took his eyes off me, continuing to stare. I reached under my boxy top in the back and patted my Glock reassuringly. "You need any man work done, give me a call." He winked.

Jami waved. "I have to run to my next job, but I'll be back this afternoon," she said, and jumped into the passenger side.

"Mac will be back from the bank by then," I told her. I didn't want anyone to know we kept cash on the premises.

People around here preferred to be paid in cash; they couldn't qualify for bank accounts and check-cashing places charged loan shark rates. We issued a check, had them endorse, and then handed over cash.

Edsel turned the key and the loud backfire made me jump. I walked slowly back to the office, keeping an eye on the Vega as it rumbled down the street. Already it was a block away and could still be heard.

"Run a check on Edsel Winer." I grabbed the bottle of water from Fab's outstretched hand. "I've got a real bad feeling about him. Reminds me of a tenant who stayed here briefly under an assumed name. The cops arrived to pick him up on an outstanding warrant and he eluded them, escaped down the beach. Under no circumstances can those two move into the Trailer Court. Tell Jami the place was red-tagged and give her extra money."

"I'll ask around about Ed, and hit up a lowlife or two; I know one I can buy off with a 12-pack. If they don't know the man then they can get the information," Mac said.

I rolled my neck around trying to release the kinks and it didn't work.

"Are Miss January and Joseph still alive?"

The two tenants requiring a ton of patience came with the property, tenants of my aunt's, and I had a soft spot for both of them. They'd both been diagnosed with cancer and were served death sentences by doctors a couple of years ago, but they flipped the medical profession the bird and enjoyed life to the fullest, boozing and smoking.

"Joseph wants to marry Svetlana, even though I told him it isn't legal." Mac snorted. "He copped a 'tude and pulled the sick-old-man card, telling me I made stuff up to make him feel worse. He ran to Shirl and she fawned over him until he felt better."

I groaned. "Drive Svet and Joseph to the courthouse and let the clerk tell him he can't marry an inflatable latex woman."

I relaxed my rule about locals and had allowed Shirl to stay for a few days and, of course, it became permanent. Best thing that could have happened; The Cottages now had its very own medical professional. She worked at Tarpon Cove hospital as a highly respected R.N.

I shook my finger at Mac. "Since she's your best friend, you need to tell Shirl that she's never allowed to move. She sneaks off and I'll send Fab after her."

Both Mac and Shirl had a girl crush on Fab and never complained about her gruff attitude. They loved when she called for favors. I knew Fab availed herself of Mac's lowlife black book— which, in her case, was purple with stickers—for information on cases.

Mac pulled her gum out of her mouth, stretching it out as far as it would go, and then thankfully threw it in the trash. "Miss January's feeling a little down. Her drunken girlfriend,

Ruby, is home sick, so she has no one to make a spectacle of herself with in public. Hence, no arrests while you were gone."

Nothing changed since I left. "Can you find a muscley guy with a car for tonight? He meets us here"—I looked at Fab and she nodded—"follows us to the airport, schleps luggage, and leaves. Negotiate an hourly rate and let him know there'll be more waiting time than actual work. And not one word of complaint that there's not much to do."

"Try for someone normal," Fab spoke up. "At least no drunks."

"Come on, Girl Wonder, I'm hungry." I pulled on Fab's arm. "I can drive."

She gave me a dirty look and wiggled her way out the door. Mac and I laughed.

Chapter Four

Dragging a chaise poolside, I grabbed a colorful beach towel and lay back, coffee in hand. There was originally a small patch of grass that ran alongside the house, but I had it dug out and replaced with bricks. My brother and I had spent summers with our aunt Elizabeth and, together, we'd search out new tropical flowers for the garden. Slowly, I'd repainted the pots a variety of art deco colors, and replanted and mulched them with seashells from the local beach. Occasionally, I would cheat and buy a sack of shells from The Shack. When having a crappy day, I found gardening a great way to sweat out my I-hate-everything attitude.

I dove into the water. Hating traditional exercise, I swam, biked, and walked the beach. After huffing out twenty-five laps, I relaxed on one of the plastic blow-up rings that floated nearby. The sound of an engine revving—my newest ringtone—interrupted my peaceful moment. Someone was blowing up my cell phone before I'd consumed my morning coffee. Multiple calls this early meant trouble of some kind.

Slowly, I made my way up the pool steps, wrapping a towel around my waist while searching for my phone.

"How did the job go the other night?" Didier asked, and winked.

He sat, feet up, in the most coveted chair in the living room because it was so comfortable, in shorts and a T-shirt that stretched across his well-defined abs, his jet black hair a mess. With Jazz stretched out along his thigh, Didier was immersed in his laptop.

"Your girlfriend didn't pull her gun once." I smiled. "So uneventful it was hard to believe the job came from Brick."

Fab had left the house early to go meet with one of her smarmier clients. She needed to dump those accounts since she rarely escaped unscathed. If Didier knew how many times she had to jump out windows, he would put a stop to it.

My phone revved again, and I struggled not to hit the ignore button. "What's up, Mac?"

"Just want to know what to do with the dead body in the shed? The old man next door already called the sheriff, almost fell off his ladder when the head kind of fell out. I'm expecting lights and sirens soon."

I sunk down onto the barstool. "The what?"

"You remember loser Edsel Winer? Well, he's dead in the shed — that rhymes by the way." Her deranged little laugh indicated she was ready to go home and have a drink. "Found him just inside the door with his head bashed in, his face uglier than before, as if that were possible."

I closed my eyes and took a deep breath. "Do not touch anything. I'm on my way." I threw my phone down and raced toward the stairs. "I have to get to The Cottages," I yelled to Didier.

* * *

I dressed in my uniform—skirt and T-shirt—in less than five minutes and flew out the door. Normally, I drove like an old woman, but in case of duress, I could stomp on the accelerator with the best of them. Two sheriff cars blew by me at the signal, so I followed discreetly and arrived right behind them.

The little house across the street was vacant again, the latest round of drunks evicted. I often parked in their driveway and sat on the front porch, watching the drama unfold on my own property. Kevin and his partner, Ivy, stood just outside my shed. I got off on the wrong foot with Kevin's old partner and was determined it would not happen with Officer Ivy.

"Did the deceased live here?" Kevin asked as I joined them. "Notice my first question wasn't 'Did you kill him?'" He looked at his partner. "Don't get me wrong, she's shot a few people, but she hasn't murdered anyone, yet."

"And to think I had plans to invite you to the

next family barbeque," I said. I wanted to give him the finger but didn't think it would promote a harmonious relationship. "And no, he didn't live here, but he had a relationship with the gardener."

"Someone wasn't very happy with him. His brains were beaten in using your shovel," Ivy commented, keeping an eye on the old man from next door as he strolled by yelling at himself. "I assume it's yours, since it's covered in blood and lying next to the deceased."

"If Mac needs a lawyer, he's in court right now but will be calling shortly." On the way over, I called Cruz's office and his assistant told me court would be in recess soon and she'd send a message.

"If Mac wanted him dead, she'd have shot him." Kevin waved to the coroner wagon.

"You're new here, Ivy. There are drinks and junk snacks in the office, nothing healthy," I said, and pointed to the door.

"I was just telling her to get used to stopping by this property." Kevin pursed his lips, arms folded across his chest.

"Edsel showed up here a couple of days ago, not enough time to become friendly with anyone. So why kill him? Joseph could find someone who knew him but don't be surprised if he doesn't answer the door. I can go with you, threaten him if he doesn't."

Ivy's face turned chilly and she said, "With what?"

"No more rides home in the middle of the night after being released from incarceration."

She laughed.

The coroner wheeled a gurney over to the shed. I didn't want to be standing here when they hauled his body out—covered or not. "I'll be in the office."

I found Mac lying on the couch when I opened the door. "You okay?"

She lifted her head. "I called Shirl and she's bringing take-out and beer." She and Shirl met in high school and had remained best friends. "There's more to this story."

I sat behind her desk for a change. "I'm afraid to ask."

"You want to see dead Edsel?" She took out her cell phone.

"You didn't!" I gasped.

"Don't tell. It might be illegal or something. You know what else? The shed had been plucked clean, miscellaneous tools and bags of potting soil were all that were left; no lawnmower, blower, or other equipment."

I finally sold the riding lawn mower after it had been stolen, pawned, and crashed in practice for a race. Besides, the two little grass strips we currently had weren't big enough for the mammoth mower.

"I'll tell Kevin so that I can get a report

number in case someone commits a felony with the yard tools. Do you think Dead Ed interrupted a robbery? Why would he come here by himself?"

Thank goodness we both have alibis.

"He's a first-class dirtball. Got the background check back and it was the worst I've ever seen. I asked around quietly about his life in the Cove, not wanting the snooping trail to lead back to me." Mac got up and pulled the aspirin bottle out of the drawer.

"I hope Jami's okay." I picked up my phone and called her number, which went straight to voicemail. "Hit the highlights of the report."

"He's a convicted sex offender, drug dealer, and has pending charges of assault and battery."

"Wow! I wonder if Jami knew?"

Mac looked at some notes she'd scribbled. "He's forty and, according to his rap sheet, was recently released from prison where he's spent most of his life. Originally he'd been sentenced to life for aggravated kidnap and rape, but the parole board felt sorry for him since he committed the crime at sixteen, so they reduced his sentence to time served for a total of fifteen years."

I stared at Mac, wide-eyed.

"He managed to stay out of trouble for a couple of years, then got busted dealing large quantities of weed. Rumor has it he did the time for the guy at the top; he could've rolled, given names, but decided to keep his mouth shut. He did almost the full eight, got released a few months ago."

"Every once in a while you manage to shock me, and this is one of those times," I said, and gave her a lackluster smile.

"Let's not forget his current charges. He's been charged with assault and battery, resisting arrest, and intoxication. I'm working on getting the events surrounding the arrest."

I closed my eyes and sighed. "No homeowner on this block has had a single murder or dead body, but we make up for all of them. Why did you go out to the shed?"

"I had my feet propped up in the barbeque, reading. I'm obsessed with historical romance right now. Got distracted by the annoying ice cream truck—should I or shouldn't I?"

"Could you focus, please?"

"I decided against the ice cream, almost forgot I'm eating healthy these days. Oh yeah"—her eyes went wide, remembering—"then I noticed a red stain under the door. I wish I'd ignored it."

"That means the killer had a key. There's three: yours, mine, and Jami's. I hope she's alive and has a verifiable alibi."

The door flew open and Fab blew in. "What happened? Didier told me you squealed out of the driveway."

"Remember icky Edsel from the other day? He's gone on to the afterlife with a bashed-in head," I told her.

"I'm gone a few hours and something interesting happens and I missed it." Fab swore in French.

I laughed because I didn't need a translation for one of the words.

"Here you go," Mac said, and held out her phone.

Fab turned the phone several times, examining the crime scene in detail. "Somebody had a hate-on for him. I bet there's brain ooze inside the shed."

Mac made a retching noise. "I'll call the crime scene cleaner dude once the shed's been released. He should give us a repeat-customer discount."

"Oh, almost forgot," Mac continued. "Jami never showed up for her advance." She handed Fab the background report.

Fab peeked through the window blind. "I bet the next stop for Kevin and Ivy — who are still out there, trying to look incognito and failing — is Jami's house."

"I wish I hadn't told Kevin she was his girlfriend but he'd find out I withheld information and there would go our truce. I didn't mention that she might be staying at the Trailer Court."

Fab scanned the report and threw it on the desk in disgust. "Don't you think the professor would call the cops?"

"If she can ask about his private parts then, no,

I don't think he would," I said. "I need to call Creole. The last thing I want is for him to find out about another dead body from someone else. It would interfere with our relationship bliss."

Chapter Five

Fab and I met up at the house. She parked the Mercedes and practically dragged me from behind the wheel of my SUV so that she could take the wheel. We rarely ever went anywhere in her car and I never got to drive. She worked some kind of suspicious deal with Brick in which he allows her to drive the hottest cars in town. But when he snapped his fingers, he expected it returned, usually with no notice.

She squealed right up to the picket fence at the Trailer Court, and Crum stepped back holding a broom handle, rifle style. All that intelligence must have robbed his brain cells. Mac needed to run a check on this one. Rumor had it he taught at a prestigious California college that one couldn't get into without perfect grades.

I jumped out of the passenger side. "Have you seen Jami?"

"Who?" he asked, a blank look on his face.

"Don't you 'who' me. I happen to know she has an unseemly interest in your body. She needs a friend before the sheriff arrives."

"You're impertinent." He raised his bushy white eyebrows.

"Haven't heard that one before. Now stop stalling."

Fab whistled. "She's right here," she said, and yanked her by the arm into full view.

"I have my own problem...need to talk to you later," Crum whispered.

"Did Edsel do that?" I asked. Jami sported two painful-looking black eyes, both sides of her face a dark shade of purple. "Have you seen a doctor?"

"Eddie went berserk and beat the hell out of me when I told him he had to return your stuff that he pawned." She fingered her bruises, a stray tear rolling down her cheek.

Fab helped her to a patio chair that wobbled when she sat. "Then what happened?"

"He left me in a heap behind the dumpster at Custer's. Crum came and got me." She nodded at him.

Custer's is a bar where locals hang out to drink beer and screw-top wine. The health department banned them from selling anything else—too dirty!

Crum left momentarily and came back with several broken-down beach chairs. After we sat down, he told us, "These were a great find. I got them out of the trash right before pickup."

I took a deep breath and tried not to concentrate on the cootie factor.

"Edsel's dead," I informed Jami.

Her mouth turned up at the sides into a faint smile.

I hoped she wouldn't have that reaction when the sheriff talked to her, which would be as soon as they could locate her.

Crum sat next to her, his mouth a grim line. Fab and I looked at one another and exchanged "What the hell?" looks.

"What happened between the two of you?" I asked.

"I told Eddie I was leaving him and going back to my husband. He knew I had car trouble on the Overseas down by Marathon Key, but didn't know that I called my husband and he came and got me and fixed the car. We spent the night on the beach. I don't know how Eddie found out, but he did and went ballistic. He threatened that if I left him, he'd kill my husband and make me watch as he fed him to the alligators."

Fab made a face, apparently that wasn't her first choice way to die.

"I told Eddie it wasn't my husband who stopped to help but my first husband, Pyle. I figured he could take care of himself. Besides, Eddie didn't know where Pyle lived."

"Do you know that if Edsel hurt Pyle you could be charged with a crime?" It surprised me to find out that there had been a first husband.

Crum went inside his pink airstream trailer and came out with a pitcher of iced tea and smudged up glasses. I wasn't sure if they were clean or not, so I passed.

His trailer was parked in the first slot just inside the fence. He decorated the outside area in an assortment of mismatched, broken-down furniture he had resurrected from the trash. The rest of the area was rundown, brought on by neglect. The previous owner liked to buy property but had no interest in keeping it maintained. There were several dilapidated trailers not fit to live in, all of them empty, not because tenants couldn't be found. I suspected Crum, the only tenant, liked it that way, and ran off anyone who thought they might like to join him in squalor.

"Why not call the sheriff? It could be your husband who is dead instead of your boyfriend," Fab said with contempt.

Jami glared at her. "This isn't my fault. I didn't know Eddie was freaking crazy."

"Is Pyle okay?" I asked.

"Eddie swore to me he'd stay sober, and then one night he got drunk, snorted a few lines, and somehow got Pyle's address. He started out by driving by their house, then got out and banged on the door, screaming mostly the 'F' word. Pyle confronted Eddie, telling him I was a flat-out liar, that he hated me and hadn't seen me in months."

"Imagine that," Fab mumbled.

"So no one got hurt?" I asked. Jami seemed oblivious to the chaos she had orchestrated.

Jami twisted her hands in her lap. To my surprise, Crum patted her on the shoulder.

"Eddie snuck back and slashed the tires on their minivan. One of the kids saw him from the kitchen window."

"Your ex has kids?" Fab asked in disgust.

"He remarried and has two children. I can't stand the woman he married."

"I bet the feeling is mutual," Fab said.

"Did the sheriff ever get called?" I asked.

"When they showed up, Eddie led them on a chase, ditching the car at a dead end and jumping a fence. The cops unleashed the dogs. He tried to fight them off and got chewed on pretty good. Once they caught up with him, he assaulted a cop who was trying to cuff him and kicked one of the dogs in the face. Did you know that's an extra charge?"

I cringed at the thought of the poor dog. "No, I didn't. But good."

"It took four sheriffs to wrestle him into the back of the car. No one thought he'd get bail but he did; his sister paid. He showed up with flowers, apologizing, I was afraid not to go back." As she spoke, her eyes glittered with tears.

We sat in silence, everyone looking uncomfortable. Fab jumped up and got us bottled water out of the back of the Hummer.

Jami broke the silence. "He'd been convicted of rape long before we hooked up. Several friends knew and never said a word. He claimed the woman cried rape because she didn't want her husband to find out she'd been cheating on him."

Crum patted her head like dog and said, "He can't hurt you again."

"I couldn't take it anymore when he stole my keys, cleaning out your shed and pawning it all. I planned to take my cash advance and disappear. He drove me to the beach and started drinking and picking a fight. I waited until he went to the bathroom and ran along the shore, blending into the tourists, jumping in the waves. Crum's been hiding me. I didn't kill Eddie but I'm not sad he's dead."

"Well, someone did and left him to die in the shed," I said.

"I have an alibi; I stayed here last night," Jami said.

"I would suggest you get a lawyer on speed dial before the cops catch up to you. There's a semi-retired one in town who takes on pro-bono cases. I'm not sure he practices criminal law, but he could do some hand-holding in a police interrogation."

Two sheriff cars rocketed into the driveway, lights flashing. Both officers jumped out in unison. I didn't recognize either one.

"Jami Richards, hands up—you're under arrest," one yelled. Both were holding their service revolvers pointed right at her.

"I didn't kill him," she started to cry.

"Don't say one word without a lawyer present," I called to her. "They have to assign you one for free since you can't pay."

"Step back," the cop bellowed. "You're interfering with an arrest. Everyone, hands up. Richards, step forward, lay face down on the ground."

I winced watching her lay her bruised face on the gravel driveway. She stumbled getting to the ground. The fun, laughing, always-smiling party girl had been replaced by a frightened shell of herself.

"Hang in there, Jami. You'll be out soon," I tried to reassure her.

"I told you once," the cop yelled, "say one more word and you're under arrest."

Jami cried out as one of the officers cuffed her and yanked her off the ground, leading her to his patrol car. I heard him read her rights as they walked away.

"The rest of you sit back down and no talking. You, with the red hair, get over here." He pointed to me. "Your name," he said as he took out his notebook.

I was an expert at this game, having been questioned more times than I could count, having mostly to do with other people's problems. My lawyer drilled it into me that yes or no answers were sufficient, only after contacting him. When that wasn't an option, I gave the shortest answer possible. I wondered how many questions it would take before I insisted on my right to counsel.

It surprised me when he only asked for our names and contact information, then the cops jumped into their respective cars and left. I didn't have a good feeling about this. With a rap sheet as long as Edsel's, any number of people could want him dead.

"Next time you're off to help a friend or stranger, I'm staying home," Fab snarked.

"I'll tell Didier," I sniffed, sticking my lip out in a pout.

I ignored her glare and took my phone out of my pocket and texted: *If you don't show up tonight, I'm replacing you.*

I turned to Fab. "I'm staying. I'll walk to Jake's and get a ride."

"To do what?" she said evenly.

"The professor said he needed to speak with me. I couldn't possibly inconvenience you a second time today." Fab hated not knowing something, so I knew there'd be no way she'd leave.

"I'm staying. You might need backup."

"You okay?" I sat down next to Crum. I almost patted him on the shoulder but snatched my hand back, reminding myself that it's the thought that counts.

Fab eyed her rickety chair with suspicion, decided on a change, and hopped up onto an old redwood picnic table that termites lived in.

Judging by the piles of dust, a rather large family.

Face in his hands, Crum slumped down in his chair. "Too much bullshit for this day." He blew out a long breath.

"What's going on?" I asked.

He looked between me and Fab. "I've heard that you two snoop around in other people's business. I need to know if I get some kind of confidentiality agreement. And an assurance you won't call the sheriff."

I held up my hand. "If you've done something illegal, I don't want to hear about it. Call a lawyer. He won't want to hear a confession either, but he'll defend you. And another thing, we don't blab all over town about anything."

"I've never in my life run afoul of the law," he said in disgust. "Follow me." He crooked his finger. "I don't know what to do about this. I figured you two would know."

We followed him into the parking lot to a dull red '60s Chevy pickup, parked next to his trailer.

"When did you get this?" I asked.

"A man owed me money and I took this in exchange. When I got home last night and unloaded groceries, I found this in the back." He pulled down the tailgate and lifted up a cardboard box. Inside sat a foot, from the part just above the anklebone and down.

I jumped back and focused on not being sick, taking short little breaths.

Fab reached out—

"Don't touch that!" I yelled.

"Look at that, someone's missing their foot," Fab said as she bent over and stared at it in detail.

"How does a foot… I mean who…wouldn't someone notice that their *foot* is missing and report it?" I stammered.

"I'd tell you to take it back to where you found it, but I suppose you don't know where that is?" Fab said.

"The sheriffs have to get involved. Because where's the rest of the person? That's the first question they'll probably ask you or, best case scenario, they already know." I grimaced and shook my head.

"No police," Crum shouted. "I'm just going to toss it in the dumpster."

"You can't do that! Wouldn't you want your foot back?" I asked. "I have a connection in the local sheriff's office and I could call him. He's a good guy."

Crum raised his brow. "You two good friends?"

"His sister dates my brother. He thinks I'm weird."

"Everybody in this town thinks I'm weird. Go ahead and call him."

I called the sheriff's office and asked for Kevin, and the harassed receptionist told me to leave a message before she transferred the call. "I think you should cover it back up and I'll keep calling until he answers. Don't go joyriding around and lose it or chance someone stealing it."

"Well this has been fun," Fab said, and grabbed my arm.

"I want to go home and get drunk," I answered.

Chapter Six

"Where are you?" Creole roared from the French doors that led in from the patio. I'd offered him a key, but like Fab, even if the doors were locked, it only took an extra minute to get in; neither went anywhere without a lock pick. He gave me a key to his hideaway, telling me he didn't want me to stand outside for a half hour begging the lock pick to work.

"Over here." I waved from the newest piece of furniture, a daybed that functioned as a bed for an overnight guest or as a second couch stacked with pillows, which was its current state.

Fab and I brought home boxes of Mexican take-out from Jake's, a pitcher of margaritas, and assorted beers. We'd both taken a swim and chowed down on the food, leaving plenty of leftovers to reheat. I was currently working on my second margarita, trying not to gulp it like the first one.

Didier walked in from the kitchen with a plate of food in his hand. He had returned earlier from an appointment in Miami. He lifted Fab's feet and sat on the couch next to her. "Food's in the kitchen," he said, and waved at Creole.

"Where the hell is he?" Creole growled looking around.

"Who?" I smiled at him, making kissy noises.

Fab rolled her eyes and made gagging noises.

"My replacement." He stalked toward me.

I started laughing.

He grabbed my ankle, stretching me out, and climbed onto the daybed, straddling me beneath his body. "Well?" he said, and started tickling me.

"Stop," I continued to laugh. "This has been a bad day."

"You're drunk. This Fab's fault?" He tangled one of his hands in my hair.

Didier laughed and barely escaped having his food upended into his lap.

Creole looked tired. As a matter-of-fact, he looked absolutely exhausted. I kissed him."I surely would have been sick when I saw the severed foot if it hadn't been for Fab. She kept whispering for me to breathe and not to think about my queasy stomach."

Creole's eyebrows went up as he said, "Severed foot?"

"Cherie, why is this the first time I'm hearing about this?" Didier frowned at Fab.

"It's not like we hacked it off ourselves," Fab sighed.

She recited her account in such grisly detail that I put my fingers in my ears and chanted, "La, la, la."

Creole lay back, pulling me into the crook of his arm. "It's not going anywhere tonight. We'll take care of it in the morning." His fingers were slowly making their way up my inner thigh. I kicked him in the butt with my heel.

"Didier," I whined, "Fab told me today that she's not helping me anymore."

Fab glared at me and said, "You are the worst friend ever."

I winked at her. "Thank you."

"She tried to blackmail me." Fab's voice was full of disgust. "She thinks you'll believe her over me."

Creole laughed at Didier. "Good luck." He scooped me up into his arms. "Say goodnight."

"Wait, I want that last bit of margarita," I said as I wriggled my fingers for the glass.

Creole handed me the drink and I downed it, waving to Fab and Didier. "If you could just work on her attitude—a little more pleasant would be nice."

"I'll show you pleasant," Fab shouted up the stairs.

Creole kicked the bedroom door shut, dumping me in the middle of the bed. He pulled the drawstring on my sweat pants, tugged them off, and threw them onto the floor. "Raise your hands," he said, and my shirt followed the pants.

I stared as he unzipped his pants.

"I'll check tomorrow, and if your gardener has been transferred to county, I'll call over and get her some jail perks."

I ran my foot down his torso, watching as his pants fell to his ankles and he stepped out of them.

"Like what you see?" He wiggled his hips.

I held out my arms. "I've missed you."

* * *

Four adults in my kitchen! You'd think that it would be crowded but we co-habitated with little friction. Fab and Didier sat across from me at the island, Creole making coffee. After complaining that Fab's coffee pot made his early morning version of the wake-up drink smell bad, he went out and got his own, taping a "Keep Out" notice on it, along with crudely drawn crossbones.

"Don't dawdle," Fab said to me. "We've got a meeting this morning."

The only thing that consistently annoyed me about Fab was how damned good she looked in the morning: hair tumbled, pouty lips, wearing one of Didier's white dress shirts. Didier dressed in only sweat pants, leaving his chest bare, which gave me a good excuse for a quick peek.

"Brick?" I sighed. "If he wants me there, it must be more missing animals or dead people." He'd once sent us to find a missing cat and Fab never let me forget that she—as a licensed private investigator—didn't chase cats or dogs or any other weird thing someone might keep as a pet.

"I installed an app on your GPS. When you input an address, it will alert you if it's an area to stay out of. If it does," Creole barked from the kitchen sink, "then you tell that bastard, Brick, to go screw himself." As he said this, he was tapping his finger, willing the coffee to drain faster into his cup.

"Oh, okay. We'll drive to a job, then call and complain about the neighborhood." Fab's words dripped sarcasm.

Creole's face tightened even more, though his early-morning look was already a little frightening: disheveled hair, day-old beard, and his blue eyes stony.

I bit my lip to keep from laughing, not wanting to be in the same trouble Fab now found herself in, with not one, but two Alpha men glaring down at her.

Didier stuck his finger under her chin, turning her face to him. "Have you forgotten that you promised not to deliberately put yourself in any kind of danger?"

She snapped back in French. He squeezed her chin, not breaking eye contact. He responded back in a hard voice I'd never heard him use before.

"Thank you, Creole," she said before rattling something to Didier that made him relax and put his arm around her.

"How am I supposed to eavesdrop when you speak in a foreign language? I'm considering a ban against it," I said.

Creole laughed. "Love, it's not nice to listen to other people's conversations," he tsked.

"Humpf!" I glared at him.

I didn't like this app idea already. When the sound went off, I'd have to remind Fab of her promise — would she ignore it? What would I do if she did?

Creole looked at his phone and said, "Gardener chick was booked last night on suspicion of murder." He didn't look up. "Doesn't look good for her; evidence is piling up."

I gasped. "I can't believe that she'd kill anyone, unless it happened when he beat her...but then how would she get the body to The Cottages?"

"Good thing the cops didn't see her reaction when you told her Eddie was dead. Smiling is pretty damning," Fab said.

"She'll be old before she gets out of jail, if ever." I looked at Fab. "Remind me to call Cruz's office and get a referral for the best public defender on the list."

"I'll put in a call for her to get some jail perks," Creole said.

"I'm booking a jail visit for tomorrow," I said and flicked Fab's hand. "You need to come with me, learn from the master so you'll know how to act if you need to go in for a little video chat."

"How are you going to make that happen so fast?" Didier asked.

"My connection bypasses that pesky one-week wait rule." I winked at Creole. "How do I get a connection inside the jail, both men and women's?"

"You don't. You bribe me and I'll do it." He put his mug in the sink and advanced on me. "Got to go, I've got a meeting with associates in a few." He pulled me off my stool and headed for the front door.

I smiled and leaned into him as he grabbed me and pushed his weight against me. As if he knew what I craved, he deepened the kiss, leaving no part of my mouth untouched.

"Be careful," I breathed into his ear.

"Send me a dirty text later," he said. He laid his finger across my lips, and slipped out the door.

I turned and Fab and Didier were lip-locked. "Hey, is this a dress-up meeting? We have to leave early to take care of the foot problem."

"Just your usual skirt-wearing flip-flopped self. Be ready in an hour," Fab said.

* * *

My daily uniform consisted of a T-shirt and a full skirt, easy to hide my Glock in the waistband or holstered to my thigh. A huge pile of flip-flops were in my closet to choose from but today I chose black and tan linen wedges.

"Kevin never returned my call, so I called him and asked him to meet us at the Trailer Court. He wasn't happy," I told Fab en route.

"Another dead body?" Kevin asked.

"Not this time," I responded vaguely, trying to work up the nerve to say, "Just a bodypart."

"Then I suggest you call the main number."

Before he could hang up I blurted, "Found a severed foot."

"I'll be right there." He slammed the phone down.

"I really have to try to win Kevin over for my brother's sake. He might be family one of these days. You need to try, too," I said to Fab.

"So who's meeting us?" Fab hit the brakes, which produced a loud screech, remembering at the last minute that the driveway had a cement bump that someone installed at the side entrance. "What are you doing about this wagon?"

The "Twinkie Princesses" had parked their lime and yellow-painted mobile kitchen roadside in the parking lot for as long as I could remember. I'd never once seen it open but they sent the rent check on time every month. Their slogan: "We fry anything."

"As long as they pay on time and there are no arrests, it adds to the rundown condition of the property."

I never understood why Gus Ivers willed me

the property, other than to thwart his greedy daughter. He'd owned the property for thirty years and never spent one dime on fix-up; everything was in a sad state of disrepair. Since I had an aversion to being a slumlord, I left it as-is under the watchful eye of the professor, while I figured out what to do. I'd had a few offers to sell, but all of them wanted Jake's included in the deal.

Right behind us, sheriffs Kevin and Ivy pulled in, and the professor was nowhere in sight. I hoped he hadn't split town with the rest of the body. It seemed highly unlikely, since his two Cadillacs—stuffed with newspapers, cans, and bottles—were still in their usual spots. The man hated to pass up a good piece of trash that he could recycle.

I barely had my foot out the door when Kevin yelled, "Where is it?" His signature uptight stare firmly in place.

It was hard to believe that out of uniform he looked like a surfer, with tousled bleach blond hair, and was in excellent shape.

Ivy smirked. "Seeing a lot of you lately."

I pointed to the old red truck. "It's under the box in the bed."

"You said on the phone you found it yesterday, and yet you didn't call it in." He lifted the box. "It's a foot all right."

"I did too. Left a message, and you never returned the call. I don't have another number."

"Then you call someone else," Kevin continued to yell in exasperation. "So, Miss Merceau, do you know where the rest of the body is?"

"No, and neither does the professor." Fab related the story in detail.

"You could be a little nicer, Kevin. We could've thrown it in the Gulf and let it wash back up like the rest of the occasional body parts," I said.

Ivy handed me her card. "If you can't get a hold of Kevin, give me a call."

Kevin finally calmed down. "Where's the weirdo who lives here?"

"He's usually leaning on the fence. I'll show you to his trailer." I led the way. Fab skirted the outer edge and leaned against the picnic table. The last time she sat on it, I held my breath, hoping it wouldn't collapse. I loved old pieces of furniture, but not if they were a hazard to a person's health.

His trailer had a piece of screen across the door opening, which stood ajar. I could see him lying on the couch and knocked.

He shouted, "Come in."

I did a double take; the inside was clean and orderly. I had expected it to be like one of his Cadillacs, overrun with trash. He'd found a couch long enough to hold his over-six-foot frame, and he lay on it, huddled under a blanket. When he sat up the blanket dropped, exposing his skinny bare chest that had spurts of white hairs running down the middle that I hadn't noticed before.

"Wait, wait," Kevin yelled. "You'd better be dressed under that blanket or wrap it around you."

Crum sneered at Kevin. "I'm always clothed." He stood up and the blanket fell to the floor. Clad in only jockey shorts, he put each foot into his signature pair of rubber boots that sat next to the coffee table. "See!"

Ivy's mouth dropped open. She leaned next to me. "You knew," she hissed, "and didn't say a word. Give me back my card."

"I'm as shocked as you are," I whispered back. "Can Fab and I leave?" I asked.

"Go!" Kevin pointed to the door. "If your stories somehow match up you won't hear from me until your next felony. If not, I know where to find you."

I pushed the screen aside, escaping outside, and motioned for Fab to hustle. "We need to get out of here before anything else happens."

"Let's go shopping." Fab gunned the engine.

"Did you forget our meeting with Brick? Besides, we always drink too much and we don't have a driver."

"When are you going to kiss and make up with your mother?"

"I talked to her this morning while getting dressed. She's coming to dinner. I have a project for her and 'no' is not an acceptable answer."

"Am I invited? Which one of you is picking up the take-out?"

"Of course; it's your house, too, and you're part of the family. She offered, so I'm sure it will be yummy and there will be plenty of it, since she knows it irritates me when there are no leftovers."

"Hang on to your hat." Fab leered at the young twenty-something next to her at the light, revved the engine, and took off when the signal turned green.

I jerked my seat belt tight and leaned in her direction. "If you don't slow down I'm going to projectile vomit."

"Joy killer."

Chapter Seven

Fab came to a screeching halt in front of the twin bookend sales agents posed on the steps of Famosa Motors. They looked like beach lizards, with slicked-back blond hair, tropical shirts, and insincere smiles pasted on their faces. They checked out the Hummer and went back to talking. They didn't waste their charm when a commission wasn't involved.

We walked through the open rolled-up door of the auto sales/rental business. Bitsy looked alarmed, slowly opening a side drawer.

"If you pull out a gun, I'm going to shoot you," Fab said, and whipped out her Walther.

"How's our favorite little stripper-turned-receptionist?" My voice dripped with insincerity.

In truth, there was nothing little about the curvy blonde, who stuffed her double Ds into a low-cut dress. She sold information on the side; the problem was, she thought nothing of selling the same info to other people—along with the name of the previous buyer—for a hefty tip. She double-crossed us and sent a stiletto-wearing ass-kicking stripper friend of hers after us. One could maybe look the other way if bullets hadn't been factored into the equation.

Brick turned a blind eye to her devious side dealings, claiming he needed eye candy for his big spenders.

Bitsy sat frozen in place and glared until we started up the curvy staircase to Brick's office.

"It's been a long time since the two of us have been here together." I hit Fab with my hip, starting a game of push and shove as we ran up the stairs.

Brick wanted his jobs done and pronto, and had a tendency to leave out pertinent details upfront that would have us refusing. I'd quit Brick for a while over his desire to use me in an underhanded eviction scheme; he failed to disclose that the building was full of senior citizens. I was back on speed dial after Fab forced a little kiss-and-make-up and we agreed to never mention the incident.

As usual, the man sat behind his enormous desk talking on the phone. When we walked up, he ran his dark eyes leisurely up and down the both of us and waved us into his second-floor spacious office that was equipped with an amazing view of the entire lot and surrounding upscale business district. He finally tossed the most uncomfortable seats ever and replaced them with buttery chocolate-colored leather chairs. He'd gotten himself a larger chair to hold his burly frame, which was a well-over-six-foot boxer physique. He didn't box for sport, just to stay in shape.

I went straight to his credenza and fingered through the snack bowl, finding two bags of mini Oreos that I loved but would never purchase for myself. I dropped them in my purse and held up a package of peanut butter cookies to Fab; she nodded, and they followed the Oreos—road snacks.

Brick banged his phone down, code for the meeting to start.

"Sit down, you two." He opened a file on his desk. "I need this car picked up." He passed a picture and a set of keys to Fab.

"Where is it?" Fab asked.

"Don't know; GPS isn't working. I'm assuming the bastard had it disconnected. Once I locate it, you two need to be ready to go. Retrieve the damn thing and bring it back here. You know the drill."

I helped myself to his notepad and scribbled Jami Richards' name. "I need a jail visit for tomorrow," I said as I passed it to him.

Brick had more connections than anyone I knew, including Creole. He owned various businesses and was well respected in the community. In addition to the car lot, he owned pawnshops around the state, recently branched out his bail bond locations, and owned and operated the Gentlemen's Club, a stripper joint in Alligator Alley. He described it as classy, but I wouldn't know.

"One more thing: for safety reasons, no more sliding down the banister," he said, directing his comment to Fab.

I had a fear of falling on my butt.

Chapter Eight

"Your mother's here." Fab nodded to the black Mercedes sitting at the curb. If you didn't drive a black automobile you didn't get into this family.

"Didier's home; you better hustle your sexy behind before Mother snatches him away from you and it will be you and Spoon sitting in the tree…" There are times when I'm so amused by myself. I laughed while Fab gave me a dirty look.

I got out and made kissing noises, staying a strategic distance behind so that she couldn't smack me. I peered in the kitchen garden window, waving to Mother and Didier who sat at the island.

Fab flung open the door and yelled, "We didn't get arrested today."

"Where's the food?" I sniffed, and kissed Mother's cheek.

"I'll call it in when we're ready," Mother said. In knee-length shorts and boat shoes, she looked ready for a boat ride.

I went into the living room and retrieved a large manila envelope off the library table that sat in front of the windows. I handed it to Mother. "You need something legal to do."

She pushed it back. "I'm busy."

"You're going to be good at this," I said, shoving it into her hands. "Open it."

"You're opening the poker room?" Her brown eyes sparkled as she thumbed through the paperwork.

"We're reopening it as a game room. The room can be reserved for private poker parties as long as" — I noticed the pink highlighted page, taking it out of the stack — "there is no cash on the table and no opportunity to win anything," I read. "Do that, and Jake's is not violating the no-gambling statute."

Mother turned her nose up. "No one's going to want to play with no betting," she said, dropping it onto the footstool, disappointed.

Didier lounged on the couch, Jazz getting his head scratched. Fab sat at the end with Didier's feet in her lap; she'd never disturb the cat. "I think it's a great idea," he said.

"There's a checklist of everything you need to do to get approved for a license." I found the paper and handed it to her.

"I'll think about it," she said in a huff. "I'm telling you, no one will be interested."

The front door blew open and my brother filled the entrance. "The prodigal son has returned. I bring fish." He held up a cooler, and before veering into the kitchen, he dropped a duffel bag onto the floor.

I eyed the bag with suspicion. I didn't want to

think about my brother sleeping on the couch and Creole walking in during the middle of the night or in the morning, small talk for five over coffee.

"We should do a barbeque this weekend," he called over his shoulder, walking out to the garage where he had recently replaced the refrigerator/freezer. I told him I'd get one. *How hard could it be?* Once he started listing his specs, I'd cut him off. "You do it."

"Is that how you maintain your pretty face," Brad said, and motioned to Didier's water. "I think I'll have a beer."

"What's up with the suitcase?" Fab's lip quirked in a smile.

"My boat's docked for maintenance. I need a place to stay for a couple of weeks," he called from the kitchen.

All eyes turned to me, waiting for my response.

I quickly blinked back my deer-in-the-headlights look. "I've got a better idea. Stay here tonight, and tomorrow you can have your very own cottage. You'll be down the driveway from Julie and Liam." Liam is Julie's teenage son, who has his thumb on the pulse of the neighborhood, somehow always knowing who does what, and when. Mother and I are crazy about him.

Brad sat down next to me on the daybed, putting his arm across my shoulders. "That's okay, I don't mind staying here."

"You'll have to sleep here and if Julie wants to spend the night, you'll have to smoosh together or she can take the couch. Liam, well…he needs to bring a sleeping bag." Let that sink in; he wouldn't have a second of privacy with his girlfriend.

Brad picked up one of the papers Mother had thrown down onto the coffee table. "Hell no," he exploded. "I refuse to visit my mother in jail. What the hell's wrong with you?" He glared at me.

"What did you do, miss every other word?" I huffed. "It's going to be a game room, licensed by the county. It's what I had planned all along until these two came up with their own plan," I said, and winked at Fab.

"Have you agreed to this?" he asked Mother.

She shook her head.

He gathered up the paperwork and shoved it back into the envelope. "I'll read everything tonight."

I looked up to see Creole standing just inside the French doors. "Mother, make that six for dinner." I jumped up and ran across the room and he pulled me outside, away from the door, to kiss me.

"Staying the night?" I whispered.

"I can stay for dinner, then I have a team meeting, but I'll be back later."

I grabbed his hand. "Hurry, let's sneak down to the beach before we get sucked in to going back inside. Why are we whispering?"

He bent down and I laughed, climbing on his back and wrapping my legs around his waist. He piggybacked me through the opening in the fence and onto the secret path that led down to the beach. It was still called "secret" even though everyone knew about it. At the bottom of the stairs, he deposited me onto the sand.

"This way," he said, and grabbed my hand. "There's a hideaway between the two boulders, we can sit and make out."

"Brad announced he wants to stay at the house—even after I offered a cottage."

Creole snorted. "I'll have a talk with him and point out his choices: Go stay with the girlfriend or I'll have him arrested. No ocean view at the jail."

"For tonight, I'll sneak out and meet you at your house."

"It's time to initiate Brad into our group. Didier and I will team up for a game of annoying. If he passes, we'll get him a bicycle."

"Brad never passes up an opportunity to torment me. But he'll be ready to fly out the door by tomorrow. Fab and I can help in the annoying department." I nipped his earlobe. "How was your day, honey?"

He pulled me onto his lap. "I hung out in a sleazy bar, waiting for a connection that showed three hours late and had nothing for me that I didn't already know. Waste of a day. Later, I'm dragging your ass into the shower to get all soapy and then into my big bed."

"You do have that wonderful aroma of cigarettes and beer."

"Don't flatter me like that," he said, and rolled me in the sand.

Chapter Nine

Before leaving the Cove we stopped for large lattes. Fab gulped hers down and shot up the Overseas Highway. We'd left the Keys behind, long past where the water hugged the sides of the highway, and everything was lush and green. She looked frustrated, having to slow to the speed limit after spotting a speed trap.

"You're grouchy," Fab informed me.

"Is it too much to ask to roll around in my king-sized bed with Creole, even if just for a little while? I snuck out last night to go to his house but Brad's truck blocked the driveway." I begged off early to go to bed, waited until the house was quiet, and snuck down the back stairs. So exasperated, I wanted to scream in the street but restrained myself, knowing the drama that would follow.

"You're an adult." Fab laughed.

"I'm not going to have S-E-X with Mother in the house. You laugh now, but you'd never do that."

"I wouldn't do it with my husband in my mother's house. She'd find out, tell Father, and— although they'd never discuss S-E-X—I'd get lectured on manners and have to hear, 'Oh, Fabiana, why can't you control your impulses?'" she mimicked in a deep male voice. "Why are you spelling S-E-X anyway? I know what it is."

"Really, Miss Ribbon-on-the-Door?"

Fab's subtle way of saying, "Don't you dare knock," was to leave a ribbon tied to the doorknob, indicating that adventurous things were going on inside.

"Creole wouldn't come over when Mother said she was staying. Brad would've flipped. It's okay for him to have hot sex, but not his sister. The best part is, I know he didn't get one minute of sleep with Mother snoring the roof off. On the way out this morning I told him to call Mac and he could have his choice of vacant units."

Mother had fallen asleep on the couch catching up with Brad's life, which I'm sure included nosey questions about his love life.

"What do I need to know about jail visits?" Fab turned into the visitor's lot and backed into a space in the last row, closest to the exit.

"It's like airport security. Nothing metal and leave your gun."

Not a single person milled around, which meant the sheriff had unlocked the door and most of the people had filed in already.

"How many times have you been here?" Fab unholstered her gun and I handed her mine to be locked in a storage box in the back under the carpet.

"Never for the free room and board, but too many times as a visitor. I'm going to leave the money I owe her in her jail account so she has money for junk food, and let her know that if she needs anything to give me a call."

"You know it looks like she did it—fingerprints, hair, and a crappy alibi." Fab was one of those people who thought Jami murdered Edsel.

"If she did, why not do it on the night he beat her? And why at The Cottages? She had to know she'd be the number one suspect." It surprised me that, with all the people who came and went and peeked out their windows, no one witnessed or heard anything unusual.

Fab jumped up the stairs to the door.

"Behave yourself," I whispered.

We breezed through the metal detector without incident and were assigned a cubicle in the far corner of the first row. Fab wasn't going to like that the exit door was in the opposite corner. No quick getaway.

I waited patiently for Jami to appear while Fab paced up and down, which rule number three—posted on the wall—strictly forbade. She checked out each cubicle and waved to inmates waiting on the opposite side of the glass for loved ones who were running late or wouldn't show at all. She had the nerve to pause a couple of times and eavesdrop on one-sided conversations.

Jami walked through the door from her pod

into the visiting area and sat down. Her orange uniform clashed with her pink hair. I waved and we picked up our respective red phones.

"I don't know what favor you called in, but thank you for the visit." She had a slight case of the shakes. "This has been a horrible day. I got assigned to a cell with a psycho bitch from hell. She had a conversation going on with imaginary voices and then flipped out, screaming and throwing herself against the wall. They hauled her to the infirmary for a shot and shipped her off to solitary. When I realized I survived my first twenty-fours, I'm not as scared."

"I put your paycheck in your account so you can place an order next time." The jail had a well-stocked commissary that sold anything from food to personal items. "Did you get assigned a good lawyer," I asked.

"My lawyer, Mr. Porter, is okay. Sucks he doesn't believe me. I don't care how much evidence they find, I didn't kill Big Ed."

I refrained from rolling my eyes at "Big Ed."

Jami waved to Fab, who hadn't stopped pacing. She'd soon be noticed by a sheriff and escorted out. "My only crime was that I didn't call the cops when we found the body."

She found the body! We?

I held up my hand. "Stop talking about your case to me, or to anyone else, except your lawyer." I pointed to the sign that read: *All visits are recorded.*

"Don't worry about me. I have friends who will visit as soon as they can make appointments; the ones who don't have charges pending."

A siren went off and all of the television screens went black. Fab grabbed my arm and hauled me out of the chair. She maintained such a tight grip that, when I stumbled, she caught me before I fell on the floor.

"I don't know what the hell just happened but let's get out of here," she said.

The siren continued. A voice came over the loud speaker and said, "Visiting hours are over. Leave orderly through the exit." The door closed behind us on that pronouncement. Fab didn't waste time, and to her credit, drove calmly out of the parking lot. It didn't matter where we went, Fab located the exit first. Good for getting out of tight spots.

"That was horribly depressing," Fab sighed. "One poor guy sat there and whoever he was expecting never showed. I thought about sitting down and talking to him."

"I think we should have a girls' night, just the two of us. When's Didier coming back?"

"Later tonight." She smiled. "He called on the way out the door, reminded me to stay safe and out of jail."

"Let's walk down the beach to that new restaurant. They have tables on the sand."

Fab picked up her phone off the console and looked at the screen. "It's Brick."

She had trained me to put all my calls on speaker, even though she never reciprocated. I punched her in the arm, making a poking gesture at the phone.

She made a few unintelligible noises, then said, "Send me the address," and hung up. "No fun tonight. We're picking up the Jaguar."

She scrolled through her phone and called out the address, which I put in the GPS and a beeping noise sounded.

"That's Creole code for stay out of that area. Now what?" I felt nauseous knowing we had a decision to make; we couldn't satisfy everyone.

"We'll lie and say we used the navigation tool on my phone. You stay behind the wheel and I'll hop out and do the drive away."

"I'm not lying to Creole about anything. He'll find out, and when he does, he'll tell Didier."

Fab twisted her hair in a nervous gesture, then clipped it in an ugly bun. "I can't do this by myself," she whined. "How bad can the neighborhood be?"

I rolled my eyes. "Take a look around…and we're not even there yet."

We rode in silence. She made a couple of turns, landing us in the middle of a ratty commercial area. Our GPS had us turn onto an access road and bounce over rotted railroad tracks. Judging by the deterioration, the area had been abandoned for a few years.

Fab hit the steering wheel. "I'll park in front of

the building. You leave immediately and go home. I'll drive the Jag back to Brick's and get a ride."

I shook my head in disbelief. "You know I won't let you go by yourself."

Chapter Ten

The paved road turned to gravel right before turning into the parking lot of a long-ago-vacant manufacturing plant. A block-long property, it was filled with old airport hangar-style buildings. They had missing doors, broken windows, and weeds growing up out of the cracks; at some point, the building had turned into a giant receptacle for hard-to-get-rid-of trash. Someone had gone to the expense of surrounding the property with barbed wire fencing only to have some creative soul hack out sections, making the area easily accessible by a car in several places. Two men, who were hunched over in the far corner of the fence, baseball caps covering their faces, looked up from sorting their shopping carts. They checked out the Hummer and looked away.

"Please tell me that the car's not parked in one of those creepy buildings." The roll-up doors were also missing, probably ripped off and sold as a resale item. I wanted to cover my eyes and pretend we'd listened to Creole and turned down the job, having gone home instead. I stared into the cavernous dark spaces, daylight casting a slim shadow to just inside the open doors.

"We'll drive around back first." Fab braked and drove slowly. "Setting foot inside the buildings is the last option."

"Fab, the hairs on the back of my neck are standing on end. Maybe we should listen for a change." My phone wolf-whistled. "That's Creole."

"Do *not* answer it. You need a more professional ring tone," Fab said in disgust. "There it is," she said, and pointed.

Someone had taken the time to park the Jaguar in Executive Parking, or so the sign read. It was the perfect dumping place for a stolen car, or anything else, since it couldn't be seen from the street.

"He's not going to give up." I pointed to my phone. Creole's call went to voice mail and instantly the phone started to ring again.

"Give me that thing." Fab jerked it off a mat on the dashboard. "Hold your shorts," she yelled, "She'll call you right back," and threw it down.

I rubbed the base of my neck where pain started to gather into a full-blown headache. *This is my fault. I should've stamped my foot and told her, "Hell no!"*

"You better hide from Creole for a while. He's going to kill you. Hopefully he'll be exhausted, because I know you'll fight him and he'll spare me the same fate." The thought of Creole's angry face gave me a stomachache.

"Make sure Dickie has me looking my dead best for my final send-off. I wonder where I'll end up." Fab chuckled. "You'll have to rent mourners since I don't have any friends."

Dickie, our good friend and the owner of the local funeral home, would give her the star treatment. I imagined a room full of Florida's finest derelicts hired to pay their last respects. I better make it mandatory that they have to be sober.

I pulled on her arm. "Let's go home. Now."

"You don't even have to get out." She opened the door. "Slide over. When I get the Jag started, I'll follow you back to the freeway, then meet you at Brick's. Try stomping on the gas so I don't have to wait all day."

Just as the door closed, my phone rang again. I hit the door locks and took a deep breath. "Hi, honey."

"When I get my hands on Fab's skinny neck, I'm going to slowly choke her to death. What the hell are you two doing over in the Tracks district?" His angry voice was on the verge of yelling.

It made me feel safe in some odd way that I wasn't alone. "Calm down. The doors are locked, I'm inside, and she's retrieving the car." I watched as Fab walked around the Jaguar, looking in the windows, and breathed a sigh of relief when the key worked in the lock and she opened the door.

"Did the warning beep go off when the map came up?" Creole clipped his words.

I hedged, not wanting to tell the truth, or to lie. "Do you—"

All hell broke loose. I watched in disbelief as an assortment of law enforcement cars converged from every direction, screaming to a halt; police officers jumped out, guns drawn, pointing them at Fab.

Another officer appeared out of my blind spot and banged on the driver's side window. I screamed and jumped so hard that the seat belt cut across my neck.

"Madison, Madison," Creole yelled in my ear.

"Help me," I breathed.

Seconds later, another loud bang and the window shattered into pieces. I covered my face and started the engine, but before I could get it in gear, the door flew open and I was dragged from behind the wheel, thrown face down on the ground, and my arms jerked hard behind my back and cuffed.

"Creole, I'm sorry." Tears slid down my face, knowing he'd never hear me, my phone left behind. He'd be going crazy wondering what just happened.

I heard Fab scream something in French, probably something about the cops' parentage. *What the hell is going on?* I tried to look up, but felt a foot pressed into my back. "Don't move," barked a man's voice.

I lay still to keep my wounds to a minimum, which meant holding my head at an odd angle with a view of the broken-up concrete. I heard male voices, but wasn't able to make out the words. The sounds of hard-soled shoes hit the pavement, going in different directions. Car doors slammed, engines starting. A pair of hands wrenched me off the ground, and I stumbled to my feet and screamed as pain whipped through my shoulders.

"What are you doing down here?" the officer asked. His badge indicated he was with the Miami Police Department. "You Madison Westin? Matches the photo we got back; the Hummer is registered to you. Where did you get the money for that ride? Better yet, can you prove it's yours?"

"We both work for Brick Famosa of Famosa Motors and we're here to retrieve the Jaguar that the customer failed to return. We've got the paperwork and the keys."

"How well do you know Gage Banford?" he growled.

"Never heard of him." I noticed he blew off my explanation.

The way he sneered, I guessed that to be the wrong answer. Out of the corner of my eye, I watched as Fab got hustled into the back of a police car. The door slammed and drove away, another car following them.

"Can you tell me why I'm standing here, cuffed?"

He jerked my arm. "I'm not the lead investigator on this." He had his hand on the back of my head to shove me into a police car.

"I'd like to call my lawyer. His number is on my cell phone inside the SUV."

"I'm sure you would but that's not my call. Now get in." He pushed me onto the seat. "Sit up," he said, and jerked me upright.

"Why am I being arrested?"

"You're being taken in for questioning. Now be quiet." He slammed the door.

I shifted to my side, trying to take the pressure off my arms, wiggling my fingers so that my hands wouldn't go numb. None of it worked. If I got out of whatever trouble I was in, I'd have to rethink working for Brick, once again.

That Gage character must have committed some major felony. In lieu of him, would Fab and I be an acceptable trade? Except, lately, we hadn't committed any crimes. Hell, I even drove the speed limit.

This cop sure as heck didn't drive the speed limit as he wound through the streets, no lights or sirens. We arrived at police headquarters where Fab stood by the back door with a plain-clothes escort holding on to her arm, and two other men appeared to also be in custody.

My door opened, a new face reached in and

helped me out none-too-gently. Fab nodded at me, and I returned a half-hearted smile.

We were both hustled up the stairs and down a corridor through an open door. The officer gave me a slight shove inside a small, uninviting conference room for criminals and sat me down in a chair in front of a severely gouged table and three other chairs. The door closed and Fab and I were separated. There was not much to look at— no snack bowl, or refrigerator for cold drinks, probably a vending machine in the hall. Would someone loan me a handful of change? The room was eerily quiet so that the slightest sound reverberated off the concrete walls. I scoped out the room, looking for the two-way mirror. All cop television shows had them in interrogation rooms. Odd. Not one single wall decoration; only a large white board, markers left in the tray.

If Fab were here, she'd have us out of these handcuffs and doing a swan dive out the window. *Such a bad idea*, I laughed to myself.

I flung my hair to the side and laid my face on it, one layer between my cheeks and the tabletop. I knew my hair was clean, but was unsure about the table. I coaxed myself to relax, like in the meditation CD I bought and used twice. I pretended to be sitting by my pool, enjoying the sun, Jazz lying next to me asleep. I crossed my fingers and hoped this wasn't trouble we couldn't get out of.

The door opened. "You can sleep once we get

you processed and into a cell," a man's voice boomed.

"I'd like to call my lawyer," I said. Cruz's voice rang in my ears: "Do not answer any questions without a lawyer."

"Whichever one of you talks first gets the best deal. You tell me what I want to know and we'll set up something sweet." He eyed me like a cat does a mouse right before springing in for the kill.

"I don't know what the heck you're talking about, whatever your name is. Miami is in the United States, the last I heard, and I'm entitled to a lawyer."

"Investigator O'Neill. Once you've been booked, you get your call. Make this easy on yourself and cooperate." He stuck out his hand with a smirk, knowing mine were still cuffed behind my back. "Tell me about your relationship with Gage Banford."

I didn't bother to mention I hadn't been read my rights. I'd save that tidbit for my lawyer. The back of my head banged up my brain stem. A migraine in the works, I needed a nap, which was the only way it would go away now.

"I'm sure you've heard of Chief Harder, call him and tell him I'm here and mention that you're denying me a lawyer after several requests."

He crossed his arms and leaned in. "You're ballsy, I'll give you that. Chief Harder's not going to walk down here for the likes of you."

"Dare you." I almost winced, sounding so immature. "Not one word without my lawyer, who, by the way, is Cruz Campion. I'm sure you've also heard of him. I'll be inquiring if I can sue for being denied counsel."

There was a knock at the door. O-whatever-his-name-is cracked it open, stuck his head out, and then banged it shut.

"Have it your way," he said as he pulled me to my feet.

A matronly woman met us in the hall; she gave me a disgusted once over, her face fierce-looking. She made me want to step back, but I had nowhere to move. She hustled me along the hall at a fast pace, not saying a word, up another set of stairs and into another room.

"Please, this is all a mistake," I tried to appeal to her. "Would you call Chief Harder and tell him I'm here?"

"You know how many times I've heard that?" She barked her instructions, ordering me to stand on the shoe outline where she snapped my photo. Then she squished my fingers across an inkpad, tossing a paper towel to me to rub off the black ink.

"Make yourself comfortable," she said, and ushered me into a holding cell.

I lay on the bed and curled into a ball, trying to stay calm and do the biggest pretend job of my life, telling myself I was sipping a margarita on the beach. I needed to pee but the only toilet sat in the corner, and the thought of someone watching freaked me out.

I tossed and turned and lay on my back and kept an eye on the crawling thing in the corner of the ceiling, at least it wasn't a roach. I turned to the wall and started counting the tick marks, wondering where someone had gotten a marker. After losing count three times and starting over, I closed my eyes. Days went by, more likely a few hours, when—at the same time—my name got bellowed by the guard and I heard a key inserted in the cell door. I rolled over and almost started to cry.

The Chief himself stood in the opening. I leaped up and threw myself in his arms. "I'm so happy to see your grumpy-ass self."

He patted me on the back. "If you get any body fluids on my shirt, I'll lock you up again."

I looked up at him and choked back a sob. "Fab's here, too."

He took a monogrammed handkerchief from his pocket, placing it in my hand. "Come on, you haven't seen my new office yet. There are perks to being Chief of Detectives. Nice big desk, comfortable furniture."

I struggled to get my emotions under control. "How did you find me?" I sniffed.

"Creole burned up my phone until I answered. He's not happy with you. Mentioned he might be committing a felony on your person.

He blew into the old rubber factory as your Hummer was being loaded on a flatbed along with the Jaguar."

"Everyone I asked to call you sneered at me. Your investigator needs personality school."

"That reminds me, I have to call Creole. Didn't take you long to have my best detective mumbling to himself."

"I don't understand what's going on. No one told me anything. I swear to you we were only there to pick up the Jaguar for *your friend,* Brick. How much trouble are we in?"

The door opened and Fab stalked in, looking like a wild mess, her jeans and shirt covered in dirt.

"Man I hate this place," she muttered.

Harder's eyes turned to steel, looking her over. "You do realize, Miss Merceau, that you owe me—and owe me big."

"Fine. Just ask her and we'll do it." Fab turned and rolled her eyes. Good thing Harder couldn't see her face.

"Did I say thank you?" I smiled at Harder. "Probably not!"

"O'Neill would like to speak with the both of you." He picked up his phone, demanding the investigator's appearance.

"What about Cruz?" I asked.

"He's waiting for court to resume, so he's sending over an associate. In the meantime, he'll be on speaker phone." Harder used his desk phone to call him. "This is just a formality," he said to Cruz. "Once I heard these two were involved, I was certain it was another case of wrong place, wrong time. I spoke with Brick to confirm."

O'Neill knocked and stuck his head in, then held the door for another man who introduced himself as Cruz's associate, Timothy Leeds, and looked fresh out of law school. He nodded at me and passed business cards around the table. He sat between Fab and I.

"I'll interrupt when I don't want you to answer," he whispered to the two of us.

Harder took the call off of speaker and handed the phone to Mr. Leeds, who exchanged a few words with Cruz and hung up. Another man in jeans slid in the door and seated himself next to O'Neill.

"You don't mind if I start." Harder glared at O'Neill. "Tell us from the beginning, when you got the call and everything you saw," he said to me.

I gave him a detailed synopsis of our morning, from when we left jail visitation to finding ourselves surrounded.

"Mine's the same as hers, except that there were two homeless-looking men slumped over shopping carts," Fab said.

Harder and O'Neill exchanged looks.

"We know about them," Harder said.

Fab continued. "I kept my eyes peeled and

didn't see a thing. We never went into any of the buildings."

"What kind of business was it?" I asked.

"It was a large rubber company that primarily manufactured tires, merged with a larger company that plucked off the good assets, selling everything else and laying off a lot of employees. The man who owns the property is old and rich and doesn't care that it's an eyesore that attracts felons wanting to dump evidence. I'm sure you noticed that there are no neighbors to complain."

Fab had her arms wrapped around her body, she'd been eyeing the door and the window. Hopefully she knew we were on the third floor.

"When can we leave?" she asked.

"The Hummer is now downstairs in the parking lot." Harder reached in his pocket and pushed the keys across the desk, then opened his desk drawer and handed over our guns. "You two are lucky these haven't been fired in a while."

"Aren't you going to tell us why you brought us here?" I asked.

The lawyer looked completely bored.

"We apologize for the inconvenience. It's an ongoing investigation." Investigator O'Neill smirked. Translation: "*None of your business.*"

I'd be annoyed later, once I was back home, floating in the pool. I said to Harder, "If you have questions, call me. We'll both be available," and nudged Fab's foot.

The attorney finally spoke up. I wondered if he thought I didn't notice him using the phone in his lap. "Call Mr. Cruz's office and we'll make them accessible."

"Come on," Harder said as he stood up. "I'll walk you out."

Chapter Eleven

Fab and I rode home, both lost in our own thoughts. It wasn't until we turned on to the Overseas Highway that Fab broke the silence. "I saw the body," she said, and shuddered.

"What body?" I screeched. "What are you talking about?"

"Someone wanted Gage Banford dead. Blew his face off. Several holes in his chest, blood splattered everywhere. Brick needs a new trunk if there is such a thing, I don't see how that mess gets cleaned up."

I squeezed my eyes shut momentarily. I just wanted to go home and have Creole wrap his arms around me, but it wouldn't be that simple after today.

"Our car retrieval job had a dead body in the trunk? That's why all the questions about Gage," I said. "I wonder if that ass-clown lawyer of ours knew this was a murder case."

"I'm just glad we're out of there." Fab weaved through the traffic.

"You do realize that without a friendship with Harder we'd be wearing ugly orange and staring through bars and not sharing the same cell." I looked at my cell phone for the time. I wore a watch, but only for decoration; I never set the time and knew nothing about changing the battery. "Ten hours of detention seemed like days. You damned well better be nice to Harder the next time you see him." I started to shake.

"Are you okay?" She pulled my hair.

"Where in the hell was Brick?" I screamed out my frustration. "He knew something went wrong when we didn't show up on time!" I paused to breathe. "Thank goodness for Creole, who is going to kill us. I don't want to go home, and we can't go to Mother's. When she hears Brick's involved that will end any sympathy. She loathes him."

"I can't believe I'm going to say this," Fab said, and made a face at me, "but getting arrested, chased, and shot at is getting old. Want a partner in Jake's? We'll cater to the unsavory sort and discourage the others."

"You know I've wanted you as a partner from day one and you turned up your dainty nose. We'd need a new name."

"We could still take the crap cases, missing animals and dead people—not surprise dead people like today. You know, like the caskets missing or bodyguard for Dickie when he does fancy funerals." She ran her finger along the bridge of her nose, admiring it in the rearview mirror, and smiled.

"Eww," we both said at the same time.

Poor thing, Fab's lost her mind.

"Didier's back?" I pointed to his car. "He got back earlier than you thought. We should've gone to Key West."

"Please don't tell him anything, not tonight anyway," Fab pleaded.

"I'm taking a shower and pulling the covers over my head. Listen to me—it would be a lot better coming from your lips than Creole's."

We walked in together. I smiled at Didier and picked up Jazz. "See you two in the morning," I said, and disappeared up the stairs before he could say more than, "How was your day?"

* * *

When I peeked into the kitchen the next morning, Fab and Didier were entangled, laughing and drinking coffee. She had a tendency to ignore good advice, and I knew the words "almost charged with murder" and "no chance of ever getting out of jail" never passed her lips.

Jazz sat on the island, Didier feeding him some treat Fab buys from the deli. "No feeding him on the counter." I picked Jazz up and set him on the floor; he meowed at me, and stuck his tail in the air, giving me the cold shoulder.

"What?" I mouthed to Fab silently, stirring my coffee.

She gave a slight shake of her head.

"What are you two ladies doing today?" Didier winked at me and put his arm around Fab.

"I'm sitting out by the pool with a book. I'm turning my phone to silent. I need a quiet day." I smiled weakly, feeling guilty Fab hadn't womaned-up.

Before Fab could answer, the front door banged against the wall. "Where in the hell are you?" Creole yelled. He blew in like a full-force category-5 hurricane. I didn't say a word and slid closer to Fab.

"What the hell, man?" Didier scowled at him.

Creole stalked into the kitchen. "What did I specifically tell you two?"

I'd never seen him this mad, rendering me speechless. I admired that no one intimidated Fab, but getting in his face with a snotty attitude would be the wrong move. Thankfully, she stayed quiet.

Creole told Didier in excruciating detail about our little adventure. How we ignored the warning beep on the GPS—along with every single other thing he said about safety—and put our lives in danger.

I gave him kudos for story recreation. He ramped up the drama to where our offense of not listening became a felony. His story-telling skills were on par with mine.

He turned his dark eyes on me. To look at them then, you'd never know they were blue.

"Come here," he demanded.

"No." I hid behind Fab, peeping one eye over her shoulder. "Where's your gun?" I felt up her back.

It took a few moments for Didier to absorb everything he'd just heard, but when it all clicked into place, he turned on Fab and yelled at her in French and the fight was on.

Her hands flew to her hips, and leaning forward, she yelled right back in his face.

Starting tomorrow, new rule: No fighting in French.

Not paying attention, Creole grabbed my arm and pulled me around the island.

"Are you okay?" he asked as he looked me over. In one swift move, he threw me over his shoulder like a sack of flour and headed out the door.

"Don't wait up," he called.

He dumped me on the front seat of his truck, and fastened my seat belt. "I dare you to move," he growled.

He hit the gas. Staring at the road, he flew over to the Overseas Highway, his jaw clenched the whole way.

I laid my head on the back of the seat. "It was terrible." I started to cry.

"You know you're not allowed to cry, so stop it." He ran his hand gently down the back of my head.

"I don't like jail," I said, and covered my face

with my hands to sob out all the fear I had stored from the day before, especially those bleakest moments when I thought I might not see him again without a barrier between us.

"We've got the whole day and night together and I'm going to make you forget yesterday."

"That's understanding of you," I sniffed.

"Did I forget to mention the part where you're going to get a lecture that sets your ears on fire, and if I suspect you're not listening, I'll call your mother?"

"I'd never escape without another torturous lecture. Once, as a teenager, I made her cry and I was so consumed with guilt that I threw myself in her arms to comfort her. I still had to go to my room."

He shook his head. I knew his father was abusive, which was how he met my aunt—hiding out to ride out the storm.

I scooted over and put my head on his shoulder.

"Surprisingly, Brad and I didn't get into any big trouble. Mostly, stupid kid stuff," I said. "If she deemed it really creative, she'd let us off a little easy."

He kissed the top of my head.

"I never did anything to incur the wrath of my father," he explained. "Too afraid. He didn't need an excuse to go ballistic. He was bad enough when he wasn't justified; can't imagine if I'd given him cause."

"Brad and I drew the lucky parent card. We pretty much enjoyed a PG growing up. I'm happy that Aunt Elizabeth came to your rescue. I still don't understand why she never told us."

"Elizabeth was an interesting woman. She led separate, clearly defined, lives and wanted it that way. I think she enjoyed the excitement of living out the life of her alter ego with no one to criticize her. She loved her summers with you and Brad and coveted that time. She would tell stories sometimes; I loved the one where you got invited out for a boat ride and threw the hostess' shoe overboard just because you felt the urge."

"I was five and it still makes me squirm. Mrs. Snow was like a fairy princess to me, so much fun. You know she laughed and hugged me. Ten years later, she died from cancer and it broke my heart. I remember bringing her favorite pink roses to the funeral."

Creole had long since slowed down, and pulled calmly into his driveway.

"When you set me on the ground, how do you know I won't run?" I teased.

I knew if I cut through the trees that granted privacy from the main road, he'd capture me where I stood bent over, gasping for breath.

"Ha! Go ahead," he dared. "Even with a head start, I'll catch you and drag you back to my lair for the ravishing you deserve."

I loved that he always helped me in and out of his big truck. He pulled me into his arms, where I felt safe, and up over his shoulder. "I'm not in the mood to run down the street," he said, and smacked my bottom.

He unlocked his door and kicked it shut, depositing me in the middle of the large bed and crawling on top, straddling me. "You're not going anywhere," he growled low in my ear. One of his hands cupped the back of my head, controlling me subtly but no less surely, as his lips captured mine in a kiss that began surprisingly sweet, and then quickly became outright demanding. I didn't try to soften his approach, but matched his fire with my own.

Chapter Twelve

Fab and I sat in the Hummer at The Cottages, watching Mac bounce up and down on the mini-trampoline she'd set-up in the barbeque area. The girls taking the brunt of the abuse, her rear followed side to side. I briefly owned one, leaving it at the curb for another exercise enthusiast after falling off and hitting my head.

Fab grabbed her ringing cell phone, looked at the screen, and threw it onto the console.

I looked at her, afraid to ask. "Who's that?"

She bit on her lower lip. "Harder."

"It's been a few days, he must have more questions about the murdered Gage." I continued to watch Mac, who'd gotten down on solid ground, hands on her knees, trying to catch her breath.

"How many times do we have to say, 'Never knew the corpse.'? I told the one cop after he showed me the pic from his rap sheet that I'd never had contact with the man." Fab pointed. "Here comes the exercise queen."

Mac waved. "Your brother's out on the beach with Liam," she said, joining us in the middle of the driveway.

"Call Harder back," I said, and nudged Fab.

"Returning your call," she said, and hit the speaker button for the first time. "I was driving and knew you'd want me to pull over to talk."

"If I were a betting man, I would have said you'd never call back," he chuckled. "Did the red-headed one force you?"

I shook my head, *no*.

"Yes," she snapped. "What do you want? Chief Harder, sir." She stuck her tongue out at the phone. She threw a mild hissy fit, swinging her hips, stamping her foot. "We're busy."

I tried to kick her and she jumped back. Mac covered her mouth and laughed.

"Just tell us over the phone," Fab amended.

"This has nothing to do with your friend, Gage. I need a personal favor and who owes me more of those than the two of you? I want you in my office tomorrow. First thing." He disconnected.

"If we were in trouble, Creole would've called. Just in case, I'll text him." I promised to text him about *all* legal issues. He'd decide whether he should don his cape and come to our rescue. At first, I would have agreed to anything to stop the lecture, but after thinking about it, I decided I liked having him as a trump card.

"You got any dead bodies for us?" Fab asked Mac.

"They show up in spurts. We're in a lull right now," Mac said. She looked around and then at me. "Love your brother. He broke up a fight between Joseph and a derelict drunk, ordered Joseph to go inside like he was a child, and then went in and kicked the door shut, making the windows rattle. Brad told the other guy he had a five-count to get off the property or he'd dropkick his ass. Joseph took it well; the next day he introduced Brad to Svetlana."

"I like Svet, she keeps him out of trouble."

Mac laughed. "I also complained to Joseph that he let Brad see his rubber friend naked but wouldn't let me."

So far, Svetlana was Joseph's longest-running girlfriend; some days he dropped his bad attitude and acted human. She managed to stay out of trouble, the sheriff never came looking for her, and she didn't shoot people or pee on the flowers.

Mac struggled into a bright fuchsia skating skirt that matched her bicycle shorts, but clashed with her lime green tank top.

"The old guy next door, who likes to pee out his bathroom window," she said, and tossed her head in the direction of the two-story apartment next door, "he thinks he saw Jami and another woman here the same day Dead Ed was discovered. When I pressed for details, he couldn't be sure, admitted to being drunk."

I sighed. *Maybe she is guilty.* "She admitted during our brief jail visit that '*we*' had seen the body. And I wondered what she meant."

"Maybe she had help," Fab suggested.

"I'll check around and find out who her girlfriends are. They don't stay besties for long; they screw each other over or sleep with the other's boyfriend." Mac looked down, adjusting her top.

"I can't imagine Edsel ever getting laid. What's the attraction? What am I missing?" Fab shook her head.

I crinkled my nose. Neither Mac nor myself had an answer to Fab's questions.

"I almost forgot," Mac said. "Miss January's got a boyfriend. They stay inside a lot. Let's hope she doesn't get pregnant. She looks eighty, but her identification says she's in her forties. Her ovaries might not be all dried up."

The thought of Miss January with a child made me cringe. She could barely take care of herself; on multiple occasions, she had gotten drunk and forgotten how to get home.

"Where would she find a boyfriend?" I asked.

"My guess is a bar or the bus stop. Where else does she go?" Fab pointed to the house across the street. "Maybe she found him in the bushes over there, where she passes out drunk on occasion."

"She found him on the beach, drug his ass home." Mac had a big smile on her face, thrilled to be the bearer of the news.

As if on cue, the happy couple came out Miss January's door. She wobbled on the stairs and he caught her arm before she fell.

"Hi, ya!" She waved her arms at us. "Come meet my beau." Her electric cigarette wobbled between her lips.

"Be nice," I said to Fab.

Miss January's new haircut made her look more worn out and grizzled, although that was a tall order, considering how she looked before. One hot day she tied her grayish mop into a ponytail and cut it off at the scalp. Now it jutted out in odd lengths.

He didn't look drunk, but when we came face to face, he reeked of cheap whiskey and looked one hundred and weather-beaten with a gray stubble that didn't pass for hair even though it grew out of the top of his head.

"This is my honey, Score," she mumbled, dropping the cigarette into the pocket of her muumuu.

I held my breath, eyes riveted to her dress in case of smoke.

Fab hit Score on his boney shoulder, causing him to rock. "Nice to meet you," she said.

Score patted Miss January's head. "Me and my gal here are going to go down to the beach and have a little sip." He showed us the brown bag he had hidden behind his back, liquor bottle poking out of the top.

They shuffled off. When out of hearing distance, I said to Mac, "Have Shirl keep an eye on those two."

"Shirl's gone incognito these past few days.

She doesn't think I know she's hiding a man up in her cottage."

"What the heck is going on here? Shirl better not go all flakey on me. I'll take care of this myself," I said, and stomped over to her door and beat on it with my best cop knock.

The door blinds moved, and several seconds later, the door opened. "What the hell, you scared the you-know-what out of me." She slid out onto the step, closing the door behind her.

"You're in violation of your lease agreement, secreting men inside your cottage. I'd like to meet him."

She didn't say anything, then stepped back. "I don't have a lease agreement."

"I'll be firing Mac for that oversight," I said. "Are you in any trouble?"

"Can't a girl get laid without everyone poking their noses in?" When I didn't say anything, she said, "Didn't think so." She cracked her door open and squeezed back inside like a woman with something to hide, and threw the deadbolt.

"Who is he?" I demanded from Mac.

"She came home early from her shift at the hospital, helped some guy with dark hair and a fine ass in a pair of blue jeans out of her car, half-drug him inside and haven't seen her since."

"Shirl does have a point, you do tend to poke your nose into everyone's business around here," Fab snickered.

Chapter Thirteen

"Where are the keys?" Fab ripped the kitchen drawers open one by one and ended up rooting through the junk drawer.

"Not in there, I guess," I said. I amused myself by watching her pace around the island and into the entryway, still searching. It pained me to end the game so quickly, but I took them out of my pocket and hung them on my index finger.

She stopped in her tracks and stared. "I can't believe you!" She stalked over and reached out to grab them from my hands.

I jiggled them, and then pulled them back just out of her reach and scooted around her.

Fab grabbed the back of my top as I reached for the front door handle. "You're the meanest friend ever," she whined. "You just sat and watched while I got all aggravated. I should've known. The smirk on your face should have been my tip off."

I frowned and made sniffling sounds, screwing up my lips so that I wouldn't laugh.

"I never get to drive my own SUV." I pointed at the window. "Look!" I said, and ran out the door.

"Where do you learn these juvenile tricks?" she yelled after me.

"I lucked out and got an older brother." I laughed.

"Please," she said, and pulled on my arm. "It's a long drive, my nerves can't take it. Next time we're going around the corner, you can drive. I promise."

"Too much drama." I shook my finger. "I texted Creole about our meeting with the chief, he wrote back that if we needed bail money to let him know."

"What do you suppose Harder wants anyway?" she growled.

"I don't know, but could you try your hardest not to get us arrested?" I looked at her and she glared. "You should enjoy life while you can; Creole said he still plans to strangle you. Luckily for you, he's been busy."

"That means you blamed our last adventure on me." Fab grabbed my arm and pulled me away from the driver's side door, and jumped in, hitting the lock.

I smirked at her, holding the keys out.

She bounced around in the driver's seat, lowering the window a smidge to stick her fingers out.

I shook my head and walked around, getting in. "Everyone knows you're the instigator and I just go along for the fun," I said, handing her the keys. "In some cases, it's clear we don't agree on the definition of fun. Don't tell me you don't use the same tactic and blame everything on sweet Madison."

She snorted. "You bet I do. I gave Didier the watered-down truthful version. He laughed in my face, and then punished me for lying."

"You okay?" I blushed deep red. "You know I hear noises sometimes."

She sniffed. "He'd never hurt me."

This was truly none of my business but I blurted out, "Then what?"

"No orgasm all night."

My mouth dropped open, and I started laughing until my eyes filled with tears.

Fab scowled at me, her mouth drawn into a tight line.

"You really need to stop reading erotica," I said, and continued to laugh. "I've seen those naughty books you try to hide, so don't deny it."

She blasted the horn, pulling up alongside a hot Ferrari, and gunned the engine. I saw the man turn and laugh before she screamed around him, flying down the highway.

"Didier's good for me. I don't want to screw up our relationship. He reassured me this morning he's not going anywhere."

I liked Didier and our newly formed foursome and, selfishly, wanted no changes. "The four of us should go out on a date night."

"You've never suggested that before." Fab looked skeptical.

"It will be fun. I'm choosing the place for our first outing. Creole's not going to agree to some flashy restaurant in South Beach where we have to do extreme dress-up."

Her blue eyes stared at me, unblinking. "I'm putting my foot down though. No drive-thru hamburger stands. The place has to have tables and chairs."

"I'll talk to him about available dates and get back to you." I liked the idea of a date night, dress-up tropical style.

Fab opened the ashtray. "I'm happy you keep this full of quarters, I'd never remember until we were out of change."

We sat waiting for another car to back out, Fab tapping her fingers against the steering wheel. Someone on the opposite side came out and Fab zipped into that space ten feet ahead of a car going the right direction.

"Why don't you ask Harder for a parking pass?" I turned and looked out the back window. "I'm not getting out, unless the woman sitting behind us waving her middle finger moves along."

Fab leaned forward, pulling out her Walther and shoving the gun into the front of her jeans. "I'll flash it and she'll move along."

"Have you lost your mind? You can't do that in the police parking lot."

Creole had a new, larger storage box installed—replacing the old one when the key disappeared—just for these occasions. I also knew and failed to mention to Fab that, at the same time, Creole outfitted the Hummer with a more sophisticated GPS. She had found the last one and drove over it several times. He harped on safety first, for which I should show more appreciation.

Fab hopped out, walked over to the woman's window, and rapped on the glass. Judging by the look on the woman's face, she decided not to fight over the space. My guess was that Fab flashed her scary face. The car jerked into gear and disappeared down the aisle.

We ran up the stairs and into the building, breezing through the metal detectors. Our passes were waiting at the check-in desk.

Fab clipped hers to her scooped-neck top, fingering it. "I've never gotten one of these before."

"That's because when you're brought in for questioning you don't get one. The handcuffs let everyone know your status."

Harder leaned against his office door at the end of the hallway, his arms across his chest. His suit pants were rumpled and he'd ditched his coat and tie. He looked better in shorts and a golf shirt; the suit made him look like a down-on-his-luck detective in a noir film.

"I knew you'd show up." He nodded to me, his brown eyes full of amusement. "But you, I wasn't so sure," he said, and stared at Fab.

I tapped her in the small of her back, a reminder not to say anything inappropriate. "Hello, Chief." I smiled, breezing by him, and took a seat in front of a large mahogany desk. The shelves behind him were filled with books on police procedures.

Harder seated himself behind his desk. "Sit, Miss Merceau." He motioned to a chair. "Your pacing gets on my nerves."

The only thing I liked about his new office was the large window, although the view of the parking lot didn't hold my interest.

"You said this meeting was personal, so that rules out the dead guy. What's new?" I asked.

"He's still dead." Harder laughed, clearly thinking his response funny.

Fab kicked my foot. We stared at him, waiting, neither one of us wanting to be the first to speak.

"This is about my god-daughter, Lizzie. She was engaged to marry this jerk, Dane Thorson, and two weeks before the wedding he disappeared." He handed over a driver's license photocopy. The man didn't take a bad photo— black hair turning gray around the edges, arrogant smile.

Fab leaned over from behind the picture, and snapped her fingers, pointing to the door. She and Harder only tolerated one another because of my friendship with the man and it stemmed from the days from before I knew her when he actively sought to put her in jail for suspected criminal tendencies he had yet to prove.

"They planned to move to the Bahamas right after the ceremony," he went on. "Hot shot got a job at a 5-star resort as their executive chef, lots of money and perks. Then he disappeared, never even showed up for the job. Hopped a plane to Switzerland and I hoped he'd never return, but he's back. Lizzie has been mildly stalking him, which worries me — but she wants answers and, so far, he's successfully eluded her. I'd like to kill him, but I'd rather play golf than sit in prison."

"What do you want us to do?" I asked.

Fab developed a nervous twitch and started kicking my calf. After the third time, I pinched the top of her leg and didn't let go until she knocked my hand away. She kicked me one last time, and got up and went to stand by the window.

"I want you to get answers for Lizzie. It would be a breach of ethics to allocate police resources for personal use. The last chief over-stepped and now is banned."

"What the hell are the questions?" Fab turned and demanded.

"You're a woman, what would you want to know?" He grimaced and looked sorry he had no one else to call. "I planned to turn it over to Brick, but he told me none of his men would take the job. Said I'd have better luck if I called you myself since you like me better than him." He gave us a toothy grin.

"That's hardly an endorsement," Fab spoke up.

"Since our short stay in your dreadful facilities, we've both been ignoring Brick's phone calls. The next day, Creole stopped by his office for a friendly chat. Brick stopped burning up our phones," I said. "Is the information correct on the driver's license?"

Harder shoved a piece of paper across his desk. "Here's all the pertinent info. I expect a deal."

Fab stood up. "Tell you what, we'll bill you triple, then give it to Brick to pay."

His phone rang. "I've got to take this," he said.

We waved, taking the opportunity to slip out the door.

"Let's get the heck out of here." Fab hit the elevator button.

"I'll call Mac and have her run a background check on Dane Thorson. He's got a Miami Beach address so let's do a drive by and check the place out. I'll knock on the wrong door and see what the neighbors have to say, worked for me in the past."

"I can't believe how neighbors will rat each other out so easily," Fab mused. "Do you think we can expense a quick trip to the Bahamas to check out that angle?"

"Didn't you hear the word 'deal'? I think if we put in an award-winning performance we could squeeze the information out of a helpful employee over the phone."

"We? Just so we're clear, you take care of the 'we' business, and I'll drive."

I quickly perused Harder's notes. "The resort name is the Ocean Club. Harder made a note in the margin. It says, 'Why?'"

The guard at the main desk asked for our visitor badges. I dropped mine on the counter and signed us out.

"I left mine on Chief Harder's desk." Fab maintained eye contact with the man and licked her lips. I thought he'd fall off his stool.

As soon as the door closed, I pulled on the back of her jeans. "Liar," I whispered. "Empty your pockets."

She jerked away. "You don't need me on this job. I'm not interested."

"Oh," I clucked, "you lamenting the fact that a gun fight might not break out? You're thinking, 'give all the boring jobs to Madison.'"

She scanned the parking lot, unlocking the SUV doors. "Sorry, but yes."

"I don't give a damn about how bored you get. Your skinny ass will accompany me every step on this job and if you don't I'll tell Creole, Didier, and Mother."

She scrunched her eyes closed. "That's mean. All three?"

"I'll have Creole go last and insist he choke you after he's done with one of his infuriating lectures where he repeats himself over and over."

She stared gloomily ahead at the road.

It didn't take long for Fab to arrive at the address that Harder gave us for Dane Thorson. She circled the building twice and slowed this time around.

"There's a guard," she said. "We'll have to park and sneak in."

"Pull in. Tell him we're interested in renting."

It was an older building, tucked into the middle of a side street in South Miami Beach. It had full amenities but lacked an ocean view.

Fab rolled down her window and charmed the sixty-ish man, gray hair, standing next to the gate arm, clipboard in hand. She asked several questions about life at The Palms, which coincidentally didn't have one palm tree. They chatted like two old friends; she giggled and batted her eyelashes. I leaned forward and still couldn't make out one word. Only after a car drove up behind us did the gate arm go up. She turned in the opposite direction of the office.

"If only you had unbuttoned your shirt a little and passed him a few bucks, we could have all the information we want on this Dane character."

"That's plan B."

There were three buildings, which were surrounded by two pools, tennis courts, and a large clubhouse. We parked along the side of building three and loitered outside the electric gate to the underground garage until someone conveniently pulled up, allowing us to walk in behind them.

Once my eyes adjusted to the dark, I scanned the entire parking area. Fab walked the perimeter. "Oh great, none of the space numbers match unit numbers. We'll need the DMV report so we can track the car that way. I sent Mac a 'hurry up' text and haven't heard back."

"We'll come back when Mac gets the reports back, snoop around, and then I'll charm information out of the old guy," Fab said as she picked the lock on a door marked, *Building 3 Lobby*.

"Let's hope he doesn't die."

"I'm thinking a little charm and some money, enough that he won't turn me down. If he jumps on the moral high ground, I'll pistol-whip him."

The way the guard lapped up the attention, I had no doubt they'd come to a deal. "What man says no to you?"

"Happened once, maybe."

"Let's check out the building mailroom, see what the set-up is, ride the elevator to the third floor. You hold the door, I'll interrogate the neighbors." I swept past her into a small area that held two worn couches and a table, the furniture on the shabby side. There were no mailboxes, indicating it got delivered to a more central spot, which I assumed was somewhere around the leasing office.

We rode in silence to the third floor. When the doors opened, Fab asked, "Do you have your nosey questions ready?"

"I'm going to knock on his door first and see what happens."

I pressed my ear to his door, where the only noise came from a television. I rang the bell and waited, staring at the peephole for any movement. A shadow crossed the opening, lingered for a moment, and then disappeared. Someone was definitely home. I knocked politely, not my usual wake-the-dead banging. Still no answer. I continued down to the end of the hall, to the last door, and rang the doorbell. Another no answer. After trying several more doors out of the line of sight from Dane's front door, I shrugged in Fab's direction and gave up.

"Someone's home at Dane's condo—just not in the mood for visitors." I glanced around to see if I missed anything before moving on.

"Let's go, there's nothing to find out here. We've got to find some busy-body to bribe or a so-called friend who won't lose sleep over a betrayal in exchange for cash."

We walked back to the SUV. "Look, your new friend is getting off of work, or so I assume since he has a lunchbox in his hand," I said.

"Wait here—and not on the driver's side." She glared and cut across the driveway.

I wanted to laugh at her. She takes that old saying, "What's yours is mine," to a new level. She's lucky her high-handed attitude didn't bother me. I couldn't kick her butt; I'd have to shoot her and then probably no more roommate.

She put her arm around the man's shoulder and walked with him to an old, but well-preserved, Pontiac. They no longer rolled them off the assembly line, but the black car looked immaculate. Miss Fabiana had a way with older men. I wanted to sneak up and listen, but the chances of her not catching me were zero.

They spoke for a long time and when Fab ran back, I rolled down the window.

"Get me a business card," she called.

Our less-than-professional business card had grown on us. It had only a phone number because we couldn't agree on a name, and to make it worse, we didn't have any ideas. I retrieved one from the console and handed it to her. He backed out and sat idling, waiting on her.

When she slammed the door, I asked, "Does he know you have a gorgeous, hot boyfriend that you're probably not going to dump for him?"

"Surprised myself and told the truth, recited the details as we know them and told him we only want closure for broken-hearted Sally."

"Who?"

"How sincere could I sound if I couldn't remember the girl's name, so I made up one up? He's never going to meet her," Fab sniffed. "If you'll let me finish, Harold is going to snoop around, see what he can find out, and give me a call. I told him pay would be commensurate with quality. He did give me a freebie: Dane calls himself a celebrity chef but Harold thinks he's full of it, says he arrogant. Boasted about being hired at Eden Roc."

"That place gets great reviews. Maybe Harder will spring for a hotel room, massage, and a little dinner. We'll concoct some story and maybe get to meet Dane Thorson." I liked my idea a lot. Too bad this wasn't a Brick job; then we could definitely expense that excursion.

"I have a good feeling this job will be bullet free."

"Harold was a big break for us. I'm impressed." I smiled at her. My phone started to buzz. "We need to swing by The Cottages. Brad wants to talk to me."

"What's up?"

"Doesn't say. If it were terrible, he'd be burning up the phone lines."

Chapter Fourteen

When we arrived, we saw that Mac had drawn hopscotch squares in an array of different-colored chalks in the middle of the driveway. Making a spectacle of herself never entered her mind. She stopped and blew a big pink bubble and waved. My bras were not made for jumping around; they were lacy and meant to show off my assets to their advantage.

"She makes me tired." Fab stared.

"Where did the portable basketball hoop come from?" I pointed to the opposite end of the driveway where Brad and Liam were shooting hoops.

Fab jumped out and headed in Mac's direction.

I waved at Brad. "You play like an old man."

He tossed me the ball. "I've got to run in and get something." Since he had an "in" with the owner, he'd been given one of the two waterfront units.

I stepped up close and shot the ball. To my surprise, it went in after it hesitated on the rim for just a moment.

"Good job!" Liam clapped me on the back.

"Isn't this great? Brad picks me up from school and we do something every day, and he helps me with my homework."

"Wait until he gets all bossy on you," I said as I brushed his sun-bleached hair back. The cut was on the long side and identical to the way Brad wore his.

Liam laughed. "He's done that already. I don't mind so much. He keeps me out of trouble."

Brad came back, manila envelope in hand. "Here's a proposal about partnering on the Trailer Court."

"Whatever this is, the answer is yes." I turned it over, eager to look inside. "Have you talked to the professor?"

"I liked him, think he's intelligent, even if he's not exactly the poster-child for normal."

"He helped me with my algebra," Liam said. "Scribbled out my problems on a whiteboard and taught me the tricks on how to solve the formulas. Did you know he used to teach math to ignorant stoops?"

Brad and I looked at each other and laughed. "I'm glad I never had him for a teacher," I said.

"Crum asked about you and Fab, as in whether you two could be potential girlfriend material," Brad said. "Took me a minute to recover from the shock and informed him you both had boyfriends who would seriously hurt him, old or not." His eyes glittered with amusement.

"That's when he told you, old or not, everything still works," Liam reminded. "I told him he'd need some pants if he was serious about dating."

"Wouldn't it be nice if he took your advice?" I ruffled Liam's hair. "We could fix him up with Mother."

"I don't think we can trick her into a blind date for a second time," Brad said.

Brad and I had gotten tired of her meddling— mostly I'd gotten tired of the annoying ambush dates she kept setting me up on to find me a boyfriend before Creole and I came out of the closet, so to speak. She never took into consideration that, like her mother, daughter also liked the bad boys. Brad and I conspired to turn the tables on her and set her up on a blind date. After that, she hadn't mentioned marriage or grandchildren.

"Since you're staying here," I told Brad, "your job is to keep the crazies in line."

"So far it's been quiet. I did tell Joseph he can't hump his girlfriend in the driveway anymore."

I covered Liam's ears and mouthed, "Hump?"

"If you don't look closely, Svetlana looks real. I feel bad for him. He told me he has crap taste in women," Liam said.

I cuffed him lightly alongside his head.

"I just repeated what he said." Liam flashed an innocent look.

"Shirl has some man sneaking in and out. He

arrives late, leaves before daylight. She's a nice woman, needs to find someone who shows their face no matter the time of day. I'm hoping all this subterfuge doesn't mean he's wanted," Brad sighed.

"You cheat," Mac screamed at Fab.

Fab laughed in her face. "You owe me and I'll be collecting."

"I don't know why Fab can't let a person win once in a while," I said. Fab had out hopped Mac. How did a person win at that game anyway?

"I've got to get her out of here before Mac quits. Barbeque this weekend. I'll assign the food to Mother," I said.

"We'll bring dessert," Liam offered. "I know what to pick out."

Liam took his dessert-bringer job seriously. He insisted on The Bakery Café, everyone in the family's favorite restaurant. He always came with at least two familiar pink bakery boxes, one a sure favorite and he always picked an untried choice.

Brad tossed Liam the basketball and they dribbled their way back to the hoop. Fab and Mac slipped off to the office. Those two, left unsupervised, could lead to trouble.

A colorful plastic pencil bag left on the cement table in the barbeque area caught my eye. Patio furniture disappeared at an alarming rate in this neighborhood, which is why I bought a large table and had it chained down. The cement benches weren't going anywhere. Some people took pride in kicking back in a stolen chair rather than buying a cheap one from the purple-haired woman who hocked tourist gear for cheap around the corner.

It wasn't unheard of for a stray person to wander in off the street and use the barbeque area for their own enjoyment. It ran parallel to the street and offered no privacy, so I had a few bougainvillea planted along the chain link fence. There was no killing that pink, prickly flower.

I unzipped the bag and heard a movement behind me, but before I could turn, a big hand wrapped me in a bear hug. Squeezing the breath out of me, he turned me slightly, his hand around my neck holding me in place.

The man's eyes were fogged and he twitched uncontrollably, clearly in withdrawal. He looked as though he'd been sleeping in the alley or someplace equally as filthy, and the stench rolling off him made me gag. I struggled not to throw up and instead concentrated on breathing.

"Give me Edsel's stuff," he barked. "And do it now," he added, holding me tight against his chest. "I have every right. I'm Edsel's brother, Ford. I want what's his." He breathed heavy into my ear. "He doesn't need it anymore. Could be worth a few bucks. I've got to have the cash now."

"He never lived here," I whispered. I gave up trying to jerk out of his grasp; he just increased the pressure on my windpipe.

"That bitch girlfriend of his did. Jami told me so herself. Said she lived in this cottage."

So that's why he'd come from the back side of the cottage, searching for another entrance perhaps and only finding a bathroom window, which the bag of bones would never be able to squeeze through. He'd once weighed considerably more, judging by the skin hanging around his neck.

He loosened his grip.

I drew in a deep breath. "She lied. Now let me go."

He doubled his fist back and I tried to move, but he landed a hit just above my cheekbone.

"Want some more?" He stuck his face in mine, blowing a foul odor at me. "No stuff, then you're going to make up for the inconvenience. Give me a few hundred bucks and I'll be on my way."

I nodded my head, pain shooting through my face. My eyes were glued to him, hoping to deflect the next punch or whatever else he might do.

"I don't think Jami killed him," the corpse spat. "Did you know he screwed everyone he met? Equal opportunity fuck—men, women, and the occasional underage kid. A lot of people knew he was a piece of shit and most didn't give a crap, looked the other way." He looked disgusted by his brother's behavior, forgetting his own abhorrent actions.

I didn't dare struggle, since it only made him increase the pressure against my neck.

"About my money," he demanded.

Ford yelped, suddenly loosening his grip, and stumbled backward.

"Get your hands off her or I'll put a bullet in your spine. Guaranteed, you'll never walk again," Fab said, cool under pressure.

I knelt to the cement, struggling to catch a full breath, my throat burning.

Ford lunged at Fab in full fury, fingers wiggling. He wanted to take her down, but she landed a direct hit to his manhood, sending him crumpling to the ground, mewling unintelligible shrieking sounds.

"What the hell?" Brad roared, racing up next to Fab. Mac puffed up seconds later.

"Make sure he doesn't go anywhere." Fab kicked Ford in his mid-section—not once, but twice—and ran to the SUV, returning with handcuffs. "You might want to call your almost-brother-in-law," Fab told Brad.

"I'm calling." Liam held up his phone.

Brad scooped me up off the ground, depositing me carefully onto a bench. "You better be okay." He kissed my head, arm around me.

"Edsel's brother, Ford." My voice came out as a croak, and I told him everything he said. "I think the bag belongs to him," I said, and pointed to the table.

He peered inside and nodded. "Probably, unless you know another crack addict. It's one way to carry around a pipe and other paraphernalia." He shook his head.

"I asked around the docks about Edsel, not a single person had a good word. Mostly they had warnings about his temper and how he got off on beating a woman." Brad grimaced.

A local sheriff's car blew in the driveway. Kevin got out, kicked the door shut, and stomped over.

"Why in the hell is my nephew involved in one of your messes?" he bellowed.

"Back off," Brad jumped up and yelled back. "This is Edsel's drug-addicted brother, Ford, looking for money. How is that Madison's fault?"

I ran my hand down his arm and shook my head, a gentle reminder that he dated the man's sister. This might be the final straw; Kevin hated that Julie and Liam lived here and constantly demanded they move to someplace sane. Julie resisted thus far, but I noticed she'd started to run out of patience for all the drama. The thought made me sad.

Kevin eyed Ford who was all curled up in a fetal position. "What did you do to him?" He kicked Ford's shoe, who responded with a groan.

"Fab kicked him in the nuts when he lunged at Madison. He came here hoping to break in and steal, and when he couldn't squeeze his ass in the window, he attacked my sister. Why is this piece of shit and his dead brother allowed on the streets?" Brad had somewhat reined in his temper.

Cottage ten had seen its fair share of drama. It had burned down when drug cooking went awry, and was used as a dumping ground for the dead body of a person no one in the neighborhood had ever seen before. And it had also been home to a nice assortment of felons.

Kevin dragged Ford to his feet and shoved him in the backseat of his patrol car. To Brad he said, "I'll be back after shift change and, if Julie's not home, I'll take Liam with me."

"I don't need a babysitter," Liam told him, standing next to Brad.

Whether Kevin liked it or not, Brad spent more time with Liam than he did, and the two had formed a strong bond.

Miss January and her boyfriend wandered up looking bedraggled, sand stuck to their legs and dirt on their clothes.

She waved and said, "Hi," in a drunken slur.

He belched.

Kevin rolled his eyes and marched around to the driver's side of his patrol car.

Chapter Fifteen

I groaned and opened my eyes when I realized the irritating noise was coming from my phone. Middle of the night calls signaled someone was either in the hospital or needed bail money. I wagered the latter since it had been a while since I'd gotten that sort of phone call.

"Can you pick me up? I just got released from jail," Joseph whined. "I'm at Homestead this time."

"I don't know why you can't get arrested locally. I'll be there as soon as I find the place."

I jumped out of bed and pulled on my favorite crop sweats and a sweatshirt. Good thing Creole hadn't spent the night; I don't know what he would have thought of the early morning jail run. I also wondered why the jails couldn't release people at civilized hours, but I suppose their guests didn't care as long as they were out, even if they had no transportation and no place to go.

I input the address in my GPS and breathed a sigh when it didn't beep that it was in Creole's no-man's land. I planned to keep quiet about this little pick-up, wait and see if he brought it up, then I'd know whether he was tracking me in general. Fab suspected as much and had threatened to have it taken out, smashed with a sledgehammer, and thrown in the back of his truck on his next visit. The only thing stopping her, I guessed, would be Didier's extreme disapproval.

Once I left the Keys, it looked and felt like another world. Gone were the blue-green waters of the Gulf of Mexico and lush greenery dotting the horizon. I was now surrounded by concrete on an efficient highway.

In the past, Joseph chose a bus bench a short walk away from the jail. They were a good meeting point since buses didn't generally start running again until daylight. This time he made it to the corner and sat there with another man, who had his head between his legs. I made a U-turn and pulled up in front of the duo.

Joseph opened the door. "Can my friend get a ride—we got released at the same time," he said and looked over his shoulder. "He's not sick, he's sore from stealing something and hiding it in his butt thinking the cops wouldn't find it." The man's face was black and blue, one eye puffed shut.

"What in the hell happened to you?" I looked him over, wishing I'd turned off my phone.

"I fell," he mumbled, his gaze sliding to the ground.

"Why is he still in a jail uniform?" I asked.

The streets were deserted but sitting at a vacant bus stop only invited trouble.

"I guess he came in naked." Joseph seemed surprised by the question.

The man poked his head in the door behind Joseph. "Please," he begged.

No good deed goes unpunished, some cynics say—and weren't they right.

"Get in," I motioned. "Where does he live?"

"Drop us off at The Cottages, Bungee lives a couple of streets over." Joseph got in the front while his friend stretched out on his stomach on the back seat.

I headed back to the Keys, just over the speed limit, keeping an eye out for speed traps.

"I'll get right to the point: What did you do this time?" I asked.

"I got into a disagreement, guy says I cheated him on a car part. I didn't guarantee it would work, stupid ass should read the fine print."

"Stolen car parts?"

"I buy really cheap," he sniffed, "and sell cheaper than anyone else. Gives me extra money on the side." He looked over the seat at his friend who had started to snore. "I threw the first punch, missed, and fell face first onto the concrete. When I came to, I was already handcuffed. Guy says I beat him up, but he doesn't have a scratch. Cops charged me with assault and various drunken charges."

"You make me tired. You're on death's door

and you're out carousing, picking fights. Couldn't you just run out the back door of whatever dumpy bar you were in?"

I didn't feel like telling Joseph that trick worked for me once in grade school, only thing was I had to be careful what part of the playground I played in for the rest of the year. The best part: I met Cheryl, who was a lot bigger than my toothpick self, and she became my bodyguard of sorts. Our friendship lasted for years until we were separated by going to different colleges.

"And what happened to the man you attacked?" I shook my head.

"Even though I told the cops I planned to press charges, they let him go." Joseph sneered.

"I don't know why you can't get in trouble in the Cove. I better not see him"—I pointed to the back seat—"hanging around The Cottages. Why didn't you need bail, when you have serious charges pending and a rap sheet of misdemeanors a mile long?"

"Yeah, about that, don't get mad…" He wouldn't make eye contact. "I heard someone talking to Famosa about bail and got on the phone before the time ran out and used your name."

Like visits, jail phone calls had a time limit and it was a good thing because they cost about three dollars a minute, charged to the receiver's bill.

It was all I could do to not pull to the side of

the road and push them both out the door. "How much?"

He hesitated. "Twenty-five thousand."

I ground my teeth together. The dentist told me to stop doing that unless I preferred my teeth to be swimming in a jar at night. "Where did you get the ten percent and what assets did you pledge for the rest?"

"I told him you'd cover it."

"You're a dick," I yelled. "I don't care that you're a sick old man, tomorrow you're going to call Brick and tell him you screwed him good."

"But," he sputtered, "what will I say?"

"Try the truth. In case I don't see you again after tomorrow, it was nice having you as a tenant—sometimes."

Chapter Sixteen

"Didier and I are taking a drive down the Keys today," Fab informed me when I walked into the kitchen, her innocent face in place, peering at me over her cup of early-morning sludge.

"No-you-are-not." I banged my can of coffee mix on the island. "Don't think about leaving or I'll drag your ass back here and cuff you to the furniture."

Didier walked up behind me, putting his arms around me and kissing my cheek. "Bon jour," he whispered against my ear.

Fab shook her head, wanting me to keep quiet.

I changed tactic and said sweetly, a hard glint in my eye, "Go, have a good time. When Mother or anyone asks where you are I'll tell them you don't really like any of them and that you're out banging your boyfriend on the beach."

Didier's eyebrows shot to his hairline, clearly not amused. "Banging is a vulgar term," he said, and glared at me.

"The author of a book I just finished used 'swive,' but then I'd have to explain the meaning to most people. Banging needs no explanation."

Didier turned to Fab, rattling something off in French.

I beat my fist on the counter. "Stop with the French. Now that's rude."

Fab stuck her nose up at me and answered him back.

Didier smiled at me. "Of course we'll be here."

He winced and I knew Fab had kicked him.

"Don't worry about bringing anything," I said to Fab. "I went to the Farmer's Market and got all these amazing vegetables for a salad. You can help me cut them up, since I know how adept you are in the kitchen."

Didier moved away from Fab and laughed. "I'll help," he said. She had on her new black bikini and sexy low-slung black and white skirt cover-up. Didier had on black trunks and a T-shirt that made you want to stare at his chest. I wanted to comment about their matching outfits, but it would suck to have both of them mad at me.

"You two act like I don't know how to put lettuce in a bowl," Fab fumed.

She looked hot, even in the middle of a temper tantrum.

Creole stuck his face against the garden window, waving. The door being locked didn't deter him; it opened less than a minute later. He tossed his bag onto the floor and closed the space between us, sweeping me in for a kiss. He took care to make sure his college football jersey didn't ride up my butt cheeks.

"Just the man I need a favor from," I said as I ran my fingers across his lips.

"Favor? What's in it for me?" He put his arm around me and walked me back to the kitchen island where he pulled me onto his lap.

I leaned in and whispered in his ear.

He laughed. "Done."

"I'll do *you* a favor," Didier said, and leered at Fab.

"Are you here to thank me for saving her life again?" Fab asked Creole.

I picked up a handful of vegetables and threw them at her.

"What was his name? Oh yeah, Ford. Brother to the pervy Dead Ed. Tried to choke her to death. See the bruise on the side of her face?"

"Fabiana," Didier chastised, and shook his finger at her.

"What the hell?" Creole turned me around to face him, gently running his fingers down my neck. "Why didn't you call?"

It made me happy to see Didier frown at Fab.

"I'm fine. Ford, Edsel's brother, let go when Fab kicked him in the nuts." I laid my cheek on his, and continued. "That's my favor. Seems Ford's a drug addict. I'd like to question him about his newly-deceased brother. Ford doesn't seem to think Jami killed him and I'd like to know who any other suspects might be. I can't go for a jail visit because I'm part of the pending case."

"I checked on your gardener and things don't look good for her," Creole told me. "I'm more than happy to have a chat with this Ford character."

"I don't want you to end up in jail," I said.

"Do you own a suit and appropriate accessories—you know shoes, tie…?" Fab asked Creole.

Didier's hand slid around to her backside and she twitched.

Creole narrowed his eyes. "Why?"

"Hold on a second," I cut in. "You're a troublemaker today. I said we'd do a couple's dinner. I explicitly said no to suits, stilettos, and those snotty restaurants the two of you favor. I agreed to a restaurant in the Keys, dress-up tropical style, no dive bar."

"Double date?" Creole half-laughed. "We get the back seat."

"You might want to rethink that if Fab is driving." I crossed myself and smiled at her.

"You need to talk to your girlfriend about speed limit signs and what they mean," Creole said to Didier. "Red lights, too, while you're at it."

"I do all the driving and Didier's never complained once." Fab gave Creole a withering look.

Didier drew her to his side, kissing her cheek.

"Come on." I grabbed Creole's hand. "I'll wash your back." Out of earshot of the kitchen, I whispered, "And that finely-sculpted butt of yours."

"What will I be doing?"

"Your hands will be over your head, against the shower wall, not interfering while I make sure every inch of you gets clean."

* * *

I rolled quietly out of bed, not wanting to wake Creole. I picked his clothes up off the floor in case Mother came into my bedroom. They needed to be washed, but I'd ask first. In his line of work, as an undercover drug agent for the Miami Police Department, clean clothes were probably frowned upon. A little quiet time by the pool before everyone arrived would be good. My favorite royal blue tankini hung on the doorknob and a flowered wrap skirt lay on the chair. I slid into them and, on the way out, grabbed my latest read.

Before I got all the way down the stairs, Mother came through the front door, her arms full of bags. Spoon was right behind her with his arms full as well.

"Nice purse." I winked at him. "Matches your outfit."

His laughter boomed throughout the kitchen. "Come give Daddy a hug." He held out his arms.

"Run that line by Brad," I joked. My brother liked Spoon, but their relationship would improve if he dated someone else's mother.

We both laughed. The smile softened the hard lines in his face.

I liked Spoon. I'd met him first and was the one to introduce him to Mother — but I drew the line at "Daddy," and Brad would flip. I'd love to be a fly in a far-off corner if Spoon tried it with him.

Liam raced into the kitchen, two trademark boxes in hand from The Bakery Café. A person had to love sweets to get into this family.

He hugged me. "You okay?" he whispered.

I nodded. "Want to help me get out pool toys?" We slipped out the French doors to the patio. "Why are you whispering?"

"Mom's not very happy about that creepy guy showing up. Kevin wants us to move. Says it's a cesspool. Said you should evict everyone and run it as vacation rentals."

I hugged him. "I don't want you to move. Don't worry, I won't embarrass you and cry. You're welcome here in my house anytime — you need anything, call. You know where I hide the key."

"I want to remind you next weekend is my first cross-country meet."

"Fab and I will both be there and we'll make a big scene when you run by. When people ask who the crazy women are, pretend you don't know us."

Liam laughed.

Mother met us at the door. "Where's Creole?"

"He's right behind you," he spoke up, wrapping his arms around her.

Creole had a special relationship with Mother and visited her at least once a week at her house in Coral Gables. I knew they never discussed his relationship with her daughter, because she was so worried that we'd breakup and he'd pull away from the family. Fab convinced me that if we didn't work out we could both take the high road and act like adults.

The doorbell rang and Brad went to answer. Hardly anyone rings the doorbell; if the door is locked, they go around the back.

I heard Brad's irritated voice but not his words.

"Now what?" I asked. Good thing I wasn't expecting an answer, no one was listening to me, all eyes focused on the front entry.

Kevin Cory barged in and looked straight at me. "Madison Westin, you're under arrest."

"What's the charge?" I felt Fab's hand on my back.

"Aiding and abetting an escaped felon. Hands in the air." He twirled his cuffs on his index finger.

"You can't do that." Liam rushed forward. "She's not a criminal."

"Tell Cruz to call back pronto," Fab growled from behind my back. It made me half-smile. Fab called the lawyer for me, and I knew how much she hated those calls.

This had to be some kind of joke, but I could see Kevin was totally serious. "Do you have a particular felon in mind?"

"Benjamin Hall. You deny picking him up at Homestead jail and helping him to escape?"

"I picked up Joseph and his friend, both having just been released and needing a ride."

"That's not what Homestead cops think. I'm here to take you into custody in response to their request. You'll be held until they send someone down to pick you up."

Creole ran in from the pool. "That's enough. Do not answer any more questions without a lawyer."

Fab's phone rang. "Sheriff's here to arrest her on a warrant." She held out her phone to Kevin and said, "Cruz would like to talk to you."

"If he wants to talk to his client, he can do it at the station." Kevin glared. "As for you," he said to me, "tell it to a judge."

"Can I change my clothes?" I looked down at my bathing suit.

"You'll get clothes to wear at the station."

"I'll make some phone calls." Creole hugged me and whispered, "You won't be in custody long, I promise."

"Stand back or you'll be the next one

arrested." Kevin's face filled with pure disgust, and then he looked at Julie and said, "He's a drug dealer"—he pointed at Creole—"and you bring your son here. It's bad enough that you live at The Cottages."

It surprised me that Kevin didn't know Creole worked undercover.

"Do you have to cuff her?" Brad asked. "It's not like she's going to run anywhere."

Kevin glared back at Brad. "I'm doing this by the book. I know she'll have expensive legal representation that will work the loopholes."

I caught sight of Liam out of the corner of my eye, angrier than I'd ever seen him, arms across his chest. He watched his uncle's every move.

"Cruz won't need tricks because you're wrong about me," I said quietly, and put my hands in the air and stepped forward.

"Turn around," he barked. "Or I'll add resisting arrest."

He fastened the cuffs with speed, tightening them beyond comfort. I'd never been thoroughly humiliated before; this was a new experience and very humbling, especially in front of my family.

Spoon wrapped his arms around Mother, who had paled.

"You're a real dick." Brad sneered.

Julie watched in wide-eyed amazement.

"Look around," Kevin said to Julie. "This will be your life. Even you might end up in cuffs one day. If you can't break off the relationship because it's the right thing to do—do it for your son."

"Don't say one word until your lawyer gets there," Fab yelled.

Didier's sad face almost had me in tears as Kevin led me out the front door. The neighbors were getting a show. I knew that by the time the story made it around the block, I'd have been seen in chains.

Jail! The second time in a month. This was a pattern I needed to break.

I heeded Fab and Creole's advice and kept my mouth shut. When I got out of whatever the heck was going on, I'd be paying a visit to Joseph. If he had gotten me arrested because one of his lower-than-life friends, he'd need to move. He could leave behind Svetlana—she'd be an ideal tenant.

Unfortunately, the ride to the sheriff's office was a short one. I thought about suggesting the scenic route to slow the inevitable. Kevin and I didn't exchange a word. He helped me out and led me inside.

"Sit." He pointed to a bench.

A few minutes later, Kevin returned. "Make yourself comfortable," he said. "Homestead is coming to pick you up, you'll be transported soon. Too bad it's the weekend. No court appearance until Monday, but I doubt you'd get bail anyway." He seemed happy to relay the last part.

I maintained my silence. It should be interesting to see how Brad's relationship with Kevin's sister, Julie, would weather this storm. This might force him to choose between the woman he loved and family. He did that once before, but we got him back when the girlfriend had to be straight-jacketed and shipped to a mental hospital. I closed my eyes and focused on my breathing, believing Creole would make good on his word and get me out of here. Then I wanted a few days with him at his beach shack.

No one spoke to me as I sat handcuffed, my fingers numb, a banging ache in my lower back. My teeth chattered. The air conditioner had to be set on fifty degrees. I wished for two beach towels, one to wrap around my bathing suit and the other for my bare legs.

I looked up when my name was called. Mary-something, a matronly woman whose name was on the door, a couple of the letters missing, snapped her fingers, motioning me to stand up and follow her into a small room to start the booking process. It went quickly, since it was understood that I would shut up and do as ordered. I mentally made a gardening to-do list, never acknowledging the flash of the camera. I relaxed my hands for fingerprints, thinking about which potted plants needed more seashell mulch. My ink-stained fingers brought me back to reality and I scrubbed them furiously with the paper towel I'd been handed. A blue uniform got tossed my way—who knew they had colors other than ugly orange?

Won't be long now before I find out if I get matching shoes.

"Hope you had breakfast. You won't see a cell until tonight. Being really hungry makes the food taste and look gourmet," Mary said, and laughed at her own joke.

I'd heard from several sources that what they passed off as food tasted like paste and was tossed on a plate in a runny, thick mess.

Mary ushered me into a holding cell that was already occupied by several women. The banging of the steel door behind me brought home the gravity of the situation in a stark way. I wasn't sitting by the pool and that sucked. Thankfully, no one made eye contact; all were silent in their own thoughts. The bunk beds taken, I slid down into a vacant corner, wrapped my arms around my legs, and buried my face in my knees. After the first time, like the rest of the women, I didn't look up when the door opened and a name that wasn't mine was announced.

The Homestead cop must have stopped for lunch because it seemed like it took hours for my ride to show up. My butt had two sore spots, courtesy of the cement floor. Finally, a female voice called my name and I noticed that Mary had been replaced by another unfriendly face. I stood up, walked to the cell door, and turned to be cuffed once again.

A male officer with paperwork in hand didn't bother with introductions, just jerked my arm and led me out to his patrol car. The drive didn't take as long as when I drove north. I shifted several times, finding no relief for the aches in my body. He parked next to the entrance, a few steps up to the door that welcomed incoming criminals. Chief Harder stepped into my path and my face almost smacked him in the chest. Cruz Campion, my attorney, gave me an irritated sigh, pointing to his watch. He was probably annoyed he had to venture outside Miami Beach for a non-celebrity client. I knew Creole had moved mountains.

"I'd like to speak to my client," Cruz barked.

The officer shepherded me into a conference room, and uncuffed my hands from behind my back, only to refasten them in the front.

"Sit," he said.

"Woof," I wanted to respond, but I managed to control myself before they added a charge of being obnoxious.

"Keep your answers brief," Cruz whispered. "You know the drill. If I don't like the questions, I'll interrupt."

I took a deep breath and swallowed back tears, biting down hard on my lip. I would not cry. "Just get me out of here," I said. "You've got relatives coming this weekend."

We had an understanding: Cruz handled my legal problems, and I entertained his visiting family members. The first couple had such a good time that word had spread throughout the extended family. There was always a Campion calling for a reservation. Their favorite reminiscence was porch seating for a fistfight that resulted in the sheriff showing up and arrests being made.

Two cops entered the room and sat across from me, one in suit pants and a shirt, and the other in blue jeans. This looked like Good Cop/Bad Cop and the bad one was a naughty looking devil. I bet he had the women licking their lips. The Chief sat at the head of the table and leaned his chair back against the wall, observer privileges I assumed.

Good Cop pushed a photograph across the table. "Do you know this man?"

"Yes…well, not exactly… 'Know' is not the right word…so no." I held back a groan at the dodgiest answer ever. "Told me his name's Bungee."

Bad Cop snickered. "Did you pick up your unknown friend the other night?"

Maybe he isn't so cute after all.

"I only came to your nice facility when my tenant, Joseph LeBeaux, called and requested a ride." I related the details from the pick-up to drop-off.

Good Cop rolled his eyes, not believing a single word. "Didn't you find it odd that Benjamin Hall had on a jail uniform?"

"He said they let him keep it since they couldn't release him naked. I didn't ask if he ever had clothes. He did say it had to do with stealing and stuffing the items up his...backside."

Cruz laughed. "Don't refer him."

Bad Cop looked me over in a way that would make most people squirm, but he hadn't been raised by Mother—and she was better at it than him.

"Hall's associate told us you held him up for a percentage off the top, in exchange he could use your property to hide out and store stolen goods," he said.

"My manager and tenants can corroborate that he's never set foot on the property. I have a receipt for everything stored at The Cottages. We keep detailed records. You should talk to Joseph about his friend."

"We can't seem to locate LeBeaux. He's either vacated the premises or he's not answering the door."

"You have my permission to kick the door down or the manager has a key and will open it. You can call it a welfare check."

"Gentlemen," Cruz spoke up. "You have Mr. LeBeaux's ride request on tape. You've searched The Cottages and found nothing. And no one confirms a relationship between my client and Mr. Hall. You have the tape from the bus stop that shows conversation took place—he didn't just jump in and drive away like other friendly, colluding criminals."

Good Cop stood. "You're being released based on the assurance from Chief Harder that if we have any more questions you will make yourself available."

Both cops looked curious about Harder's and my relationship.

"My cell phone is on twenty-four hours." I smiled weakly.

"Call my office and I'll make her available," Cruz said.

* * *

I changed into my bathing suit in record time, dumping the uniform in a laundry basket and somehow managing to walk to the exit instead of running.

"More relatives coming to town," Cruz reminded me. "I expect the full entertainment package. If you can't arrange a brawl, take them to that seedy bar that seems to be a big hit. I think they come here to see you more than me. Next time you get arrested, I suggest Miami." He climbed into a black Testarossa and sped off.

"Thank you," I said to Harder. "Creole must have some incriminating pictures."

"He never says no to any of my requests, so I thought it was about time I returned the favor. I wouldn't have bothered if there was a chance you aided an escaped felon. One question, how could you let him sit on your backseat?"

"He'd lain down. It's due to be detailed, I'll mention it to Spoon's guy; he keeps the Hummer looking like new."

We both laughed, having the same aversion to ickiness.

"Get me an appointment with Mr. Spoon. He never returns my calls. I have a sixties MG Roadster that needs a couple of impossible-to-find parts. I've heard he's the man."

I laughed. "I'll be using Mother to deliver this favor. Where's Creole?"

"He'd better be in the Cove. I ordered him to stay there until you got back."

I peered up at him and said, "I need a ride."

"Your girlfriend is parked in the back, as far away as she can get from the building while still being in the parking lot."

Harder walked me to my SUV where I said, "We made a connection with a security guard on your case, or should I say, Fab flirted and charmed him until he agreed to help. Older men love her. I know you're here because Creole asked and I want to tell you I appreciate it because I know you have way better things to do."

As we approached, the Hummer appeared to be empty. I knew Fab was slunk down behind the wheel, keeping an eagle eye on the comings and goings.

Harder rapped on the window. A second later,

the click of the door lock sounded. "Try driving the speed limit, Miss Merceau. I hear it's character building." He helped me in and closed the door.

"You okay?" Fab tossed me a sweatshirt. "Joseph's a dead man."

She picked up her phone and hit a button. "Here," she said, and handed it to me.

"Are you on your way home?" Creole asked.

"Just leaving the police station. Before this I had fond memories of Homestead—they host the last NASCAR race of the season and crown the champion here."

"I'll be waiting for you."

Chapter Seventeen

On the way home, Fab told me that Brad and Julie got into an argument, and then Mother burst into tears. Liam refused to speak to anyone. He and Didier ended up going for a run on the beach.

"Look who's standing in the street." Fab pointed, and I saw that the headlights illuminated Creole's face.

"I don't want to be mean, but I wish everyone had gone home." I looked at the cars parked in front of my house. "This is going to be weird, facing everyone after being arrested."

Creole held up his hand, and Fab hit the brakes. "He couldn't wait until I got in the driveway."

"Thanks, girlfriend," I said. "I appreciate you."

"It's unwritten code: The one who doesn't get arrested picks the other one up."

Creole jerked the passenger door open and slid me off the seat into his arms, planting a quick kiss on my lips.

"Fab, you tell the family she'll talk to them tomorrow." He kicked the door shut and opened the door to his truck, dropping me on the front seat before going around and climbing behind the wheel. By the time Fab got out of the SUV we were at the corner.

"You just might be the best boyfriend ever." I scooted over so that I could put my head on his shoulder.

"You just wait. I've got plans for you. First, a long shower. We'll use every drop of hot water. Then I'm whipping up a frozen gourmet pizza and whisking you off to bed early."

"To sleep?"

He gave a deep rumbling laugh. "By the time I'm done with you, you'll sleep soundly."

* * *

Creole and I sat at an outside table at The Bakery Café, sipping coffee. My leg draped over his, I flicked his finger through the whipped cream and licked it off. We stared at one another with stupid smiles. He reminded me regularly that I was "his" and I realized I wanted him to be "mine."

Creole had taken a call from Fab earlier and arranged to meet her here. He told me earlier, "If it weren't for evidence against Jami, there would be a list of people who'd be happy to see Edsel depart life early."

Fab created a scene in front of the restaurant, cutting another driver off as she sped into a prime parking space. Everyone sitting on the sidewalk looked up from their coffees to stare. She slid into a chair, lifted the lid off her coffee, and gave it the sniff test.

"Did you eat all of the pecan roll?" she asked.

I laughed at her. This was a regular stop for mornings when things went awry or we just needed a sugar fix. Trying to choose one item from the display case took concentration.

Fab set my phone down in front me and the screen informed me I'd missed a dozen calls. I turned it off before it could ring.

"I've got information for you two on Edsel. Not a nice guy; no one's mourning his death," Creole said.

Fab gave an unladylike snort. "Great—one dead guy and a dozen suspects."

Creole flagged down the waitress and gave her an order for three kinds of breakfast rolls and reminded her to bring a knife.

"We're going to share?" I smiled up at him.

Fab made a retching noise before sputtering, "Stop with the public display."

"Dead Edsel has got a criminal record as long as your arm. Got an early start and it's all he's ever been."

The waitress set a dinner plate with the rolls on it in front of Creole and leaned down, giving him a full view of her cleavage. Then she winked.

Irritation spread through me and I gave her a dirty look. Before I could jump her and pull her hair out, Creole gripped his arm around me. "Thank you," he said to her. After she moved on, he whispered, "Were you jealous?"

"Of course not," I sniffed.

Creole continued. "Edsel caught a couple of breaks and blew them, ending up back in prison. I read Mac's report and hers didn't mention him terrorizing a girlfriend with two small children who left him to reconcile with her husband. The threats got so bad she thought he'd kill her whole family. He did two years and once again got an early release—bad decision."

"Good riddance to him," Fab said.

He broke off a piece of cinnamon roll and pressed it to my lips.

"He worked on a construction crew consisting of ex-cons. He had a hot temper and was on the verge of being fired. He hung out at a hole in the wall called Dawg's. What are you going to do with the information?"

"Ferret out a few people who knew him, kick over a rock, see what crawls out—unless you have the names of those other people interested in hastening his death," I said.

I eyed the half-full plate, not able to eat another bite. I would stuff the rest in a napkin before I asked that waitress for a bag.

Creole cupped his hand under my chin. "Be careful. Not a scratch, scrape, or bruise."

"Yes, sir." I rolled my eyes. "It's not like we go out of our way. You need to work on keeping the same promise."

"I've got an appointment." He licked my lips. I giggled and he kissed me. "Don't look now, but Zach and his ugly sidekick are over in the corner. I'm very happy he turned out to be a stupid ass because I got the girl." He sing-songed the last part, laughing.

I gripped his T-shirt and jerked his face to mine. "You be damn careful." I kissed him. "There's more where that came from."

I watched as he walked to his truck. Before getting in, he turned and made a smooch face.

Fab smirked at me.

"What?" I asked.

"I'm happy for you, happy that he makes you smile and laugh. You sparkle when he's around. Happier for me because this one doesn't demand that I move out every five minutes."

"I think we're a rockin' foursome. We're not breaking up anytime soon."

Fab checked her watch and said, "Time to go meet Harold Munce, the security guard. He left a message, has info on the chef. We need to do a good job on this one."

"This just got reassigned to being a freebie. It's the least we can do."

I knew she hated the word "free" but she didn't seem upset. Actually, it looked like she'd come to the same conclusion before I had.

Fab jerked on my top. "We should've snuck out the side door. Zach and Slice are headed in our direction. We still have time to run."

I didn't have time to answer before they both hovered over us.

"Hey, ladies." Slice winked. "Heard you got arrested. You okay?" He bent down and kissed my cheek. Slice, like Creole, used a nickname.

Both he and Zach were well over six feet, walls of muscle, ex-navy seals who were currently partnered in a security business.

"Charges were dropped," I said to Zach. It surprised me not to be bothered by smiling at my most recent ex-boyfriend, Zach Lazarro. He hated that I ran around minding other people's business, which was how he referred to it. "How are you?"

"Business is good. Learning to manage my time better now that I have a son. Don't want to miss any milestones." Zach's blue eyes softened and lit up when he mentioned his son.

There was a time when I'd brush his jet black hair out of his eyes, but these days I only wanted my fingers in Creole's hair. I smiled at the thought.

Fab nudged me under the table, a gentle reminder, and said, "Let's get out of here."

There was no love between her and Zach. In the past they partnered up on occasional jobs, but no longer since he and I broke up. Luckily for me, Creole came along to help me move on.

I looked at Slice. "You and the lady D. A. still tangoing?"

"Sigga and I are what's known as a 'hot item.'" He laughed. "For some reason she looked past my ugly mug to the sweetness inside."

Fab made a gagging noise. Both men glared at her.

I didn't see any girl lunch invites coming my way from Ana Sigga, the hard-nosed district attorney, since Fab was my best friend. She had caught her ex-husband and Fab in flagrant delicto, *doing the nasty*, having failed to mention he was married.

"You're so shameful, digging for a compliment about how smoking hot you are, scar and all."

Slice had a scar that ran along his right cheek from his eyebrow and disappeared under the collar of his shirt. Details unknown. He didn't generally entertain questions.

"You might need a reminder, Madison. If you need anything, call anytime." Zach's eyes darkened. "A word of warning, you need a better boyfriend. His job is damned dangerous and will end up hurting you."

My jaw clenched hard and I had to consciously make the effort not to grind my teeth. "Like you did," is what I wanted to shout. He bottled his feelings of discontentment until he'd had enough. No warning, just over.

Fab shot to her feet and got in Zach's face. "Eff you, asshole," she hissed, and hauled me out of my seat to the Hummer before anyone could spit out another word.

"It wasn't so much what he said as the look of disgust on his face," I told Fab when we got into the SUV.

"I don't get Zach. He and Creole grew up together, they were best friends."

"Zach had been convinced for too long that Creole was a drug-dealing dirt bag and when he found out he worked undercover, originally for the DEA and now for the Miami Police Department, he didn't want to believe he'd been wrong. Creole gave him the cold shoulder after he assumed and never asked about his life. Their relationship got worse when Creole told him he wanted me and would wait patiently for him to screw up."

"Any regrets?" Fab asked.

"I mourned our relationship, the what-ifs. In the end, Zach only wanted to change me. Turns out, he chose a fixer. Since Creole, I only think about him in those rare times when I run into him. Creole has made good on his promise to erase him from my thoughts."

"Didier and I are team Creole. We like him, think he has integrity, and he gets along with everyone, he's not a stirrer of trouble. Did I mention, Didier being a ten, Creole's a nine?"

"Nine? You're crazy!"

"You know who else really likes him—walks between his legs, swishing his tail against his skin? He knows Jazz isn't allowed on the counter, so he holds him and Jazz eats out of his hand. So sweet."

Fab's phone rang. She hit the speaker button.

"Where is she?" Brick demanded.

Finally, she'd gotten into the habit of letting me listen in on phone calls without my having to make threats.

"I'm right here," I sighed. "Remember, you've been cut off. We don't work for you anymore."

He paused and said firmly, trying to contain his temper, "Be in my office tomorrow. I've got a delivery job."

I liked the last delivery job—easy, no drama, and great pay. "Where to?"

"Pensacola."

"Forget it, it's too far. Find someone else," I said. I reached out and hit the disconnect button.

Fab wagged her finger. "He'll call back. He can get away with hanging up on anyone he pleases, but doing it to him? I bet he threw the phone across the room."

As if on cue, her phone started to ring.

"Don't answer," I said.

Fab answered before I could finish my sentence. She held the phone from her ear while he yelled. "I'll do it," she told him.

"You tell her tomorrow," he continued to yell. "It's a one-day damned job." And then he hung up.

"I'll blame it on the boyfriend, tell him he said no. Brick won't confront Creole."

"I love that. I'll be using that trick." Fab looked momentarily lost in thought. "I'll go to Pensacola, no big deal."

"Let him send Bitsy. He's always bragging on her man skills. She can flash her double Ds and get a signature at the same time."

Fab pulled up to the guard gate at Dane Thorson's condo complex. Harold stepped out of the booth and raised the arm when he recognized Fab. She rolled down the window and he pointed where to park. He said he'd be a few minutes since he was waiting for shift change.

Fab watched her rearview mirror and when Harold started in our direction, lunch box firmly under his arm, she jumped out.

I took up the mirror vigil. Fab scoped out the property, moving him out of the sight of security cameras behind his car. When she kissed his cheek, I knew the meeting was at an end.

"Another serial slug," she said, slamming the door. "Harold really came through. I had a little chat with him about under charging and paid him accordingly. The story he told he got from Dane's neighbor, an older woman, who never minds her own business. Keeps a chair at the peephole and uses a glass on the wall when either of her neighbors fight. Harold invited her to lunch and pumped her for information, and got the low-down on all the neighbors on the floor. Turns out he likes her, so I encouraged him to ask her to go for a walk on the beach and another lunch."

I squeezed my eyes shut, tension gathering behind my eyes. "Surely you didn't pay to hear about his love life?"

"Where's your sense of romance?" Fab teased.

"What did you get?" Since a nap didn't appear to be in my near future, I grabbed the aspirin bottle out of the console.

"If Dane planned to move to the Bahamas, he didn't tell anyone, didn't even hand in a notice to vacate. He did ask the nosey neighbor to look after his girlfriend's cat while they flew to Norway to meet his mother and get married. Then, when they got back, they remarried at the local courthouse to make it all legal."

"Why not break up with Lizzie? Do you suppose there are other fiancés out there? He'll end up dead and we'll be the suspects."

"I've got a new goal—stay out of jail for the rest of the year." Fab smirked.

I stared at her and we burst out laughing.

"Saturdays, our boy can be found at the track—dogs, horses—he loves to gamble. Snoopy neighbor lady was surprised he married the tall, dark-haired ice queen who looked closer to his age than the blonde with the riot of curls, Lizzie, who I presume was half his age and looked at him like he was a prince. She liked the blonde because she always had a friendly word and helped carry her groceries a few times. Her impression was that the one he married had money."

"Mac reported no criminal history and not much of a credit file," I told her. "He only has one credit card, not even a car loan, and yet he's got a new BMW registered to him. Do you suppose he paid cash or the new wife bought it? I'm sure Harder already perused his criminal record."

I fished through my purse, which always had a ton of junk in it no matter how many times I upended the contents on the floor and forced myself to clean it out; whatever I wanted was always on the bottom. My fingers glazed the spiral notepad and I grabbed hold before it could disappear.

Pen in hand, I snatched up my phone. A friendly voice answered at the Ocean Club in the Bahamas, and I asked to be transferred to Human Resources.

A harried-sounding man answered.

"I'm calling to speak to an employee by the name of Dane Thorson."

"We don't have an employee by that name."

I spoke quickly before he could disconnect. "I'm sorry to bother you but he left this number for contact and I'm calling on behalf of his mother, who is trying to get him a message. She doesn't speak English."

The man sighed heavily into the phone. "He interviewed and accepted a job, and the day he was supposed to show up for work, he telephoned, and his words were slurred and foul. He sounded drunk and told us to stick the job. I've worked in this industry for over twenty years and have never been more fooled by a man's character."

"Any idea where he went?"

"I did a review of his entire application, double-checked references to see what I missed, and nothing changed except that he quit his current place of employment. As I recall, the emergency contact number he gave us belonged to a son in California. You might try him."

"Thank you, I appreciate you taking the time to talk to me."

"I hope this is the last I hear of Thorson. Good luck," he said before disconnecting.

"They speak English in Norway," Fab said smugly.

"He probably doesn't know that, I sure as heck didn't," I said as I made a couple of notes. "Now we know he burned the Ocean Club and couldn't bother to be professional. He's got a current wife, ex-wife—or baby mama—and a son. Sucks to have a broken heart, but Lizzie is way better off."

"We're here! I'll run upstairs and take a look around." Fab was already out of the SUV.

"He's married, that's all we need to tell Harder. Case over." Neither one of us needed a breaking and entering charge.

Fab shut the door and sprinted across the driveway as the underground gate opened. That woman never listened. I tried to follow, but the gate closed before I could sneak in. The door to the lobby locked, and no one was in sight. For several hundred units, it was a quiet property, not even a single person at the pool on this near-perfect day—warm, clear, baby blue skies. Unlike my friends, I didn't carry a lock pick in my pocket; I left it in my purse.

"Just great," I mumbled. My phone had no signal. I sent Fab a text, not knowing if it would go through. I hustled back to the gate, unsure whether or not to loiter inconspicuously waiting for a car to go in or come out.

I returned to the SUV, angry with the fact that there was no Fab in sight.

Damn that woman!

My phone meowed, signaling a message, which was a one-word text from Fab: *Help*. I pocketed my lock pick, this time making it through the gate right before it closed. Last time we were here, I tried using my fake keycard on the front lobby door and it didn't work. I needed to remind Fab to get us updated cards. This turned out to be my fastest time. After popping the lock, I waited for the elevator.

"I'm looking for my cat," I practiced, for whoever answered the door. "That's lame." Thank goodness there was no one around while I talked to myself.

I pondered potential stories. Hurricane in the garage? Boogie man in the hall? If Dane had half a brain, he'd be suspicious and call security. I looked around and my eyes rested on the fire alarm; I used that trick in the past and it worked. The big drawback is that it scared people and there was at least one older person on this floor. I twisted my fingers in my shirt and, since the handle was missing, used my fist to break the glass, which hurt like the devil. Expecting shrill sounds to fill the hallway, I got nothing.

Two men in tennis gear emerged into the hallway. Having nowhere to go, I got in the elevator with them, stood in the back corner, and hoped not to be noticed. A silent, short ride down, the doors opened and they went out the lobby door.

I stared out to the parking lot, mulling my options. Most came with the risk of someone calling the police. Harder would kill us.

Fab sprinted out of the garage. Almost in front of me, she slid behind the wheel.

"Where in the hell have you been?" I was out of breath so I couldn't yell. "I briefly considered calling the police, after rejecting the idea of shooting Dane Thorson."

"Hiding in the entry closet, which nearly had me gagging at the overpowering stink of moth balls. Figured it was the safest place, full of winter coats. Can't remember the last time I wore a coat. I hid behind a full-length leather coat, which was nice but it also stunk like mildew."

Fab took a long drink of water. "I knocked and got no answer, figured the coast was clear, so it surprised me when I heard the shower running. I thought I had time to search the living room. Then he called out, 'Baby,' and I was certain he didn't mean me—I barely got in the closet when I heard him outside the door. He made a few business calls, boring stuff, problems with a food delivery. He rattled around in the kitchen and got another call. He unleashed a long string of colorful words, and then ended the call with, 'I'll be there in fifteen minutes.'"

"Let's get the hell out of here," I said in exasperation.

"I couldn't help but remember the last time I tried to bluff my way out of some guy's house and damn near ended up dead." She grimaced and took a side street over to Collins Avenue that ran along the ocean.

Chapter Eighteen

Fab honked at two men beating on one another. "Why are we here?" She slid around them. They staggered out of the way at the last second, both with blood streaming from their noses, Fab giving them little choice. One swayed and crumpled to the ground, the other man kicked him in the ribs and stumbled to a battered pickup where he lurched over the side and fell face down in the truck bed.

Dawg's, a dingy rat-hole bar that catered to lowlifes, sat in a dark corner under the Intercoastal Bridge. The only part of the neon sign that worked was the arrow; no other lights except the lone bulb that burned above an old ship captain's door. An old screen door, the screen removed, banged intermittently with the wind, the inside track trimmed with large multi-colored Christmas lights. If you weren't a local and you were drinking here, you were probably lost.

"Edsel drank here. You know local bars are a great source for gossip. Maybe we'll run into an old friend of his or someone willing to claim a relationship," I said.

"You do the talking. Me and my Walther have your back. I will shoot our way out of here if I have to." Fab looked down at her jeans. "I'll bet you we're overdressed."

I held out my hand. "Hand me your knife. I'll hack them off so your butt cheeks show."

"I'll tell everyone, look what she did to my expensive jeans," she sniffed and dabbed her eye.

I laughed at her and lifted my skirt. "Surprise. I've got my Glock," I said and undid the strap.

Fab caught the screen door mid-bang. I nudged her so that she wouldn't jerk it off the hinges. The jukebox blared an annoying tune and several heads turned and stared as we walked in. One scruffy-looking man stared at Fab and smacked his lips.

I grabbed her shirt and whispered, "Just because he's a member of the swine family doesn't mean you can kill him for thinking you're hot."

"What will you have?" the mustached, platinum-blond bartender asked—rail thin, bikini bathing suit top showing off a pair of pancake breasts, overly tanned, and skin like shoe leather.

"Two of whatever you have on tap," I said before I slapped down a fifty. "You can keep the change if you'll answer a few questions."

"Sure, hon." Her nicotine-stained fingers

reached for the bill.

I covered the money with my hand. "Answers first."

When she set our mugs down, Fab arched her brow at the beer running over the side and scowled at the woman.

I shoved a grainy booking photo across the bar.

"Have you seen him in here?"

The old man next to me leaned in. His bristly whiskers brushing my shoulder, I damn near fell off the stool. I relaxed my fists when I realized he'd be my grandfather's age if I had one.

He flashed a toothless smile and said, "I like redheads." He whiffed of fish stink.

"Never seen him." She pushed the picture back, busying herself behind the bar.

Liar! Why would she pass on the money? Tips can't be that great in this drinking hole. Maybe I should tell her the key to selling a lie is eye contact.

The old man reached his boney fingers across the bar. "Let me see that, Rita?" he asked the bartender. I handed it to him and retrieved my money.

"Too bad," I said to the woman. Her eyes hardened to black pin dots. Clearly, she hated us both.

Fab turned her back to the bar and rolled her eyes at me.

"This is Ed," the old guy said. "Used to drink

here before his girlfriend rearranged his brains," he laughed. "Are you going to drink that?" He pointed to the beer. "You know Ed brought her in here a few times."

I grabbed Fab's and slid them both in his direction.

"Did he come in with anyone else?" I asked.

"He hung out with the same guys at the table in the corner. Heard they all had prison records. The women didn't hang around long. They all had a heavy hand with the ladies."

"They still come around?" Fab asked.

"They've avoided this place since two of them got arrested on parole violations in the parking lot. Give me your number," he said, and held out his hand. "What kind of information are you paying for?"

I dug a card out of my pocket and cash and handed it to him. "Anyone with a reason to kill Edsel."

He looked around. "Careful who you talk to, you could end up hurt or worse, no one likes a snooper."

I nodded my head. "You be careful, too."

"You know we got a pool going," he wheezed. "Does Jami fry, or free room and board the rest of her life? I've got five dollars that says she walks," he said, only after he downed his beer and reached for another. "I never liked Ed. He peed on the bathroom wall one night. Worst aim I ever saw."

Rita finished with the customers at the end of the bar and came back to listen. "You cops?" she asked. She'd written me off as harmless, but it was Fab that held her attention and she catalogued her every move.

"We believe his girlfriend is innocent and would like to speak to people who knew Edsel, possibly come up with some other suspects."

"I'll ask around," Rita said, and eyed us. "Leave a card and I'll call when I get something, but you'll have to pay. No freebies."

The old man leaned across the bar, almost face down. "You're pretty, too," he slurred to Fab.

She tugged on my arm and glared at the bartender. "Don't waste our time. Call only if you have good information."

"I hope she never calls," I said as we walked out the door.

Fab yelped, moving backward.

A burly man had his hand wrapped in her long hair, pulling her in his direction. She struggled and he yanked harder. When she winced, I drew my Glock.

"Get your filthy hand out of her hair before I shoot your left eye out," I growled. "And while you're lying on the ground sniveling, I'll put one between your legs."

He threw her away and she stumbled but landed upright.

I cocked my gun. "Take one step and you're dead. In fact, if you move before we've cleared the parking lot, I'll shoot you."

I rolled down the passenger window and leaned out, Glock in hand. "Another one of your admirers," I said over my shoulder.

"I don't think so, he called me Glow."

"I know Glo-worm, she likes the worm in the bottom of the rot-gut tequila—lets it go down slow so she can savor the taste. If I had known that, I would've shot him just because."

Fab squealed the tires and blew out of the parking lot.

"I need a shower," she said.

"Let's go for a swim, the pool water is warm. I'll wax you in a game of basketball?"

"If it ever happens you beat me at something, I get a re-match," Fab grumbled. "Beer is the only thing you could order?"

"A margarita and vanilla vodka doesn't say, 'blending in.' The locals at Jake's order beers, most of them with a chaser of something."

She slowed going over the bridge, and as usual, a sheriff hung his hand-held radar out the window. "Thanks for the cover," she said. "I love when you use the Madeline Westin you're-in-trouble voice. The only thing better would have been if you had shot the guy's little friend off and we could watch him bleed to death."

"It's a good day when I amuse you and when I annoy you, especially the latter."

"Have you thought that Jami really is guilty?" Fab asked. "There's no evidence in her favor."

"Nothing more than a gut feeling. I've known her for a few years now. She works hard, plays hard, never violent. A new public defender, Droll, got assigned her case. I called him and offered our services. He didn't seem impressed— then threw out that he was exploring a plea bargain.

"I asked Droll, 'What if she isn't guilty?' And I got dead silence. I waited for a response and got none so I asked him, 'Do you think she's guilty?' His response? 'I never ask my client that question.' That's a standard lawyer answer, so I left my phone number and I could feel his relief getting off the phone. I let him know we'd check out anything he wanted. I don't expect to hear from him."

"If he's like most public servants, he's got a caseload for two people," Fab reminded.

"His idea of a plea bargain is probably life in prison over death. If the court believes she murdered Edsel, then I highly doubt she'll ever see her family again except from behind bars. I don't know what good it does if I'm the only believer."

Chapter Nineteen

Fab pressured me into playing nice with Brick and taking the damn delivery job. I coerced her into coming along with the philosophy that what Brick didn't know, he couldn't complain about until he got the bill. He ended up delaying the trip by a day since the Bugatti hadn't arrived and I refused a ten-hour ride along in a hauler with the car.

To make sure there weren't any misunderstandings, I purchased two tickets to Panama City Beach and booked 5-star hotel accommodations. When Brick mentioned Bitsy would make all the arrangements, I laughed and told him, "No, thanks." I rejected the help, knowing she might pick a crummy motel for which I'd be subjected to endless complaining from my travel partner. Brick had a driver at the airport to take us to the hotel, where he'd made a rental car available.

We arrived the night before and indulged in massages and room service. That's when I found out Fab's ugly little secret: She liked horror films and found one on the pay channel she hadn't seen before. I covered my ears, turned away, and read a book.

"The auto transporter is downstairs waiting, the Bugatti loaded on the flatbed. This shouldn't take any longer than two hours," I said to Fab.

"I'm coming along. I'll hide in the back seat."

"Last time I did one of these deliveries the guard checked my car before I got out. You stay here and behave yourself. That's code for 'don't shoot anyone.' Get another massage."

"Give me the address, just in case." She wiggled her fingers.

I handed her a piece of hotel stationary that had the pertinent information. "I'll be fine. The last one went smoothly. I was escorted in, signed docs, collected cash, and left."

At least I'll get to drive the rental car, I thought. That would have been impossible if Fab had been along. I pulled out of the hotel driveway and waved to the driver, pulling in front of him for the half-hour drive along the oceanfront panhandle. I ran my hand over the white leather, which did not have a single food or soda stain. Brick had a cherry red two-seater convertible Mercedes delivered as my rental car. His rich clients wouldn't find it amusing if I arrived in an old Buick, blowing smoke.

There was little traffic on the highway, which made it easy to enjoy the scenery as I approached the exclusive community. It surprised me when I pulled up in front of an ugly dark yellow castle on the beach, complete with turrets. A solid-wood ten-foot fence ran across the front of the property, including the driveway. Before I could cut the engine, a man appeared, arms across his barrel chest, glaring at me. Holding his hand up, he motioned for me to stay in the car. He accessorized his tropical shorts and shirt with a shoulder holster.

He exchanged a few words with the driver of the transporter. Suddenly the fence opened, he turned, and directed me inside ahead of the delivery truck. I grabbed the briefcase off the seat courtesy of Brick, which held the paperwork.

The guard opened the door. "Welcome, Miss Westin. Step out." He held out his hand, indicating the briefcase. He took it and opened it for inspection using the hood of the Mercedes — which I found disrespectful to the car. He thumbed through and handed it back.

"I'm Gunner. Put your hands on the hood."

"For what reason?" *What's with rich people?*

"Security. Just a quick check for weapons." His smile indicated he enjoyed this part of the job.

I took a step back. "Do not touch me."

"It will only take a second. Unless you have something to hide."

His smile made my skin crawl.

"I'd hate to report your lack of cooperation back to your employer. He may have lax standards, but we do not. Do not make me tell you again."

I stepped back closer to the car and my hand reached for the handle. "I'm leaving," I said.

His eyes were now beady brown. "It's a cursory pat down to determine if you're packing."

I lifted my navy mid-thigh full skirt to my waist—thankful I'd worn pretty black lace bikini underwear that showed nothing—did a twirl, and shoved my skirt down. "Satisfied?"

He pointed to my navy and white short boxy jacket. I unhooked it and pulled it open and down to my waist, turning around. My black demi bra showed off my assets and kept my nipples covered. I officially hated this job.

I'd never want to be left alone with Gunner. I fiddled with the hooks and got myself dressed. We stood silently, watching the car being unloaded. The driver parked it into its assigned space in the six-car garage. Gunner grabbed my arm, his fingers digging deep, which would leave a bruise. I jerked away, and was surprised he let me.

"Follow me."

The double-door entry opened into a stark white living space that overlooked the water. The furniture, rugs, and accents were all white; the only color, if it could be called that, was the chrome accents on the furniture. The room was devoid of personal items, sterile and ice-cold looking. Standing at the open patio doors was a man who I assumed was the client, Anthony Dunbar, jet black hair, emotionless, chilly dark eyes.

"Sit." He indicated an uncomfortable straight-back dining room chair, pulled back from the square glass table.

Mr. Dunbar and Gunner apparently attended the same charm school. This was nothing like my first experience. I briefly entertained the idea of kicking off my heels and running for the door.

I set the briefcase on the table, snapped the locks, and removed the paperwork and the exquisite Mont Blanc pen the client got to keep. I held it out to him.

"Sit down," he growled. "I'm not signing anything until my mechanic goes over the car and makes sure I'm getting what I paid for. Make yourself comfortable, it will be a few hours."

I suddenly felt like a prisoner, no longer feeling the protection of Brick. "I'll leave you my phone number and you can call me when you're ready to sign."

"I'm not going to tell you again." He pointed to the chair. "Now give me the keys."

"Per Mr. Famosa's orders, I'm not supposed to relinquish the keys until the paperwork has been signed." I struggled to keep the fear out of my voice.

He advanced on me, hand out; and, frankly, he scared me.

"Give them to me."

Gunner cleared his throat. "Boss, I already turned them over to Victor, he's got the Bugatti jacked up already." Putting his hand on my shoulder, he shoved me down hard on the chair.

What the heck was happening? This was supposed to be a simple delivery job. I would pass on to my successor a word of warning: Never leave their keys in the briefcase.

Dunbar nodded. "Make sure she doesn't go anywhere."

He stormed from the room.

"Do you mind if I call my family and let them know I'll be late?" I asked Gunner.

"You can call them when you leave."

He had a threatening stance, arms at his side, flexing his hands into fists. "Bathroom is next to the bar. If you set one foot outside, the alarm will go off, and we wouldn't want the guard to shoot you. Your every move will be monitored."

"This is kidnapping."

"Such a harsh word." He shook his finger and left through the same door as his boss, a key twisting in the lock.

Damn. I'd thrown my phone in the briefcase and short stuff took it with him on his way out. I hated this chair and had only been sitting here a few minutes. I stood back from the open doors, hoping the fresh, warm beach air would have a calming effect on my nerves. I wandered around the room, running a finger over everything, every so often checking for dust and not finding any. I helped myself to a bottle of water from the bar and, of course, he had the brand I despised because it tasted like dirt.

As much as it might be fun to open the cupboards, I restrained myself; I didn't want another visit from Gunner. I pushed an armchair in front of the door. There wasn't a single throw pillow in the room, unlike at my house where I had several on each chair, most of them with a painted tropical design.

I kicked my leg like I had a nervous tick, careful to make sure I didn't breach the threshold, unlike Fab, who would've vaulted the fence already, leaving Gunner in a heap on the floor. How long would it take for Fab to realize that something had gone wrong? Then what? She could hardly storm the castle.

The door flew open and Gunner filled the doorway. "You were told to stay inside."

"I am inside." The space between me and the door had to be at least two feet. "How about letting me sit out by the pool?"

He flipped the chair around, and in one swift move, I ended up back on the dining room chair. He whipped out zip ties.

I knew where this was going—I was about to be tied to a chair for hours. "I have to go to the bathroom."

"You should've thought of that before acting like a willful child." He jerked my arms behind me.

"Fine, I'll pee on the chair." I wasn't going to resist even if I could, this had to be over soon.

"There's the bathroom," he said, and pointed. He looked at his watch. "You've got two minutes."

I slammed the door behind me and pushed the lock. I peed first, in case I ran out of time, and then sprinkled cold water on my face. No escaping through the bathroom window since there wasn't one.

Gunner knocked on the door. "Time's up. Come out or I'll kick the door in."

"I'm not done yet."

"Okay, if that's the way you want it. Stand back. On a count of three, the door will be open. It will be your fault if you end up unconscious."

I reached over and unlocked the door. A lot of people—well a few, anyway—knew I was here. How could they hurt me, or worse?

"If you let me sit on the couch, I promise not to move."

"No. You should've thought of that before dicking me around. I've got better things to do than to babysit." He placed the dining chair in the middle of the room and fastened my right wrist to its arm.

I moved my wrist and the plastic cut into my skin. "This is too tight."

"Then don't move." He twisted his fingers in my hair, pulling until I yelped. A strand got caught in his ring and he yanked it out, making me wince. "I'd better not have to come back." He slammed out of the room.

Whoever designed this chair should be shot. I don't know how long I sat without fidgeting but it had to have been a record. I couldn't relax because the top of the chair hit at the base of my skull. I misjudged the size of the seat and, squirming around, my butt slipped to the floor and tipped the chair at an odd angle. A sharp pain let me know that the zip tie had embedded in my skin, which started to bleed. It made me smile half-heartedly to see a few drops of blood dribble on the pristine marble floor. No getting comfortable now.

I lay there for what seemed like a long time, pressing my temple against the cold floor, listening to my stomach rumble. If Dunbar had someone monitoring the room, they didn't have any sympathy for my situation. I began to doubt if I'd ever be allowed to leave in one piece.

Why? Did Brick screw Dunbar? Would I be a casualty? I shuddered at what could happen if the answer was yes. The door banged opened, and I heard the footsteps of more than one person. I didn't say a word.

"I want this floor cleaned up now," Dunbar barked, walking around me. "Get her a Band-Aid."

Gunner leaned down and nicked my skin when he cut the tie with a switchblade. "Get up."

As hard as I tried, I couldn't suppress the

small scream.

"Looks like you'll be spending the night," Dunbar informed me.

"I'm the delivery girl," I pleaded with him. "Let me go and take your issues up with Mr. Famosa. I'm of no use to you." I rubbed my wrist.

"I disagree." He gave me a tight smile.

Without thinking, I blurted, "You're a piece of shit."

He cleared the space between us and slapped my cheek so hard that my head whiplashed to the side. "You will speak to me with respect, do you understand me? Your response better be, 'Yes, sir.'"

I blinked several times, my brain feeling foggy.

"Yes, sir," I mumbled.

"Look at me—and louder," he boomed.

I looked into his hard cold eyes, which sent a shiver through me.

"Yes, sir."

"Put her on the patio and tie her to a chair. I don't want any more mess in my house."

Gunner shoved me into the bathroom. "Hurry up and don't close the door."

My doubts about ever being released were escalating. I washed the dried blood off my arm and fresh blood pooled around the gash. Gunner came back, throwing down a gauze bandage. He unscrewed the top off a bottle, but I couldn't see the label. He held my arm over the sink and poured the clear liquid over my skin.

I screamed.

"This way it won't get infected." He unrolled the gauze and rolled it around my wrist.

Tears leaked out of the corners of my eyes.

"You got your wish. You're going to get to sit outside. Go ahead and run, you'll be very sorry."

I had all of the smart-ass sucked out of me. I didn't make eye contact, just walked ahead of him and sat in a chaise, hoping he'd leave me there.

His eyebrows went up at my choice of furniture but he didn't say anything.

"I'm hungry." My voice was just above a whisper.

"You get one bottle of water and that's it. You should've thought about food before making Mr. Dunbar mad."

"I've done nothing to deserve this kind of treatment and you know it. Your mother would be so proud."

"Say one more word and I'll gag you." He zip tied my good arm, this time not quite as tight, I tested it and found some play. He came back and threw a bottle of water onto my lap. I didn't say a word, and stared straight ahead.

"This is your last chance," he said quietly. A few moments later, I heard his footsteps retreating across the marble floor.

I turned on my side and curled into a ball, closing my eyes.

Chapter Twenty

"What the hell? I'm worried about you and you're asleep."

My eyes flew open to find Fab crouched down by the side of the chaise, the last rays of daylight slipping away.

She ran her hand over my bandaged wrist. "What's going on?"

"Ow. Keep your voice down." Whatever Gunner had poured on it had taken forever to stop burning. "Get out of here before you get caught, and go get help."

She slid a pocketknife from her jeans and cut the tie. "We've got three minutes before the security cameras go back on. I recognized the system and got a little help. Follow directly behind me, nose to my back, and they'll never know how you got out of here."

My lip quivered as she helped me up. "Did I tell you I'm very happy to see you?"

"Hurry up, we're running out of time. I'm going to remind you of your gratitude later."

At the far end of the property, a second gate stood open about a few inches. We barely cleared the opening, when the motor on the fence whirred and the backyard floodlights came on all at once. The exterior of the house was awash in lights, including along the street.

"No car?" I looked at the empty street. "Run! Leave me behind and get help." I was headed for a panic attack at the thought of getting caught.

Fab grabbed my hand. "Move your ass." We jumped into the ivy, a four-foot wide strip that ran along the front of the house. From behind a tree, she pushed a baby blue Vespa to the street and hopped on.

"Don't just stand there," she said.

I slid on behind her. "Where did you get this?"

"I…uh…borrowed it."

"You stole it?" I hissed.

She stomped on the gas, and for something I thought was a bicycle with a motor, it shot down the road.

I wrapped my arms around her middle. "I'm in awe," I whispered in her ear. I hid my face in her back, afraid to look. She gained speed as we rolled along the oceanfront in the pitch dark. I said a silent prayer, knowing we were about to die, run over by a large auto that didn't give a damn—or worse, Gunner had tracked us. Since talking was impossible, I held on for dear life. Taking a quick peek back, the wind slapping my face, something thumped the top of my head and I hid my face again.

Fab surprised me when she put on her signal and pulled into a convenience store and whipped out her phone. "I've got to send a text and then we're off. We don't want to stay here any longer than necessary."

"We missed our flight."

"Did you hit your head? We still have a hotel room." She smacked my butt. "Let's go." She merged back onto the highway and pushed the scooter to sixty. *Who knew?*

I shook with relief at the sight of the hotel. Fab blew past the driveway—what was she up to now? Special parking for scooters? She circled around to the far corner and followed a path that ran down to the beach. I raised my eyebrows when she pushed it around the back of a Tiki Shack, parking it next to its cousin scooters.

"I had to return it. I don't want to face charges of grand theft scooter."

"That would blow your bad-ass image." I wanted to hug her, but more than that, I wanted to be safe inside the hotel room.

"Does Dickhead Client know which hotel you're staying at?" Fab grabbed my arm.

"I didn't tell anyone, only gave Mother the information. I'm happy that I left you the info, ignoring Brick's demand that you not know the location. Screw him."

True to form, Fab knew how to get around the building without using the front door and traipsing through the lobby.

"This time, I was the one with the bad feeling," Fab said, leading me around the pool area, through some ground cover and into a service elevator. When the doors opened on our floor, she looked out and scanned the hallway.

I breathed a sigh of relief when she slammed the room door shut and threw the bolts.

She turned and faced me. "Why do you have a bruise on your cheek?"

"Dunbar hit me. Didn't like my attitude," I said as Fab helped me with the hooks on my jacket. I shrugged it off and tossed it onto a chair. "Order me a pitcher of margaritas and an enchilada. I'm in desperate need of a shower." I headed to the bathroom, only stopping to step out of my skirt and kick it out of the way.

The water gushed over me in a waterfall effect. I stood underneath and released all my pent up emotions in gulping sobs. I lathered the Plumeria-scented shower gel, courtesy of the hotel, all over me, making a mental note to boost some off the maid cart. I wrapped myself in one of the white cotton robes that hung on a hook, cinching the belt tight. Looking in the mirror, I ignored the slight bruising and pulled my hair up into a ponytail.

"I want you to know I'm never trading you in for a shinier model. You know, less miles." I smiled at her, refusing to get teary since she hated it.

"That's good timing," Fab said at the knock on the door.

"Take your gun just in case." I looked for my

purse and realized Dunbar had everything, my purse, my phone, and too much personal information.

A hunky, barely-legal beach boy pushed a cart into the room. Blond hair, blue eyes, big dimples. He knew he was cute. He ran his eyes leisurely over Fab, enjoying himself. She flashed him a sexy wink, tipped him generously, and then with one hand on his chest, shoved him out the door and closed it behind him.

"You remembered the salt and the wedge of lime." I filled my glass to the top with the delightful green beverage and savored the first sip, took a slight breath, and then downed half. "Girl hug?"

Fab rolled her eyes and pointed to the king-sized bed. "Have a seat." She handed me the delicious-looking enchiladas, settling on the bed across from me. "What in the hell happened?"

"I don't know." I related the details from the moment I stepped out of the rental car. When finished I said, "Thank goodness I had nothing to do with renting the car I drove. The last thing I want is an arrest for grand theft. Not to mention my Glock was a gift from Brad that I want back. I don't care about Brick's overpriced car, that's his problem.

"I'm impressed with the way you disarmed the security system," I added.

"About that" — she paused — "I had to call Zach, then Slice, since Zach wouldn't answer my calls." She held up her hand. "I knew in an hour something went wrong. I waited an extra hour just to be sure. Then I burned up the phone lines, no one answering their phones, and believe me, I tried them all."

"Creole's going to hit the roof. I didn't tell him about this trip because I thought it would be like the last job—no problems."

Fab refilled my drink. "Creole's calls went to voicemail. To show you how desperate I was, I called Harder and he'd gone to an all-day conference."

"Where the hell is Brick?" I held out my hand. "Can I use your phone?" Voicemail annoyed me, especially when I was mad.

"Call me, now," I growled. Then I texted him: *911.*

"Without my ID, I can't get on a plane and I'm not staying here."

Fab's phone rang immediately. I looked at the screen before tossing it back, shaking my head.

"She's asleep. This wasn't overreaction on my part. Dunbar—you know, another one of your sleazy clients—had her tied to a chair. And she's sporting a black eye thanks to him. Apparently, business must not be very good for you if you're taking on clients like him. He needs an upgrade to his security system." She held the phone away from her ear while Zach yelled something unintelligible, and then she hung up on him.

"Turns out Dunbar's a client of AZL's," Fab

told me. AZL Securities is Zach's company that he'd built into one of the biggest in the state.

Zach could be a little more gracious, since I nursed him back to health a time or two in our relationship. I knew him well enough to know he was just worried; he thought I took too many risks, which was another reason for our breakup. I'd give him a sincere thank you and a free meal at Jake's.

"Zach thought I was using him on a personal job, he didn't believe you were involved. Once I convinced Slice, he passed the news on. I stayed on the line while the tech guy engineer arranged interruption in service and walked me through what to do."

Her phone rang again. "Brick," she said after looking at the screen, and handed me the phone.

My voice fluctuated between calm and angry. I detailed my day. He exploded in a string of colorful language. When he found out I didn't have his car or money in my possession, he sputtered a few words in English, so I pretty much knew his line of thought, and he ended in a flourish of explosive Spanish.

"You need to get my purse, phone, and gun, and have them delivered to the hotel before morning. Leave them at the front desk; I'm not giving out the room number. Our flight leaves at 8:00 a.m. and I need my identification. You might mention that if Dunbar doesn't return them, that I'm not without friends. I'll press kidnap and assault charges and I have the bruises to prove my claim. You and I both know I could get the cops to knock on his door tonight."

It surprised me when he said he was sorry, admonished me not to overreact, and assured me my belongings would be there by morning.

"Any idea why Dunbar screwed Brick?" Fab asked.

"Dunbar was definitely paranoid over not getting what he paid for, but tying me to a chair?" I thought about the phone call. "I got the impression Brick wasn't expecting any problems. He seemed surprised and he's smarmy enough to mumble some pitiful excuse. Would you call Didier and tell him that if Creole calls, I'll be home tomorrow?"

"I called him while you were in the shower, had to promise we'd be low key until we got back home."

"I'm so happy that we're this weird, happy family."

* * *

Fab called down to the front desk and found out a package had been delivered. She ordered me to stay put and ran down to retrieve it.

She returned and sat cross-legged on the bed, slicing open the box with her pocketknife.

"Doesn't that package have my name on it?" I asked.

"I'm only speeding up the process. You're not good at these things." She upended the box Brick had delivered. Everything was returned, including an envelope of cash, his way of saying he felt bad.

Wait until he receives the expense report.

Even my fun red slides that I dropped—and they'd disappeared one at a time in the bushes—had been returned; but they didn't suffer the abuse well. First priority: Go shoe shopping.

Fab threw her bathing suit in the suitcase, snapping it closed. "Brick arranged for a car to take us to the airport and the man is downstairs waiting. Let's leave early, we can shop at the airport, surely that's a business expense. I'll feel better when we're out of here."

"Let's stop at Lincoln Road when we land in Ft. Lauderdale, there's at least two shoe stores I'd like to run through."

"You have enough shoes." Fab let out a long-suffering sigh.

"Now's not the time to go all meany on me. It won't take long, you know I shop fast."

Chapter Twenty-One

We hadn't been home long when I got a frantic call from Mother saying she needed a ride home from the sheriff's office.

"It was all a misunderstanding," Mother stammered.

"Do I need to bring bail money?" I laughed.

"Madison Elizabeth Westin, get over here right now," she snapped. "Hurry up."

Oops, she used my full name. I was in trouble now. Growing up, my brother got his full name yelled out a lot more than I did, mostly because I covered my tracks better.

Fab arched her brows at me. "What?" was on her lips. She and Didier were laughing in the kitchen, making some sort of culinary mess.

"Didier," I called. "I need a favor."

He looked around the corner and I batted my eyelashes, not wanting to move off the couch and disturb Jazz from his nap.

"The answer's no. I don't do jail runs," he said, and laughed.

"But it's Mother." I can't believe that Westins were turning out to be jailbirds.

"Sorry, Cherie, you're on your own."

"I'm busy, too," Fab yelled.

"Sorry, Jazz, you'll have to move. No one wants to be nice to a girl who's had a bad week," I whined loudly, and slipped into my flops. "I'm going to tell Creole you were both mean to me." Didier glared, I thought he would come after me and wring my neck. I closed the door and hurried over to my SUV. No competition to drive today.

* * *

As soon as I slammed the door of my SUV shut, my phone rang. I looked at the screen before answering. "It's about time," I mumbled.

"Do you know who you're speaking to? You must have drawn the short straw."

"Yes, Chief, sir, I do." I ignored his reference to Fab not being the one to call. "Did you get the report?" I had suggested she call, in a gesture of showing that she'd had an attitude change, but she made a face and walked away. Even when I threatened to tell Didier, she only laughed.

"Yes. I have another job for you," Harder said, clearly not amused. "By the way, where's the invoice?"

Rather than blurting out, "No," I'd wait until he made his pitch and then turn him down. My intuitive sense kicked in, and his "job offer" didn't surprise me.

"Are you still there?" he asked.

"We took a vote and unanimously decided to give you what's known as a freebie. In appreciation for everything you've done for Fab and I."

He snorted. "I want you to call Lizzie, take her to lunch, whatever, and tell her what a piece Dane Thorson is," he blurted.

Men were such cowards when it came to emotional issues.

"No! I don't know Lizzie, and believe me, you don't want Fab to do it." I almost laughed at the thought. "Trust me. It's better coming from someone who loves her."

"Double pay?"

"This is what you're going to do: Invite her over, just the two of you, and sit with her while she reads the report. If she bursts into tears, wrap your arms around her and hold her close, you don't have to say a word. Pat her head a couple of times. Do not complain that she's getting your shirt wet or admonish her not to use it as a Kleenex." I smiled at the thought of him being the comforter; I had faith he'd do a good job.

I broke the silence. "It will give you a special bond."

He blew out a long breath. "I suppose you're right," he said.

"We're available anytime."

"Did you check with your cohort before making that offer?" he said, and laughed. "You two did a good job."

"Rip off the Band-Aid and call her."

"Yeah, yeah. Thanks again." We ended the call.

Lizzie wouldn't think so at first, but she was better off without Dane Thorson and she'd move on to find a nice guy, not a fraud.

* * *

Mother had given me an address I didn't recognize until I pulled up in front of the Fish and Wildlife building. It had been a long time since I'd been here; Fab had a friend who used to work here but he'd gotten promoted and moved to another office. Mother fidgeted, pacing just outside the fence, scowling. Her hair was a knotted mess, not her usual impeccable self, but rather more like a cat toy after it had been drug all over.

She flung the door open. "This is not my fault," she yelled loudly enough that a couple of officers turned around and stared.

I leaned over to kiss her cheek and she drew back. "Bail money, indeed. I am not a criminal."

"What is it you used to say to me? 'Why don't you start at the beginning and don't leave out one damned detail.'" I scowled back at her.

Mother's cheeks turned the same shade as a tomato. "Can I use your phone? I need to call Spoonie."

I groaned. "Jimmy Spoon is a grown-ass man.

One who no one in their right mind would challenge...one who slays lesser men with his growl, sending them into a run for their lives—and you give him a baby name?"

"He's such a teddy bear." She grabbed my phone off the dashboard. "Straight to voice mail. I know he didn't get arrested—I asked. If that wet-behind-the-ears officer had paid attention, we'd still be out on the water, enjoying the day."

"The beginning, Mother," I sighed.

"Before you take me back to your house, swing by the docks where Spoon parks his boat. If he's there, you can drop me off."

"I'm not dropping you anywhere, until you tell me what the heck happened."

"Spoon's boat got pulled over on the water for a safety check. Two officers boarded, they had a list to check for life preservers, that sort of thing. The one hinted that the licensing might not be up to date, which I knew was ridiculous and told them so. Then the other officer leaned down to look in the lockers. I wasn't paying attention, and the tip of my cigar caught his pants on fire."

"Mother," I shrieked. "Is the man okay?"

"Him? What about me? He jumped in the water."

I'd never seen her throw a fit ever—she stressed manners and no public outbursts to me and my brother while growing up. It amused me. Thankfully no one was hurt. *Wait until I tell Fab.*

She continued in a state of indignation. "I

couldn't believe that the Coast Guard has the right to board a boat, especially for no reason. It's called a suspicion-less search. The main guy told me to be quiet and Spoon gave me one of those faces of his that he uses when he's not pleased with me. I gulped down the rest of my Jack, and the next thing you know there was a fire."

I covered my face and laughed, which sounded more like a coughing fit.

"He kind of did put his butt in my face, doesn't that make it his fault?"

"I'm surprised you didn't get arrested." I took a long drink of water before I succumbed to more laughing.

"I apologized and then burst into tears. He believed it was all a mistake."

"You cried." I stared at her.

"Not real tears, but he didn't know that. I rubbed my eyes hard so they looked red."

"Did you and Spoon have something to hide and you created a diversion?" As long as I'd known Spoon he'd been a law-abiding citizen. I wanted it to stay that way.

"How can you ask that?" Mother squinted her eyes.

"You didn't answer the question."

"No, we did not. We were minding our own business and the other was an unfortunate accident. I peeked when he got out of the water and the fire didn't go through his underwear."

I took the loop down to the docks and pulled

into a parking space. "Spoon hasn't brought the boat back," I said, and pointed to the empty slip. "Or is he in custody and you haven't been notified?"

Mother glared at me. "I told you we didn't break any laws." She reached for the door handle. "I'll wait here."

I grabbed her arm. "You get out and I'm calling Brad. You're not going to stroll the docks waiting for lover boy." I didn't waste time. I put the SUV in reverse, flying backward, figuring she wouldn't get out of a moving automobile.

"Shouldn't he have been back by now?" She turned in her seat, staring out the back window. "Take me back."

I ignored her. She'd never allow me out of the car by myself. "Spoon can pick you up at my house."

She picked up my phone and pushed redial. Frustrated when she got no answer, she left lover-boy a terse message.

"Spoon will come to my house first. He knows you'd stay with me." On the verge of yelling, I struggled to stay quiet. I wanted to go home. "Call him back and tell him you're at my house."

I rounded the corner of my street, happy to see my driveway. Although Mother complained all the way, I thought it prudent not to remind her that at least her day didn't end in cuffs.

Before she got out she said, "I did get a ticket to appear in court. Can you make an appointment with your lawyer?" She grabbed my arm before saying, "Our little secret." She zipped her lips.

I walked in ahead of her and claimed Jazz, then threw myself in a chair with my feet over the arms. Fab and Didier lay on the couch watching something riveting on television with the sound down. Reminded me of college when we'd get drunk and watch muted Shirley Temple reruns.

I looked at Fab, my lips a tight line, a slight shake to my head. She knew to ask later.

Mother poured herself a Jack on the rocks and paced the floor relaying her story to Fab and Didier. Fab looked at me and rolled her eyes in a gesture that she wanted confirmation it was all true. I didn't think Mother would exaggerate this story.

Didier gave her a hug, whispering something in French, which seemed to calm her frantic pacing. He finally got her to sit down, thank goodness. I'd grown weary watching her flitter about the room. He murmured something else and she stayed put, leaning back and putting her feet on the ottoman. Good thing Brad wasn't here; he had no such power over her. It always irked him when someone could get her to do something he couldn't.

The doorbell rang so Didier answered it and carried the pizza into the kitchen.

Mother cleared her throat. "Neither of you

will say anything to Brad. He's still on the fence about my relationship with Spoonie," she said to Fab and Didier.

Didier assured her neither of them would say a word.

Fab stuck her finger in her mouth.

It startled me when Spoon walked in through the French doors without making a sound. It made me wonder if he'd been standing outside listening before making his presence known.

Mother squealed, jumped up, and ran to him, pushing him back out onto the patio. Fab and I exchanged looks. She started to get up to eavesdrop, but Didier pulled her back down.

"How are we going to find out what really happened?" I glared at Didier. "Let Fab go listen, she's good at it."

"That is your mother," he admonished. "You really need to stop doing that," he said to Fab.

We both looked at one another and exchanged the same thought: *Like that's going to happen.*

"Wait until I tell Creole that he's short on the details because of you." I smirked at Didier.

He frowned and shook his finger, and from the tone of his voice, I knew I was getting a short lecture in French.

I said to Fab, "You can translate later."

The patio was turning out to be a busy place; Creole's voice drifted through the door before he entered.

I jumped up. "How was your day, honey?" I

pulled him into the kitchen and pressed my body to his for a much-needed hug.

"What the heck is going on around here?" Creole kissed me.

I popped the top on his favorite beer and handed it to him. "It's a surprise."

Mother and Spoon came inside holding hands, and she announced they were leaving.

"Not so fast, Mother. I'm sure Creole would like to hear about your day," I said.

His hand slipped under my skirt and he pinched the bottom of my butt cheek. Thankfully, I only squirmed a little.

"I do not," he whispered in my ear.

I felt his hand moving to the other side and jumped out of his embrace. He jerked me back and held me firmly against his chest.

"Yes, I'd like to hear her retell the story. I thought later would be better, but now is good. Be sure you don't leave out a single detail." Spoon glared at Mother.

Fab covered her mouth and laughed. We both took perverse delight in watching Mother squirm; this was the same thing she did to us on occasion.

"Refreshments anyone?" I asked.

When Mother finished her latest version, we learned she'd been argumentative and disrespectful to the officer in charge and just about got them both arrested.

Creole laughed until he had tears in his eyes.

"That's a good one. And you" — he pointed at Mother and continued to laugh — "set his pants on fire. Surprised you're not in custody."

"She burst into tears and sobbed how sorry she was," Spoon said, and squinted at her.

"Cried?" Creole looked at her and started to laugh again.

Even Didier, after recovering from her newest version of how her day went, laughed.

"All of you stop laughing. This was a serious situation." She smiled up at her boyfriend. "I'm sorry. I didn't like the way they talked to you or treated you." She slipped her hand in his. "Come on, Spoonie, this is an unsupportive bunch. And none of you tells Brad. I will do it in my own time."

"Spoonie?" Creole and Didier said in unison, and the laughter started up again.

Spoon turned and glared at both men, put his arm around Mother, and banged the door closed.

"I'm afraid to ask about your day," Creole said, and turned to Fab. "Make sure you get all of the coffee made in the morning." Then he dipped his body and quickly slung me over his shoulder.

Fab gave him a dirty look. Everyone drank something different in the morning, which required two coffee pots and an espresso machine.

I wiggled my butt against his cheek.

"Be still." He smacked my bottom.

I waved as he carried me up the stairs.

Chapter Twenty-Two

Creole slipped out of bed and left before the sky thought about getting light, but before sneaking out of the house he left me with a thorough kiss. Sleep eluded me so I decided to go grab egg soufflés from The Bakery Café. This early, I'd have my pick of breakfast pastries. My first stop: The Cottages. Just a quick drive by to make sure all was quiet. We had good tenants for a change, but I never knew when I'd get a call about a new felony having been committed.

I loved that there was no traffic. After rolling down the window, a salty sea breeze whipped through my hair while I continued to drive along the beach. I turned the corner and saw a man come out of Shirl's cottage and close the door. His eyes darted around, hands stuffed inside his pockets. I recognized the scruffy-looking man before he noticed he was being watched. How in the heck did he hook up with Shirl? This must be her new man; no wonder she kept him hidden. Did she know he was an undercover cop?

It had been a while since I'd run into "Help," who was a friend of Creole's.

I leaned out the window, letting out a low

whistle. "Get your butt over here and don't think about making a run for it or I'll drive over you." I couldn't make out his reaction because his baseball cap was pulled down. He donned large dark glasses, and his clothes were not as dirty as usual.

"Creole can piss off before I do him another favor," he growled through a clenched jaw. He delivered a message for Creole one day, but thinking he was a prowler, Fab and I pointed guns at him. I'd run into him only a couple of times since, always going out of my way to say hello, knowing he wanted me to ignore him.

"You want a ride?" I smiled.

He shook his head and flipped his glasses up. His eyes narrowed to slits. "What I want is for you to drive away and forget you ever saw me. And keep your mouth shut."

He looked clean, his hair was still wet around the edges.

"That's so unfriendly," I admonished. "Does my tenant know about your disreputable self?" I wanted to laugh at the frustration pouring off him. "You tell me your real first name and I won't bother you until the next time."

"Jim Bob. Now go." His eyes constantly swept the street on the off chance that, at this hour, someone might appear.

"Your lack of accent would suggest otherwise." I wagged my finger at him. "Do not break Shirl's heart. Or Fab and I will feed you to the alligators."

"Are you threatening me?" He'd had enough of me for one day.

"Just be honest with her. I know that's hard for your sex, but give it a try," I said. I didn't know the man at all, but Creole vouched for his character and that was all I needed to know.

Knowing Shirl, he could whisper, "Lose the damn skirt," and she would be naked in half a second. He'd be hard to resist; he fit her type of bad-boy good looks, longish dark hair, and the palest pair of indecent blue eyes which could strip you bare.

His jaw clenched. "I'd hate to complain to Creole about you."

"Stop by sometime and I'll give you lessons in making up good threats."

He stared at me for a long moment, turned without a word, and shuffled down the street a few houses before turning in and disappearing. I sped up to see where he had gone and it surprised me to see a path that cut straight to the beach. I drove slowly down the rest of the block, looking for more secret paths, but found none.

I need to pay better attention.

The neighborhood was typical of a small beach town, this street and the surrounding neighborhood full of charming fifty-year-old beach houses and a few multiple units. Limited grass, some favored rocks. Well maintained, more tenant-friendly than owner-occupied.

My phone rang. "What are you doing cruising the block like you're looking for criminals?" my brother asked.

"Did you know that there's a secret path to the beach a few houses down?" I looked in my rearview mirror to spot where he was loitering.

"That's what you get up early and do? You were never this weird before."

"When did you become the poster child for normal?" I liked having my brother around and wasn't looking forward to when all the repairs would be completed on his boat.

Something tapped the passenger-side window and I screamed. Brad had smooshed his face against the window, gesturing to let him in.

I clicked the locks.

"Isn't this tint illegal?" he asked.

"Look, I have a scary-girl rep to maintain. Have you seen Joseph?"

"He's been hiding out since the night of your near-arrest. I don't know who he's more afraid of, you or the police."

"He can't hide forever."

He laughed. "What's for breakfast?"

"Damn, I forgot. I've got to go get it," I said and stomped on the gas. The highway was still not heavily trafficked and I knew the back roads.

"Let me out," he said.

"To do what? You got in, you're staying. Besides, we need to talk business."

"You're interrupting my run on the beach."

"You can do that with Didier and boy bond, unless you're intimidated by the fact he's better looking than you." I winked.

He slugged me in the arm. "Julie thinks I'm a looker. I want to learn a few French phrases for my own perverse needs."

"If you start talking about your sex life, I'm going into detail about mine."

"Being your brother, that's the last thing I want to hear about. I know you have one but I'd rather pretend that you've never been kissed."

"One of your friends was the first," I said, and laughed.

"Which one? I'll kill him."

I pulled into a parking space in front of The Bakery Café and, judging by the empty spaces, the morning rush hadn't begun.

I cut the engine and turned to face him. "Does this mean you and Julie are okay after the whole arrested-in-my-living-room thing?"

"So far, there are no lasting issues. If I could get Kevin to keep his opinions to himself that would help. I confronted him and he's fine with me, it's the rest of the family."

"I hope you're not forced to make a choice. That would mean I'd rarely see you."

"I already told Julie not to ask. I'm an as-is guy and that includes my family. It didn't help when Kevin showed up the other day to pick up Liam and he refused to go. He called his uncle out on the whole arrest—he wisely observed that

Kevin enjoyed handcuffing you. That, Liam didn't like."

"Telling Kevin 'no' is a big red flag. Did they work it out?"

"Kevin started to grab him to force the issue and I blocked him."

"Maybe suggest a guy outing to Kevin—he and Liam could go somewhere of Liam's choosing and talk out their problems."

"Probably not while he's grounded. Kevin told on him."

I gasped. "That blows. He should have addressed the anger one on one. Remember when we made a pact, no telling on the other?"

"It pissed me off. Liam and I are going fishing when he gets off of home detention."

"You have always been the best big brother." I blew him a kiss. "Let's talk about the Trailer Court. I read your prospectus and approve your plans for renovation." He put together a detailed report, turning the run-down lot into a fifties-themed trailer court—complete with restored Airstream trailers—with the intention of making it a tourist destination.

"Heard through the gossip grapevine, while restoring that old Airstream on the back of my property, that Spoon had a couple of them rotting away on his auto body lot. I mentioned my plans to him and he indicated he'd like to be an investor."

"You don't even like him. What happens if he

and Mother break up? They're still in the honeymoon stage of their relationship, although I like the idea of a family venture."

"I didn't comment one way or the other. We need a sit down to go over the plans and costs. As for Mother, she could do a heck of lot worse, and it was you who pointed out how happy she looks. How can I ignore that?"

"Have you ever met a man who can keep up with her? Even when you fixed her up with Doc, he wanted to make a few changes. Trust me, a woman hates that."

"And does Creole want to make changes?" Brad eyed me closely.

"He never tells me not to do something, just to be careful and not to scratch up or bruise what belongs to him."

"Which one of us is going to get pregnant first?" Brad raised his eyebrows.

"Probably not you; most likely Julie." We laughed.

Three cars pulled up to the bakery at once. "I'll get the food. You run down to Sherman's Market and grab some orange juice."

Chapter Twenty-Three

Tropical Slumber Funeral Home had the most interesting history of any business in the Cove. It got its start as a drive-thru hot dog stand. Long-time locals claimed that on a hot day you could still get a whiff of a fully-loaded dog. When the parking lot was empty, as it was then, Fab insisted on parking on the red carpet that ran under the overhang up to the front door.

"How rude is it to show up to a funeral that we know is over?" I looked around wondering if we were early or late.

"We didn't even know the deceased, and what we've found out since is that the world is a better place. Besides, I talked to Raul and told him we were stopping by for information."

Raul and Dickie purchased the business a few years back. They couldn't be more different. Raul schmoozed the clients and handled all the business details, while Dickie's talents lie in making the dead person look their best for their final hurrah. And looks-wise, they couldn't be more different, either: Raul the body builder, Dickie thin and pale, never looking quite comfortable in his own skin.

It surprised me that the door stood wide open. You usually had to ring the doorbell when there weren't any send-offs in progress.

Raul came rushing forward. "You're in time for left over funeral food," he said to me. "I heard you call it that once."

The entry was decorated in red brocade, with plastic slipcovered furniture and a large gold-gilded mirror that hung over a round table that displayed the food. I helped myself to a sandwich triangle and thought briefly about stuffing a couple in my pocket like people do at real funerals. Fab reached around me, picked one up, and sniffed it before she bit in.

I noticed the look on her face. "Swallow. Don't you dare spit it out."

She pushed the rest of the sandwich in her mouth. "Just kidding."

Raul laughed. "I've missed you," he said, and hugged Fab. "Stop by sometime, I miss playing cards with you, even if you do cheat."

"I can get you an invitation to a private game at Jake's. Not a criminal in the group." She opened a drawer and withdrew a note pad, scribbled something, and handed it to him.

I settled back in a chair, careful to make sure I sat on my skirt; otherwise, the backs of my legs stuck to the plastic and made an unfortunate sucking noise when I stood.

"You're so snoopy," I said to her. "Did you ransack the place when you stayed here?"

I met Dickie at my aunt's funeral, with no expectation of ever seeing him again. Then we became friends—the kind who will hide you when the police are looking to have a chat.

"Where's Dickie?" I asked.

"He's got a headache; still shaken up over a... well... misunderstanding." Raul grimaced.

Chances were high that his story had something to do with a dead person, but a girl could hope.

Fab had the attention span of a child. She moved about the large foyer looking into all of the viewing rooms, at two of them she jumped back from the door. Oops, must be occupied. She never ventured out of hearing range.

"Anything we can help you with?" Raul waved Fab to a chair. "Dickie went on a body run, brought it back, and was excited to get started on the preparations. You know him, he always looks forward to a new job. A new challenge. He'd done his preliminary work and was setting up the embalming process when the deceased, Mr. Simmons, started talking to him. Poor Dickie fainted. I ran for the smelling salts, which brought him around, but he refused to go to the emergency room. Luckily, he's only got a goose egg on his head."

Fab and I exchanged looks.

"So what happens when the dead don't stay dead?" Fab asked, moving closer, the conversation finally grabbing her full attention.

"Mr. Simmons wanted to call his family. We were trying to talk him out of it, as hearing such news over the phone might be too much of a shock. The bell rang and his wife and kids had come to reaffirm arrangements that he'd made in advance."

Fab patted Raul's shoulder, and whispered something that made him smile. They had become good friends when she stayed here.

"How is the Simmons family?" I asked.

"After the shock wore off, and the tears dried, we wanted to take Mr. Simmons back to the hospital but they refused. They wanted to take him to a different one that wouldn't declare him dead when he wasn't. Can't blame them. I did insist we call the sheriff and report him alive." Raul looked frazzled.

"Don't worry about Dickie, he'll be back to his old self," Fab reassured.

"He needs a few days away from dwelling on dead people, we both do," he said, and half-laughed.

Fab turned to me. "The Cottages," she mouthed.

"I have a great idea," I said, and almost laughed at the dirty look Fab gave me.

"Be our guest at The Cottages. Choose whatever days you wish and call Mac. We're beachfront, you can barbeque out by the pool. We just got beach cruisers for the guests. And you'll be close by if an emergency comes up."

Raul looked uncertain. "I'll talk to Dickie."

"Talk to me about what?" Dickie appeared in the doorway. His suit pants and white dress shirt looked slept in, his brown hair disheveled. Their Dobermans, Necco and Astro, were by his side. Both dogs were rescued when their first owner got murdered.

"You and Raul come to The Cottages for a few days' get-a-way," Fab said. "You can walk to anything you want to do."

Whoever thought Fab would become good friends with the local funeral director? Dickie no longer jumped when Fab came around. Since becoming friends with his partner, she made an effort not to scare him.

"It would be a nice way to repay you for the favors you do us," I said.

"Anyone show for Edsel Ass's funeral?" Fab asked.

"I believe Winer was his last name." Raul smirked at her.

Dickie took a seat on the bench next to Raul.

"We figured this would be a freebie send-off." Raul snorted. "We donate our services to the indigent. It surprised both of us when his sister, Nina Winer, showed up—a tall blonde, awkward, unkempt—and wanted our cheapest plan. 'Something to keep the bugs out,' she mumbled."

"Even cutting corners I do a good job," Dickie argued.

"Nina told me she'd be the only one in attendance, and to keep the service short. A few words might keep him from going straight to hell but she doubted it," Raul said. "From what we heard, she was probably right, but we never mention that word."

"That's some sibling love." I hadn't thought about funeral arrangements, but I hoped if left to Brad he wouldn't be thinking about my final resting place being hell.

"She mentioned a crack-head brother who was in jail and she refused to post bail *again*. According to her, Edsel's only friends were cellmates from prison," Raul said.

Fab held up a sandwich. I mouthed, "No," not feeling comfortable eating in front of people. Food in hand, her arm went back. I covered my face and ducked. I looked up laughing. "She's threatening a food toss."

They smiled indulgently, thinking her antics amusing. I shook my head. Necco and Astro sat at her side, knowing their best chance for a sandwich stood in front of them.

"The brother and his wife did show up. I heard part of the conversation he had with Nina and he fessed up to begging for money from a family friend. He originally planned to go to rehab but changed his mind, thinks he can handle his problem at home. Nina looked ready to explode then spit flew. 'Great, another one of my friends who'll never speak to me again,' she said, and then she stomped out the door.

"Two homeless men showed up to pay their last respects, said they knew him from prison; one indicated they were cellmates for a short period. They were looking for food and liquor and they seemed disappointed to find out we didn't serve alcohol." Raul shook his head. "We would prefer to serve only non-alcoholic because in the past fights have broken out. It's not good for business if we have to call the sheriff."

"Almost forgot," Dickie said. "There was that odd woman who showed up to visit Mrs. Murray and I found her leaning into Edsel's coffin."

"What did she look like?" Fab asked.

"Hard to tell. She had several layers of clothing on, a weird knit cap, and dark glasses. I wouldn't have let her in, but she walked in behind another couple to make final plans for their loved one and I didn't want a scene," Dickie said.

"Did you ask her what she was doing?" Mac had told me it turned out that Edsel had several girlfriends, maybe it was one of them. "Did you get her name?" I asked. *A mysterious woman*, remembering Jami's mention of the word, "we." Or another woman wanting to make sure he was dead so that she didn't have to worry when he might show up again.

"That was something else I didn't like. I asked her name twice and the first time she ignored me and the second time she mumbled something unintelligible. She did say, when she walked by the door and saw Edsel, that he reminded her of her father and felt the need to say a little prayer. Apparently, I interrupted her and she hurried out. I checked and she didn't do anything unseemly. He had nothing to steal," Dickie said.

"Anything unusual when you picked up his body?" I asked.

"Since one side of his head got bashed in, I had to arrange it just right on the pillow. Other than that, there was no other trauma to his body. Some nasty scars, which I assumed to be from old fights. Our coroner friend told us they got his killer locked up; pretty cut-and-dried, with fingerprints, shoe prints, hair, and fiber. The motive as of now: He beat her up and she retaliated a few nights later by killing him," Raul said.

I still don't think she did it, evidence or not. Crum believed her, too. In Florida, you needed to convince six jurors; I didn't know four more people who believed her to be innocent.

Fab had taken her place by the front door, indicating it was time to go. I stood up. "I expect to hear from Mac that you called and reserved a cottage."

"Thanks for the info," Fab said as she hugged Raul.

Dickie and I waved. He knew I didn't bump body parts with anyone, the few exceptions being family and Creole.

Chapter Twenty-Four

I grabbed one of my retro shell buckets and walked the beach in the early morning. Looking across the white sand, I noticed that I almost had it to myself. I splashed through the water, drenching myself before finally sitting down alongside a large pile of shells that had washed up. I picked through them, letting the warm bathtub-like water wash over my ankles.

After filling my bucket, I kicked my way back home through the water, diving into the pool to wash off remnants of my sandy outing. I finished my swim and stretched out on a chaise. Jazz jumped up with his "pet me" meow, and lay by my side.

I texted Creole: *Don't forget family dinner at Jake's.*

My phone rang back immediately. "Why in the hell do I have to hear from someone else that you were out of town, held hostage, and returned with bruises?" Creole barked.

I squeezed my eyes shut. I never meant for him to find out from anyone other than me. "I planned to tell you that night but Mother stole all the drama, you left early, and I haven't seen you since."

"What happened to total honesty in our relationship?" he demanded.

"Who in the hell told you?"

"Is that all that matters to you?" His voice was clipped and angry, showing no signs of slowing down.

This was our first fight and it was not even face to face. "Listen to me, I'm not hiding anything. It wasn't my intention not to tell you." I stood up and paced the patio.

"Tell me now."

"Do you believe that I planned to tell you every detail?" If only he were standing in front of me, he'd see I hadn't meant to jerk him around.

The silence lasted so long, I thought he'd hung up. I looked at the phone to see if we were still connected.

Finally, he said, "Are you going to tell me what happened?"

I pressed my cheek against the wall and took breaths to stave off my mounting frustration. "If you need more information, go back and ask whoever told you. I'll make an excuse as to why you're not showing up to dinner," I said, and hung up, tears rolling down my cheek.

Who would tell him by accident, or otherwise, and not give me a heads up? This relationship had zero chance if he thought I was a liar. My phone beeped.

Oh, I'll be there, Creole messaged.

Maybe Brick told Harder and that's how he found out. I felt ambushed. I had plans to steal away with him down to the beach after dinner; it would be another low tide tonight so we could walk in the water.

I needed a nap before going to Jake's. I picked up Jazz and snuggled. He could always be depended on for a sleep partner. It wasn't often I found myself with an empty house, so I lay on the couch, Jazz resuming his nap. Listening to the whirring of the ceiling fans, I wondered if Creole carried a grudge, or worse: saved up old offenses and threw them in someone's face. Tonight I'd know if we could get back on track or if this would be a deal breaker. The liar issue was huge for me. I wouldn't be able to overlook him not taking my word over someone else's. My word, my promises, meant something to me. Damn him! At least I'd have given him a chance to explain.

The front door opened and I groaned in Jazz's neck, using the beach towel to dry my tears and blow my nose. So much for peace and quiet. Fab's giggles floated back to me as she and Didier headed into the kitchen. Before I could call out, I heard snippets of their conversation, "Panama Beach," and turned on my side, burrowing back against the cushions, listening intently. I just ripped off a trick of Fab's. How would she take being eavesdropped on?

Silence, then Didier said, "I felt bad when I joked with Creole over the car fiasco. Shocked me he didn't know anything. I was certain Madison would've told him."

"Don't worry about it, they'll work it out," Fab said, brushing it off.

I heard them kissing, my stomach in knots. I slid off the couch, taking Jazz, and scurried upstairs. I understood something slipping out, but not giving me a heads up? That, I didn't get.

* * *

I woke up with a headache and swallowed two aspirin before stepping under the showerhead and attempting to force my bad mood down the drain. I chose mango body wash, a fragrance that I enjoyed.

I favored black for nights out and tonight was no exception. Rooting through my closet, I came up with a flirty, very short black skirt and black slides that would show off my tanned legs. To go with that, I chose an off-the-shoulder long-sleeve top and some sexy underwear I'd stopped and bought the other day as a surprise for Creole: a black lace bikini and a matching midriff camisole with a shelf bra. I accessorized with gold jewelry—a wide cuff bracelet I recently found in a quirky resale store, and earrings.

I'd become friends with Shelly, the spiral-curly blonde who owned "Fishy Treasures." When she got something in she knew I'd like, she called. Her instincts were always right on.

The top of the armoire was where I kept my shell purses displayed. Stepping up on a small chair, I grabbed a favorite, a black pica clutch, another fun find in an out-of-the-way store.

I kissed Jazz and left him sleeping in the middle of the bed. Fab had tied the "do not disturb" ribbon on her door. I'd be early to Jake's, but I planned to spend the extra time with a pitcher of margaritas.

* * *

I parked to the side of the building and wandered in through the kitchen door of Jake's, waving to the cook, who managed to do his job and talk on the phone. Currently he was making animal sounds to his four-year-old. Phil, the bartender, didn't look happy. She frowned at me instead of her usual laughing hello.

"Pitcher of margaritas and one glass with salt." I banged my hand on the bar. "Why the pissed-off face?"

"I told those two to stay off the deck." She pointed over to the two men at the corner table. "They opened the door and plunked their asses down anyway. I've ignored all requests for service."

I walked over to the jukebox and turned it on; the owner didn't have to stuff it with quarters. I bypassed Jimmy Buffet in favor of a random selection.

"Who's this for?" Phil asked, setting the pitcher on the bar.

"It's all mine and I'm not in the mood to share a sip."

Phil watched me down the glass and refill it the top. "You have a designated driver?"

"I can sleep it off on top of the pool table," I said, and laughed. I remember the night I spent on the men's room floor, an attraction for college boys stopping to stare on their way to the urinal.

I turned and glared at the two poachers. How dare they sit at my favorite table? It needed a permanent Reserved sign. Remove the chairs like at the burger stand, I giggled. The two men had the audacity to yell, "Hey," and wave their menus in the air. I rubbed my hands together; I'd enjoy evicting them. Besides, the time had come to set up for the party and they needed to get out.

"The deck is closed," I said, and waved to the sign on the floor. "If you want service you'll have to come inside." I pressed my lips together in a line, barely restraining my hands from going to my hips.

"Look, sister, that's not until later. We have plenty of time." He looked at my legs, coming back to focus on my chest.

His menu brushed my hair; I jerked it out of his hand. "Get out now or I'll shoot you both."

He kicked back his chair, stepping forward. "You bitch."

"There's the door." I pointed.

Phil stepped into the doorway, the sound of the bar's Mossberg shotgun being racked. "Need any help?"

Both men's eyes widened, moving around Phil and I, eyes rested on the rifle. They left without a word and several of the regulars clapped.

My heels clicked across the wooden floor; I grabbed the pitcher off the bar and went back to the deck.

"That was fun." Phil smiled. "I told Daddy about the last guy who caused trouble. My parents want to come for dinner."

"Maybe we should arrange entertainment…or not." We both laughed. "Dinner is on the house."

I grabbed the Closed for Private Party sign and taped it back on the door. Everything I had requested was sitting on a side table. I went to work rearranging the round tables down the center of the floor, for seating on both sides. I drank and set the table, first with the tablecloths, a contribution from my aunt that I brought from home for the occasion. Next were the place settings, each in a different color of Fiestaware that I had scored from a factory outlet. I put out glass votives from my own collection, which ran down the middle of the tables. I was obsessed with outdoor lighting and had a tendency to overdo; I flipped the switch and white Christmas lights lit up the deck and along the roof eaves year round.

The sounds of "Beer for my Horses" drifted out the door; three women who'd been drinking made the country music selection, thumbs stuck in the tops of their jean shorts, gyrating around the dance floor and singing along.

I snatched up my almost-empty pitcher and twirled across the floor to the bar, straddling the stool on my knees—a rather unladylike pose, but I ran my hand down my backside and smiled knowing that my underwear didn't show.

"I'll have another!" I banged the pitcher.

"You need to slow it down. We have a limit in this bar." Phil eyed me.

"I'm queen of this joint." I tipped my glass in the air and turned at the sounds of giggling and the use of fun vulgar words. How dare they have so much fun and not invite me. I went over to reprimand them and one of them looped my arm and whirled me into foot-stomping moves that left me dizzy and laughing. *I must be drunk, I never dance.*

The next selection started up, and all four of us belted out the lyrics to "We love this bar," singing and twirling as Mother walked in the door.

"You're drunk," she hissed.

I escaped her outstretched hand, going the other way. "You want to meet my new friends?"

Chapter Twenty-Five

Mother glared at me and pursed her lips. She looked younger these days in her mid-calf-length tropical dress.

She doesn't look happy. I made a sad face. "Hi, Spoonie," I said loudly.

Mother closed the distance, her hand pressed to my lower back, and shoved me down the hall to the bathroom.

"You're making a spectacle of yourself," she yelled over the music.

"At least no one's ass caught fire." I wiggled my nose at her.

She screwed up her eyes. "Throw water on your face and sober up," she said, and stormed out of the bathroom.

I waited until the door slammed shut, stuck my head out, and wobbled toward the kitchen, thinking briefly about kicking my heels off. I bent over at the waist, admiring my legs and how good my shoes looked, and decided they needed to stay on.

Cook told me my family had started to arrive and he'd sent out appetizers. I grabbed a mug, filled it with black coffee, and reached in a drawer, helping myself to aspirin. I hated the idea of surrendering my buzz. I took a sip and threw the rest down the drain.

"Everyone's here," Phil whispered. "You okay? You're a fun drunk." She patted my back.

Phil held my hand all the way back to the bar. I watched as my family converged through the door at the same time, wondering if they'd all arrived on a bus. I wanted to go home.

Fab glided in the door toward me. Didier hung back talking to Brad. "You look fabulous," she said.

I looked at her unflinching. "Are you my very best friend in the whole world, including France?"

She squinted at me, and put her hand on my shoulder. "You know I am. Why are you drunk?"

"Creole's mad at me," I said softly. "Really mad. I planned to tell him tonight what happened up north but someone beat me to it. He thinks I'm a liar."

"We can fix this." She hugged me. "Look who just walked in the door."

Creole scanned the room, finding me, and nodded in my direction. We both met up at the entrance to the deck, staring at one another.

"We'll talk later," he said, still sounding mad.

No kiss. No hug. This day totally sucked. I walked back to the bar. "When we sit down to dinner, send another pitcher of margaritas," I told Phil.

Kevin showed up with a bubbly brunette with a gigantic chest, wearing six-inch stilettos that brought her eye level to him.

"That's Darla," Phil said, and tossed her blond mane in the laughing woman's direction. "She's a favorite dancer out at the Gentlemen's Club."

"How do you know this stuff?" I asked in awe. *The sheriff and the stripper!*

"There isn't much I don't know about what goes on in the Cove, and what I don't know I can find out in short order, for a price, money-back guarantee. Do your other snitchers offer complete customer service?"

It shocked me that she sold information. I'd rather work with her than some low-life. "Unless you can clone yourself before you graduate law school, you can't go anywhere. As for your new service, expect to hear from me or my manager, Mac."

Liam put his arms around me and kissed my cheek. "I know I'm fourteen but maybe you could tell Phil I'm twenty," he said in my ear.

"Have you lost your mind?" I hugged him back. "You're going to have to wait for an older woman until you're eighteen."

Everyone had drifted out to the deck and taken places around the tables. Drinks were served, and Cook had delivered food to munch on until our main dishes arrived. I slipped into the only vacant chair next to Creole. He put his arm around me and briefly played with the ends of my hair, engrossed in conversation with Didier planning a killer bike ride. I liked riding but the two of them were too competitive and it was no fun struggling to keep up.

Brad spoke up. "So, Mother, have you been behaving yourself?"

Would she confess her latest escapade? I doubted it, too many people knew the truth and she'd want Brad to hear a watered-down version. I refilled my glass, and flashed her an "I dare you" look, which she returned with a scowl. Although completely drunk, I managed to hold myself together, resting my hand on my chin.

"You've had enough," Creole whispered.

"Why did you come, anyway?" I asked. "So you could sit back and ignore me, or better yet, you needed a sympathetic audience to commiserate, 'Oh, poor Creole.'"

"Why don't you ask about Madison's behavior?" Mother pouted. "She's drunk!"

Every pair of eyes turned on me, some amused, a couple judging; the pros able to keep their thoughts from showing.

I flew out of my chair, sending it flying backward to the floor. "At least I went to see Brad at The Cottages and told him all about my psycho trip up north. Did you happen to mention that you got arrested?"

"Arrested," Brad shouted, crimson with fury.

Everyone sat quiet and wide-eyed. Kevin checked out the distance between the table and the front door.

"I was not arrested. If that little sissy hadn't complained so much about his pants being on fire, they'd never have taken me in for questioning," Mother yelled, mostly in my direction.

"Did he die?" Brad demanded.

"Is it too much to get some family support? It was a horrible ordeal," Mother sniffed. "You'd think I did it on purpose."

Kevin leaned in Spoon's direction. "What did you do to get your boat boarded?"

"Not a damn thing," Spoon said, and glared at him. "Routine inspection."

"When I asked you about behaving, I meant the poker room." Brad looked around. "How many people at this table already know?"

Creole snorted.

I whipped around to face Creole. "We Westin women are deceitful, aren't we Creole? You know that first-hand."

"I never said that."

"I heard you think it," I said.

"Sit down." He made a grab for my arm.

"Creole's right. Sit down," Mother snapped. "I knew you two getting together was a bad idea. You're already fighting."

"Why not get everything out into the open?" I nudged Liam's leg. "That way Brad can catch up, he's always lamenting that no one ever tells him anything," I said, and stepped up onto his chair and stood on the table. "Do I have everyone's attention?" I wobbled.

Brad reached his hand out. "You okay?"

Creole stood, reaching for me, and I jumped away, knocking silverware to the floor. "You touch me and I'll kick you."

He stopped, let out a short chuckle of surprise, and sat down. *I'll be damned. He's enjoying me making an ass of myself.*

"Spoonie, do something?" Mother stared at him.

"Good grief, Mother," I said as I looked at the two of them. "Spoon, how old are you?" Not waiting for an answer, I said, "You let her give you a baby name?"

Spoon didn't contain his enjoyment of the unfolding drama; he sat back, arms folded across his chest, and winked at me.

"You see, Mother, I didn't get a chance to tell Creole what happened to me up north before someone else told him, and now he believes I never planned on telling him. That I broke my word and I'm a-big-fat-liar."

Mother's mouth formed an O.

"You excessively handsome, loathsome French man—you blabbed first." I pointed to Didier in case the new guests hadn't been introduced. "And you," I said, turning my attention to Fab, "who just promised this afternoon that I was

244

your best friend ever, knew he ratted me out and kept silent. Does he know you stole a motorcycle?"

"What kind?" Liam asked.

Julie raised her eyebrows to her hairline and shook her head in disgust.

"Fab rescued me from the bad guys on a Vespa." I smiled at her, making a *vroom* noise.

"Hey, Kev, I know you don't like me but I'm happy that you showed up. And thank you for coming, Marla."

"Darla," she mumbled.

I bent down in Creole's face. "I'm replacing you."

I straightened and stepped back. Liam stood with his hand extended to help me. I looked over my shoulder at Creole and said, "Tomorrow I'm making calls putting out the word that I'm available.

"Order whatever you want." I turned up my nose at Creole and walked to the deck doors.

"You stop right where you are," Creole growled.

Everyone sat silent in their chairs, not taking their eyes off the unfolding scene.

I growled back. *Damn, I will miss him.*

He caught me before I got through the doors, and no one said a word.

"I'm not going anywhere with you." I shook off his hand.

Suddenly, he bent and swept his arm under

my legs to lift me into his arms and over his shoulder.

Outraged, I kicked at him, landing my knee in his mid-section. His hand slid under my skirt and pinched hard where my bottom met my leg.

"Fab," I screamed. "I'll forgive you if you bring home leftovers." I kicked again, this time connecting with his thigh.

He pinched the other side even harder as he stomped through the middle of the bar.

"Ow," I yelled.

The bar erupted in laughter and applause.

He practically ran across the driveway, dumped me onto the front seat of his truck, and seat-belted me in. "You try to make a run for it and I will catch you and you'll be very sorry."

He climbed into the driver's side. "What are you giggling about?"

"A little game of chase sounds fun."

"When I get you home, I'll chase you around the bed."

"You'll catch me," I sulked.

He laughed. "Honey, listen up, I could catch you running down the street but in the bedroom I don't have to worry about you getting hit by a car."

I put my feet on the dashboard. "It shouldn't take too long to find your replacement."

"Not gonna happen. I believe that you're not a liar or a promise breaker."

"Really?"

"Come over here." He pulled me closer and gave me a quick kiss. "Yes."

* * *

I woke up but had a hard time opening my eyes, the sunshine streaming through the window made me groan. I clamped them shut and lay perfectly still. I rolled to the side of the bed, pulling myself to a sitting position. I shook my head, hoping the vise-like grip would lessen.

Creole gave me a look of amusement. "You feeling okay?"

"Why are you yelling?"

He picked me up, set me on my feet, and led me to the bathroom, stripping off my clothes. "You'll be feeling your tequila hangover today." He pushed me into the shower. Even though I wanted to lie on the floor to keep the room from spinning, Creole was insistent. He stood me in the corner of the shower, face against the cool tile, and bathed me. He finished and helped me out, rubbed on body lotion, and dressed me in one of his T-shirts.

He led me over to a bar stool and handed me a green drink. "Close your eyes. Don't smell it, just drink, it will shorten your hangover."

I downed the drink, took a couple of short breaths to keep it down, and handed him back the glass—it was truly disgusting. I rested my head on the counter, willing myself not to blow the muck back up.

I eyed him. "What are you smiling at?"

He clapped his hands. "I enjoyed your drunken show. I couldn't believe you drunk yourself into a stupor. When you first sat down, you kicked your foot in a manic fashion and made an assortment of irritated voices, sniffing and growling." He laughed. "I'm so happy I got to see firsthand, it's always better than the retelling. You spitfire."

He washed the glass and, over his shoulder, said, "Don't think you're replacing me either. I'll put the word out, 'Stay away.' The first stupid one to defy me disappears and no one else will ask."

"My bottom still hurts," I whined.

"I didn't pinch you that hard. Come over here and show me." He held out his arms. "I'll kiss your cheeks and give you something else to think about."

I buried my face in his chest. He lifted me and I wrapped my legs around his waist; he carried me into the bedroom. He did that a lot and I remarked on the fact.

"It's easier to keep track of you that way." He smiled. "You'll feel better after a nap. I'm going to keep you in my arms, make sure you don't go anywhere but to sleep."

I didn't want to admit that the room had begun to spin a little. He lay me on the bed, and I nestled against his chest and fell asleep.

Chapter Twenty-Six

When I got home, the smell of coffee led me to the kitchen. I slipped onto a stool at the island, and my favorite brew appeared in front of me. I had a serious case of bed head, my hair sticking out in all directions; my face reddened and bristled from a rash that covered my cheeks. If asked, I'd pass it off as a food allergy and not whisker burn. Make-up sex had been intense and had me thinking an occasional argument would be a good thing.

"I don't understand why one of you can't leave your telephone on," Fab muttered. "Leftovers in the fridge."

"I've sworn off Mexican food and margaritas for a while. I hope my drunken spectacle didn't kill my love for Tequila." I downed half my coffee. "Where's the boyfriend?"

"Didier felt bad about what happened. I haven't seen you that drunk since that time we got snockered at lunch and went shopping, and you made a loud scene in every store we went into." She laughed. "Enjoyed the show."

"I remember you encouraging my obnoxious behavior during our shopping spree. Don't tell anyone, I enjoyed purging my soul until I woke up at Creole's feeling like a steel bar had been rammed into my head."

Fab turned. "Is Madeline speaking to you yet? Has she gotten over your drunkcapade?"

"We've exchanged text messages. I need to go tell Mother I love her and she's the best. She did open the game room. It was supposed to be open to the public, but so far, it's private parties only. She's not interested in making waves with the owner right now. We'll take her out for a two-daughter lunch and some shopping. That should smooth the waters."

"You two solve more problems with food and shopping than anybody else I know. I'd never get off so easy."

"Do you miss your parents?"

Fab had a strict upbringing and she rarely spoke of her family. She'd rebelled when she became an adult and they seemed to be unforgiving.

"Not so much now that I've been adopted by your mother. If I went home, I'd be forced to live under their rules and prove myself as an obedient daughter, and then all would be swept under the carpet only for as long as I never defied their authority. My guess is that they'd arrange a marriage to someone suitable—code for having nothing in common with me."

"I need something stronger." I stared at my empty cup. "It has to have caramel and whipped cream, with a pecan roll on the side."

"Mac called, wants you to come to The Cottages."

I looked Fab over before running upstairs; judging by her black ankle pants that I loved, and silk top, I'd have do better than sweat shorts and ninety-nine-cent flip-flops.

* * *

"We should've taken your car," I told Fab as she pulled out of The Bakery Café after we chugged down lattes and wolfed down rolls. "I might throw up and don't want to do it in here. It's hard to get the smell out and on a hot day it whips up a fresh scent."

"I don't even want to know how you know that." Fab grimaced. She pulled on one of my curls. "You hair is falling out of the clip and not in a good way." She studied my hair, looking amused.

"Two signs the humidity level is wretched: my hair is bushed out and my scalp itches."

Fab laughed at me, not an ounce of sympathy on her face. Her long brown hair never frizzed. How unfair is that? And anti-frizz products are full of it.

"I told Didier that if there is ever a next time that something accidently slips out, we fess up, because you would do that for one of us. I promise you he didn't do it on purpose."

"Poor Didier. Is he mad that I outed him in front of people?" I shook my head, feeling my cheeks turn red.

Fab chuckled. "He feels initiated into the family. He worries you're mad at him. I told him you're not a grudge holder."

"Creole and I made up, and kept making up, so all's good. We worked on a couple of trust issues and now we have a new system. I call or text with, 'I'm fine.'"

Fab pulled into the driveway of The Cottages and Mac sat in the barbeque area sunning herself. Apparently, she'd been to South Beach—she sported pink boa-feather flip-flops and matching sunglasses. The flashing lights around the lenses made me queasy.

"It took you long enough." Mac met us at the office.

"Just remember who works for whom here," I said.

"You're surly this morning. Still hung over from the royal ream you gave your family?" She looked at me unsympathetically. "This problem needs your expertise, sure as hell not mine." She put her hands on her hips, sticking her double Ds out. Mac dressed in layers; she pulled her long skirt out of her shorts, ready to go back to work.

She better not put my eye out.

"What already?" I asked.

"Miss January lost her cat again and she's terribly upset, pacing around, drunken-mumbling." Mac looked over at her cottage as though she might hear; even if she was outside she'd be drinking or passed out.

"How can a person misplace a dead cat? Was she pushing it around in the stroller again?"

"There's not a damn word about dead cats in my contract." Mac shuffled nervously. "I heard you got drunk and stood on a table and yelled at everyone in your family. Sorry I missed that."

I glared at Mac and cut across the driveway. Miss January's door stood wide open. She lay passed out on the couch, one leg hung over the side and resting on the floor. I twisted the lever on the glass-front screen door and, to my surprise, it opened. She snored softly, drool running down her chin. I ransacked the place. Finding Kitty in the oven, I covered her with a dishtowel and put her back in her usual place on the couch.

Not a single personal item sitting out, her tiny cottage was immaculate as always. I'd enjoy seeing a photo or two. A lump in the bed caught my eye, and I recognized the grizzled face as belonging to her boyfriend. I was pleased he didn't sleep in the buff. I left him to his peaceful snooze and went back in the living room and straightened out Miss January, who stirred a little, slurred her words, and went slack. I threw a light blanket over her. Hopefully, when she woke up, she wouldn't remember any kitty drama.

I took the dish towel with me, and when I got back to the office, I balled it up and slam dunked it into the trash. "Put dish towels on your shopping list and give them to Miss January."

"How are the love birds?" Fab asked.

"Drunk and sleeping it off. He's got nice legs for an old dude."

"What did you do?" Fab looked shocked.

"Not what you're thinking." I laughed.

"Next time you complain about some lunatic I rent to, I'm going to remind you how weird the new gardener you hired is." Mac shook her head.

Fab and I stared at her. "What are you talking about?" I asked.

"Mr. Crum is doing a good job for a certified snobby nut case." She took an emery board out of her desk drawer and proceeded to saw on her fingernail. "I'm surprised you hired a man who wears a skirt—and a very short one."

Fab started laughing.

"I never hired him," I said, trying not to yell.

"I've got his bill here. I'm going to pay for the plants even though I think he dug them out of someone else's yard. They didn't arrive in containers; he had fisted them, roots exposed." Mac slid the invoice across her desk.

"Nervy bastard. Pay him and fire him."

Stolen plants? Good grief.

"You might want to hold off until we find someone else. I'm having a hard time, the locals want to mow and go, no plant service."

"Your decision, but I don't want word to spread that the sheriff came here trying to identify stolen flowers."

Out of the corner of my eye, I saw Joseph darting up the driveway. Without a word to Fab and Mac, I chased after him. The closer I got to his cottage, the more my anger grew. I beat on Joseph's door, leaving him no doubt it was either me or the cops. He had avoided everyone since he'd gotten me arrested. If I had known that he'd just met that Bungee cretin in jail, I'd have left them both at the bus stop and sped home without a glance in the mirror.

If Joseph thought he could ignore me forever, he was mistaken. I yelled at the top of my lungs, "Get out here so I can kick your ass."

Fab and Mac, who had followed me out of the office, laughed.

I turned and glared at them. Fab drew her Walther, waving it in my direction. I stared for a few seconds, finally realizing the message she was sending. I my put my heel to the door in short kicks. The longer he dawdled and hid out, the more it annoyed me.

I yelled again, "You open this door or I'm shooting the lock off. Count of three: one…"

He didn't need to know I had no intention of filling the door full of bullet holes when I could go to the office and get the key. Besides, the doors had been an upgrade that I installed when I first took over the property, single French glass doors with roll-up plantation blinds.

"Two…" I yelled again, feeling it in my throat this time. Maybe Creole would find a hoarse voice sexy.

Joseph cracked the door opened. "I'm calling the sheriff. This is harassment. I'm a sick old man, a Veteran."

Reminding me of his service to the country made me feel bad, but not bad enough to stop from unleashing a tirade on him.

"Get out here." I pointed for him to stand in front of me.

He opened the door and stood on the threshold. "I'm sorry," he mumbled, his eyes staring a hole in my knees. "I just wanted to help the guy out. I swear I didn't know he broke out of jail." His boney shoulders started to shake.

The anger evaporated out of me seeing him so upset. "Where is Bungee now?"

"Not in custody, judging by the phone calls I ignore," he said.

I groaned. "What does that mean?"

"Your lawyer sent his lackey over for a statement, and he showed up with a detective. They asked questions and I answered everyone truthfully; I met Bungee in the holding area for the first time." He slid into the chair next to the door. "My ankles were swollen bad that day and I might have exaggerated my health issues a little, but I didn't want to get arrested."

"And what else," I demanded. He still hadn't

made eye contact and fidgeted in the chair.

"Two other detectives showed up, banging on the door a couple of times, and I didn't open up and invite them in. They've got to have a warrant to kick the door down. I figured if I didn't leave my place, they couldn't take me into custody."

"You might as well face your possible felonies. The worry will kill you instead of the cancer."

He scuffed his shoe back and forth on the cement porch. "I called Mr. Famosa to smooth things over. He was totally pissed at being lied to and even angrier when I told him I didn't have any money."

I did a mental eye roll. It surprised me Joseph was still breathing to tell the story and that the cops hadn't found him dead or that he hadn't just disappeared. No one screwed with Brick without unpleasant consequences.

Joseph cleared his throat. "He was more concerned that it would 'F' up his relationship with you." Joseph shuddered. "Then he made a clicking noise, told me that would be the last sound I heard before dropping dead."

"How did the conversation end?" I asked.

"He hung up on me."

Signature Brick! Nice to know I'm not the only one who gets hung up on. I'd have Fab call and smooth things over.

I peered over my shoulder at the sound of male voices at the opposite end of the driveway. Bad Cop and Good Cop stood conversing with

Mac and Fab. All four stared in my direction.

"Looks like the cops are back." I motioned to Joseph.

He kicked his chair back, ran into his cottage, and turned the dead bolt.

I picked up the chair and waited for them as they ambled up the driveway in form-fitting jeans, both in all black. "Hello, officers." I flashed an insincere smile. All I could think of was going home; if only I'd left a few minutes sooner.

"We'd like to speak with Mr. LeBeaux. We see he's finally home," Bad Cop said, and knocked on the door. Rather civilized in comparison to my obnoxious pounding.

They both did a leisurely perusal over my body. I glared at both of them.

"Are you here to arrest him? Does he need a lawyer?" I asked.

Good Cop frowned at me. "It's none of your business."

I forced myself not to sound snotty. "Do you want him to open the door or not? You can't kick it in without a warrant."

"Just get him to open the door," he growled. "We have more questions about his friend Benjamin 'Bungee.' Have you seen him?"

Bad Cop returned from looking around the side of the cottage. They had to know by this time that the only two exits were facing the front.

"Hell no. I would've reported him immediately to the local sheriff." I pulled out my cell phone. "You better not be lying," I said while texting for Joseph to open up: *They're not here to arrest you. Only questions.* "Or I'll complain to Chief Harder."

The lock turned from the inside. Joseph opened the door and motioned them in.

"They said they just wanted to talk and I believe them," I told Joseph.

I turned to the cops and said, "Have a nice day."

"What was that all about?" Fab asked when I joined them.

"Still looking for Bungee," I said to Mac. "Put out the low-life alert and see if anyone knows where he's hiding out. The sooner he's picked up, the sooner these impromptu police visits will stop."

Fab snapped her fingers at Mac. "You owe me five."

"What did you two wager on this time?" I asked.

The unmarked police car had caught the attention of the snoopy neighbor next door, who hung out his bathroom window about ready to fall.

"I bet Joseph wouldn't answer the door and you'd shoot it off the hinges. Your friend here laughed in my face and took the bet."

"We have a new policy," I informed Mac. "As owner, I'm leaving the dirty work of informing tenants about policy changes to you."

"What about her?" Mac tossed her head in Fab's direction.

"Requests for bail and rides home from the jail go through the office during regular business hours. If they get released at the crack of dawn, they can wait or walk."

"About time," Fab said, and grabbed my arm.

I let her drag me to the Hummer. "Thanks, Mac," I said over my shoulder. "If you get word on Bungee, call me no matter the time."

We backed out and Mac untied the jump rope from around her waist, which I thought was just an ugly belt, and started jumping. I winced as her body moved in several directions at once.

Chapter Twenty-Seven

I felt the mattress dip. Smiling, hazy with sleep, I stuck out my hand and ran it over Creole's leg. My eyes flew open and I was to about to scream when a hand hit my shoulder.

"Shh, it's me," Mother whispered. "Were you expecting someone else?"

I ignored her smirk and squinted at the clock. "A little early isn't it?"

"But I brought goodies. I got a little carried away, but nothing seems to go to waste around here. You never have any food, unless it's vegetables." She wrinkled her nose.

Mother and I shared the same dislike for most vegetables unless disguised in a cheese sauce or something that cut the healthy level. Didier was responsible for the green foods that he turned into slimy juice in the morning.

Mother brushed my hair out of my face. "I don't like it when we fight. Spoon—notice I didn't say Spoonie? I'm forbidden to call him that unless we're in private. Spoon and I argued over something stupid right before we got to Jake's and I took my frustration out on you."

"That's what started my drinking binge—a

misunderstanding with Creole. I don't know why I can't be a happy little drunk in the corner instead of a scene maker." I rolled over and put my head on her chest. "Been staying out of trouble?"

"Thanks for letting me have the run of the game room, I christened it already. It turned out to be really fun and I know it's supposed to be for all the customers but I don't want anyone grubbing it up. I want it available to private parties only."

"You have complete control and I trust you." I smiled up at her.

She tugged on the ends of my hair. "I want you to know I think you and Creole are a great match."

"Why the turn around? You were so worried we'd break up and none of us would be friends anymore."

"There are no guarantees. I should know that, your father died too young. I'd have to be blind not to see the way you two look at one another. And when he threw you over his shoulder and carried you out of Jake's, it was so romantic," she sighed.

"That means a lot to me and will to Creole. We won't have to sneak around anymore, although I think it's fun, so we'll probably continue."

"Spoon also reminded me that you supported our relationship when no one else did. And he likes Creole."

"I have something to confess," I said, although I couldn't quite meet her eyes.

"It doesn't matter what you did, I love you. Is there a warrant for your arrest?" Her eyes big as saucers, she hugged me.

"Really, Mother." I heaved a sigh. "I didn't go to Marcy's wedding; she's been married for two years. I never got an invite, some friend."

She frowned at me. "Where did you go? I'm more interested in with whom?"

"I snuck out of town with my pretend cousin." I turned red.

"I knew it! Besides I never liked that loud mouth Marcy girl, snotty thing, even in high school." She brushed my hair out of my face. "Did you have a good time?"

"I like him a lot." My cheeks never stopped burning.

"This reminds me of the time you threw a party when I went out of town for the weekend and told me a year later."

I giggled. "That was a really cool party." I rolled off the opposite side of the bed. "Let's go downstairs for coffee and rolls."

She looked at Creole's football jersey that I had on and chuckled. "When I came down the hall, Fab had a ribbon tied to her door handle again. Do you suppose they…you know…all the time?"

I felt my face get warm again. "Probably."

"You know she left a book open on her tablet last week and I started to read." Mother looked embarrassed. "Romance novels aren't what they used to be, you know, separate beds and all. She wasn't happy to see my eyes glued to the screen and took it back."

I hugged her and said, "You're a second mother to her and she doesn't want to disappoint you."

"Good thing I remembered the title of the book. When I told Spoon about it, he bought the book for me. I've been reading it to him." She blushed.

"Please, please don't ever tell Brad," I said.

We both laughed.

"We're made up now aren't we?" Mother asked.

"We can have tiffs but nothing more than that." I kissed her cheek. "Love you this much," I said, and held out my arms.

* * *

Didier looked at his watch for the tenth time, tapping the dial. How he and Fab never broke up over time issues mystified me. He was always punctual, more often early, while Fab arrived when she felt like it.

"It's date night," I gushed to Fab as she floated down the stairs in a mid-calf strapless black dress that tied just above her breasts, a deep slit showing her legs from mid-thigh.

I had on a black wrap skirt with a large

tangerine hibiscus print, tied to the side exposing a generous view of my leg, and a spaghetti strap top to match the flower print.

Didier let out a low whistle and devoured Fab as though she were one of those new margarita cupcakes I'd seen at the bakery.

I stood at the garden window over the kitchen sink, unashamed to be staring out impatiently. "He's here!" Creole's truck rolled into the driveway parking just behind mine.

Fab half-smirked. "Let's hope he knows how to dress outside of work, ditched the crummy clothes and washed his dirty feet."

"Why don't I kick you to the floor and beat the hell out of you?" I balled up my fists.

"Good luck with that." Fab rolled her eyes.

As the front door opened, I ran to meet him. "Look at you, so damn delicious," I said, and planted a kiss on his mouth. My voice rising, I added, "And to think, Fab thought you would show up looking like a roady in a beach band, you know, skeevy."

"I'm going to rip your hair out. I didn't say that, exactly," Fab huffed.

"Exactly?" Creole growled. "I'll have you know I can dress myself. I even own my own tuxedo. And look, Didier just gave me the thumbs up. He ought to know."

Didier laughed.

Creole and Didier were dressed almost alike, Creole in black pants and tropical shirt, Didier opting for taupe-colored pants and shirt.

I gave the address of The Fish Co. earlier to Fab since we agreed to meet at the restaurant I insisted on being able to choose, just so that we didn't end up in formal wear like the two of them did on a regular basis.

"Since we'll be getting there first," Fab started as she fingered the new black diamond heart pendant Didier surprised her with, "if this turns out to be a dive bar or some crummy broken down restaurant we're not even getting out of the car."

"I'm not driving, so we might beat you down to Islamorada," I challenged.

Creole and I left first, since he'd partially blocked Fab's Mercedes.

"Is this supposed to be a race?" Creole asked.

I laughed. "Didier makes her drive the speed limit or somewhere close, anyway. She listens to him. As for me, she only slows down when I threaten to throw up."

"If you so much as have a twinge of sickness, hang your head out the window. I'll hang on to your leg so you won't fall out."

* * *

Mother recommended the restaurant, raved about the food, and told me to request table number ten by the window; it had the best view of the inlet. The outside looked a little worn, which drew a groan from Fab.

The inside had been totally modernized to seaside chic. In the center of the room under the tiki-hut ceiling, sat a ginormous round fish tank, an assortment of tropical fish swimming freely with no fear of ending up on someone's dinner plate. The walls were hand-painted in a soft green seascape with muted tones of yellows and oranges. Tables were set in white linen and shell-decorated candleholders with lit votives.

Mother had been right; the inside corner table had a view of the entire length of the water. A few boats parked nearby, their outside lights on, which danced off the water.

"No Tequila?" Fab asked.

I wrinkled my nose, looking at the red wine I ordered. "My favorite alcohol and I need some time apart."

"You should try my vanilla vodka, you'd like it," Fab said.

"I hung my head in a toilet for hours over a fifth of vodka. Stayed sick for five days. The thought makes my stomach jump."

"Really, Madison," — Fab channeled Mother — "is that appropriate dinner talk?" She shook her finger.

Creole and Didier laughed.

"Good imitation." Creole gave her a thumbs up.

Didier looked between Fab and me. "How did you two meet?"

"She interrupted a breakfast meeting and created a scene in the restaurant by pouring a pitcher of water over her boyfriend's head, who happened to be sitting across from me. I kept an eye on her from the time she stalked in, and moved out of the way just in time. Imagine that?" Fab said.

I shook my head. "I remember our first meeting a little differently."

Imagine that!

"I came home from a lousy day," I explained, "and there she stood in the kitchen window, waving. Hard to believe, she picked the lock and made herself at home." I made a face at her.

"No need for surliness. Didn't I teach you to pick locks?" Fab asked.

"She built this door-lock contraption as a get well gift. I'm practicing again."

Didier pulled her close and kissed her cheek.

"Let me guess, she moved in the next day?" Creole asked.

"Not right away, but once again, I came home and her suitcases were at the bottom of the stairs, boxes in the garage, feet on the couch, Jazz asleep on her chest. Best day ever."

"I never wanted a friend, but she hounded me. Then came the bribes of shoe shopping which wore me down."

We must have timed it right because our food arrived lightning fast. We toasted to friendship. My first bite of scallops was heavenly. Everyone was happy with their selection.

"How did you two hook up? She kick your ass and drag you home?" Creole asked Didier.

Didier leaned over and whispered in her ear, "...cave woman..."

I gazed up at Creole and laughed. He winked. I knew he also heard Didier.

"We met briefly at a party. And I thought she was exquisite." He blew her a kiss. "To my disappointment she vanished. Imagine my surprise when I opened my wallet and a card lay on top with her name and number scribbled down."

Fab smiled at him. "He was an easy mark. Getting inside his jacket, I had to restrain myself from marking his chest with my fingernails, reminding myself there would be plenty of time later."

"You couldn't just stick out your hand and say, 'Hi, I'm the fabulous Fabiana,'" I asked. "What if he had never called?"

"I'd have tracked him down and 'drug his ass' home, as he so eloquently put it." She glared at Creole.

Didier smiled at me. "And you two?" He looked at Creole. "Did he arrest you?"

"He had the use of a cottage when I inherited them. I don't think he actually lived there; he just came and went at random times. My aunt had put a 'no eviction' note on his file. He skulked around, an occasional glimpse now and then.

One day he showed up at my house and introduced himself, that's how I found out we were cousins."

"You have to stop with that story." Creole pulled on the ends of my hair. "Some people will think…you know what they'll think, and spread it around town."

"I lived in a hotel when I met Fabiana." Didier patted her hand. "She invited me to Madison's one night for dinner and a swim and I never left. A few days later, when I had an appointment, she went back to the hotel, packed up my clothes, and checked me out. It surprised me when my keycard didn't work in the door. After a chat with the front desk, I called her and she said, 'Did I forget to tell you?'"

"I remember meeting you that first morning over coffee," I said. "You were half-naked, had terrible bed-head, and spoke to me in French. I nearly swooned. Since then you've charmed your way through every woman in the family."

Didier looked embarrassed. "It always surprised me you never asked where I came from or when I was leaving. Now I feel like part of your family."

"Mother adores you. Spoon, on the other hand, glares a lot but only because you make her blush and giggle."

A scruffy, middle-aged man with mean, beady eyes hauled a chair up to the table and plunked down. Tall and lean, his ill-fitting clothes hung on him. He brandished a gun and pointed it at Fab. "Remember me, Fababean?"

I squinted at him. "Wouldn't that be fava bean? I tend toward greasier foods myself." I groped my thigh, remembering none of us had accessorized with guns. We'd have to get creative.

"Shut up. In fact, all of you keep your mouths shut and listen or my first bullet will find its way to her throat." He waved the muzzle in Fab's direction. "I can watch the life gurgle out of her." He made a choking noise.

I gave a quick glance around the restaurant; no one seemed to notice. He had his back to the room and had attracted no attention. I didn't see that as a plus for our side.

Fab spoke up. "You and me, let's go outside, nice and quiet-like. We'll have a chit chat over old times."

Creole pushed his chair back, and the man cocked his gun. "Sit back. Don't be a dead hero."

"Where are your manners?" I said to Fab. "Aren't you going to introduce us?"

"What do you want, Devil?" Fab quirked her brow, she was assembling some kind of hasty plan.

"Family name?" Didier glared at him. "I'm sure we can come up with an amicable solution that doesn't leave anyone bleeding or dead."

"You, Fababean, all the ways I planned to make you pay, slow and methodical. In the beginning I wanted cash, but I think I'll settle for revenge." Devil grinned at her, two bottom teeth missing.

"Listen to me, Devil, I had nothing to do with your going to jail," Fab said.

"You helped set me up, drugged me, or else I would've been long gone when the cops showed up, instead of waking up surrounded, the briefcase of cash missing, and under arrest for the stolen goods in my possession."

"You were a thief. Did you forget you stole all those items?"

"You're such a liar. This is nothing but revisionist history. Remember your client, Harry Newlin, biggest scum hole ever? He bragged to me during his brief stint in jail; you delivered the briefcase and he had bail money."

"This matter can be solved in a civilized manner. We can get you another briefcase," I said.

Creole kneed me under the table so that I knew something was about to happen, but what?

"You really are a dumb bitch, you know?" Devil scowled at me.

I cocked my head. "No, I didn't know that," I said, and caught the tail end of a hand signal between Didier and Creole. Devil missed it in his show of disgust.

"Devil," Fab said, "you get up and leave nice and quiet and I owe you one. If you shoot me, you'll end up in jail for the rest of your scrawny life. You get one shot and then I promise that these two" — she motioned to Didier and Creole — "will beat you to death."

Creole radiated controlled anger. He never took his eyes off Devil. "You've got a three-count to get up and leave or I'll send you to hell." He nudged me and pointed downward.

"You remind me of a pimp I knew, worked the girls around North Miami. On slow nights he had them selling drugs. Go ahead, move, it will be my pleasure to kill her," Devil said as he eyed Fab.

The waiter arrived with a much-needed distraction, dessert menus. Devil was momentarily distracted. Didier flipped the table, sending food and drink flying. Devil's gun dropped to the floor. Creole leapt over the table like a feral tiger, planting his shoe in Devil's chest and sending him to the ground. Lying face up on the floor, Devil wiggled his fingers in the direction of his gun. Didier's foot came down on his wrist, and kicked it toward Creole.

Devil screamed, his hand hanging at an odd angle.

Fab moved from behind Didier, raised the hem of her dress above her knees, and kicked Devil in the groin with the toe of her high heel.

Creole flipped Devil from his fetal position on to his stomach. "Hey, model boy, I'll take your belt."

Creole grabbed Devil's wrists in one hand and

he passed out. He secured his hands with Didier's belt and his feet with his own, leaving Devil face down. He dropped a white linen napkin over the Smith & Wesson handgun, depositing it onto the only chair that had not been overturned. He turned his back, and took out his phone.

Fab and I exchanged looks, neither one of us happy that we couldn't hear a word.

"A free side show is always good for business." The manager approached and introduced himself, clearly not unhappy about the mess. Not a single customer left; the ones close by watched and continued to eat. When Devil was secure, a smattering of claps followed. "Do you mind dragging him outside to await the cops that are on their way?" He toed Devil roughly. "Free meal next time you come back."

Chapter Twenty-Eight

Fab and I changed into bathing suits and took our morning coffee down to the beach, sitting on the bottom step, toes in the sand. I bent over and sifted my fingers through the white powder.

"I'll go find out what the new crisis is at The Cottages," I told her. "I'm not the one who stared down the barrel of a gun last night."

Fab hesitated, lost in thought. "How soon do you suppose it will be before Devil is on the loose again?"

"Creole assured me last night that we'd seen the last of Devil." I put my arm around her shoulder. "You and I are a package deal. He looks out for the both of us."

"My only regret is that I couldn't kick his little friend up to his tonsils before the cops drug him off," Fab said.

"You're coming with me." I grabbed a hold of her arm. "I'll drive, you can sit back and relax."

In one swift movement, she had me sitting in the sand while she ran up at the steps. At the top, she yelled down, "I'll drive, you whine for me to slow down."

It was worth picking myself up and slapping

the sand off my skirt and legs to hear her
laughing.

* * *

It surprised me Mac wasn't sitting outside
soaking up the sun. We found her sitting behind
her desk, legs propped up, reading a romance
novel for which she had a voracious appetite. I
appreciated that she wore shorts under her
bohemian-looking dresses and skirts.

"You better sit for this one," Mac said, and
motioned to the chairs in front of her desk. Fab
had already claimed the couch.

The door banged against the wall and Shirl
rushed in. "You don't mind if I listen in do you?
Mac has a tendency to leave out details in the
retelling. They dribble out later."

"I do not." Mac kicked the top of the desk.

"Do too." Shirl plopped into a chair next to
me.

"Stop! You're making my head hurt. Do we
act like this?" I said to Fab, who feigned sleep.

"When do you two go anywhere without each
other?" Shirl smirked.

I wrinkled my nose at Fab, who opened one
eye. "We've found it to be a health hazard not to
travel as a pack; safety in twos."

Fab flipped the shutter up and looked out the
window as a car missing its muffler bumped
down the street. "And a needed sounding board

while trying to figure out what the hell to do next."

Mac sat up, throwing her feet on the floor, looking at me. "Miss January is in jail and she's not getting out anytime soon."

I covered my ears with my hands. "I don't want to hear this," I said, and sighed. "What, no bail for a serial drunk?"

"Try felony drug possession, obstructing an investigation, and resisting arrest," Mac said.

Shirl spoke up. "I talked to a friend at the sheriff's office and he said they already offered her a deal, but she claims not to remember anything about last night, and is adamant she didn't know what they were talking about. She blacked out during booking and then got transferred to the hospital where she regained consciousness, and was transferred to a medical unit where she'll be for a few days."

"Miss January doesn't do drugs. Is there a beginning to this story you could start at?" I asked Mac.

"You're not going to like this next part. It seems as though she decided to party with her old friend Carly and her friend Ruthie. Since Miss January drinks all day, I assume she was pretty well hammered when they came and picked her up. They spent a few hours at Custer's and then left for an unknown location. Not long after, they got pulled over in a residential neighborhood by the roundabout. Carly was behind the wheel, Miss January in the passenger seat, and Ruthie in the back. All three got arrested."

"Where do the drugs come in?" I asked.

"Carly got charged with drunk driving, Ruthie resisting arrest, and when they helped Miss January out of the car, she had a pocket full of eight-balls. The cops say she tried to dump them in the bushes, and then became belligerent when confronted."

"She doesn't have the money to buy any quantity of cocaine," I said. "Those two remind me of when you were a kid and not allowed to hang out with someone because all you ever did was get into trouble."

"Don't look at me," Fab said. "I wasn't allowed to have fun friends. I got into trouble once in grade school and we were separated and never had contact again."

"She won't be allowed visitors until she's transferred to a cell." Shirl's phone beeped. She smiled, answering a text.

"I'll bet you they're Carly's drugs and she didn't want to go down for the charge because of her extensive rap sheet," I said.

"How are you going to prove that, Nancy?" Fab asked me. "Especially with Miss January's faulty memory."

"I've read every Nancy Drew book five times." Shirl smiled at Fab in a way that was akin to hero worship.

I shook my head. Fab could tell Mac and Shirl to do some outrageous things and they'd hop to it.

"Any idea what bail will be?" I knew Miss January could never come up with bail of any amount.

"My friend said no bail for now," Shirl said. "With no previous record, they don't want her, they want dealer information."

"You might as well know that Carly is out of jail. She spent a grand total of five hours in a holding cell and was released when her mother posted bail," Mac informed us.

I poked my finger over Mac's shoulder, until she turned. "Please," I said, pointing to the snack bowl.

She dug around and pulled out another of my favorites, a mini Snickers.

"I can't kill Carly," I said, although I liked the idea. "I need to squeeze information out of her, then she needs to take her wacked-out mother and move to some other part of the Keys, or rather, some other part of the states, which would be more preferable. They should try Washington."

Fab grabbed a handful of darts and threw them. Three landed in the bull's eye, the other two went wild. "Carly's not going to rat out a dealer if the guy is anything like the ones I've known in the past. Shortens your life span."

"If I make my own jail appointment, I have to

wait a week. Brick is out of the question. You could ask that favor for me," I pleaded to Fab. "I don't want to owe him anything."

"If you were nicer to the sheriffs around here, you'd have more connections," Shirl said, and smirked.

"I'm working on my attitude. I invited Kevin to dinner, and that turned out to be a fiasco. Cornered your new boyfriend the other day," I said to Shirl. "Besides the sex, how is the rest of the relationship going?"

"I'd like to go out and show Steven off, but I know he's tired after a long day at the office. He doesn't really like selling insurance," Shirl told us.

So Help's name is Steven. Probably not; most likely another lie. Insurance—couldn't he make up a more exciting job? My guess was that he didn't own a suit, so how could he pass himself off as a businessman?

"Have him give me a call." I smiled. "I'll review my insurance with him, throw some business his way."

"I think he may be the one," Shirl gushed.

"How did you meet him?" Fab asked. She'd only had one encounter with Steven and that was when she threatened to shoot him in my driveway.

"I met him at the hospital when he came in as a patient, head trauma. He'd gotten mugged. I thought he and Creole were friends. Thought I saw him visit Steven, but he said no. He makes me laugh. We have the best time together."

Who knew Help had a sense of humor? He's going to break her heart and I'm going to feel scummy watching it happen. I couldn't tell her he was an undercover cop—that had to be his call.

"Would you find out what you can about Miss January and how she's doing?" I asked her. "Let me know when she gets transferred. Free dinner to your sheriff friend and anyone else he wants to bring into Jake's."

Mac looked thoughtful. "I wondered why the sheriff would be staking out a residential neighborhood in the middle of the night. I thought about this and I thought that maybe the cops had the location staked out, house under surveillance, and the women got popped when they drove away having concluded business."

"I'll call Creole. Once she's transferred to county, he can get someone to keep an eye out for her; hopefully she won't get into any trouble. How's she going to deal with being sober?" I closed my eyes, hoping she wouldn't die in custody.

"She needs to detox under supervision or any number of complications could arise and she could end up dead. The worst thing for a body is to go cold turkey," Shirl said.

I looked at Fab. "I'll have to find out who her attorney is so I can apprise him of her problems and hopefully he won't let her linger in jail if it can be helped."

Fab pulled on my arm. "Come on, we'll go get lunch."

"We have to get her out," I said, and laid my head on her shoulder.

Chapter Twenty-Nine

I peeked in the window of the courtroom to see who had arrived, before slipping unnoticed into the back row. I had shown up to Miss January's court hearing early, and to my dismay, her case had been assigned to Ana Sigga, chief prosecutor and damn good at her job. Her reputation as a hard-ass was well deserved, and she didn't offer up sweet plea deals.

Miss January and several other defendants were handcuffed and paraded in and led to seats in the jury box. An armed bailiff stood guard in case one of them was stupid enough to attempt an escape. She looked pale and disoriented, unsure of what the heck was going on around her. Her prison orange hung off of her like a sack, and she looked more like a coat hanger for the uniform.

A dark-haired man stood, identifying himself as her public defender, fresh faced, dark circles under his eyes. I'd guess he was newly graduated from law school. He'd need every skill he learned in college to go up against Ms. Sigga. I suspected she'd chew him to bits and spit him out as a snack.

It further depressed me to find out that Chief Harder had decided to take a vacation. Not that he owed me any favors, but that wouldn't stop me from asking.

Ms. Sigga stood up and walked to the defense table. As she tossed a file down, my eyes went straight to her shoes. Another pair of red-soled Louboutin spike heels, different from the last ones. The lady liked her expensive, designer shoes.

Miss January stood silently in the jury box, her attorney by her side, where he answered all the questions on her behalf. She entered a plea of not guilty and the bailiff escorted her to the holding area for her ride back to the jail.

I wanted to talk to her, but it was forbidden for anyone to talk to the prisoners. I had no in with her lawyer but now that I knew who he was, I could go badger him at his office. Someone I knew must know him, so they could speak on my behalf. As I snuck out, mulling options as to how to help Miss January, my thoughts turned to Carly and how to get the truth out of her.

* * *

I called Mac and Phil to see if they could come up with any information about the night of the arrest and who the drugs were purchased from. My head ached worrying about Miss January. I made sure to leave enough time to take a nap before dressing for a family dinner at the Crab Shack.

Mother wanted to celebrate her poker room being a huge success. It was making money and there had been no raids. I didn't expect any since the group was private, by invitation-only. The regulars didn't miss a game. We'd had a couple of inquiries from the general public about booking it for parties, and so far Mother had ignored those requests.

A horn blasted behind me. Fab blew past and into a parking space. The Crab Shack sat off the main highway that looked out over the blue waters of the Atlantic Ocean; it was everyone in the family's favorite restaurant.

I kissed Didier's cheek. "I know I have you to thank for her showing up."

Fab looked like her usual hot self, with a black slip dress and ridiculously high heels. I wanted to hide my low-heeled linen wedges from view, but my dress wasn't long enough.

At least I won't fall down.

Fab rolled her eyes. "Do me a favor and get drunk again. I need a good laugh."

"Ow!" Fab jumped, glaring at Didier.

"Pinch your butt cheek, did he?" I smirked. "Creole does that all the time."

Didier put his arms around the both of us. "Both of you behave," he admonished. "Where is the boyfriend?"

"I texted him but haven't heard back." I checked my phone again, just in case. "Still working, I suppose—and not getting into trouble, I hope."

Spoon spotted us, stood, and waved. Mother didn't choose a restaurant without a water view and tonight was no exception.

Mother hugged us. "Where's Creole? You two aren't fighting are you?"

I sighed. "We don't fight." We were a pretty compatible couple and that surprised me as I stood there thinking about him. Another thing I loved was that he got mad and got over it, no grudge holding. We were alike in that way.

We ordered our drinks and I decided it was time to reacquaint myself with my old friend— Tequila. I chose a margarita with the intentions of sipping it, not downing it in a gulp or two. I managed to sit in the best seat at the table. With my back to the wall, I could scan the room and enjoy the water view. The restaurant had a low-key atmosphere, decorated with fake palm trees and fish mounted on the walls, rope lights strung around the ceiling.

"Did you invite Brad?" I asked.

Mother looked around. "He's at Liam's track meet, and he didn't know when it would end. Wouldn't it be nice if—"

"Let me guess," I said, cutting her off, "he got married. You need to let it be their decision to trot down the aisle."

Mother blushed. "Really, Madison. I wasn't intending to meddle."

Everyone laughed, knowing that Mother liked to manage her kids' personal lives in the spirit of wanting grandchildren.

"Look who's cuddling in the corner." Fab made a gagging noise.

Mother looked relieved that Fab changed the subject and she didn't have to answer. Surprised me that Fab didn't get "the look" for inappropriate noise-making at the table.

I turned and, sure enough, Ana Sigga and Slice were kissing. "She must be stalking me. I saw her earlier in court, didn't get a chance to say hello. I think I'll do it now."

"Court?" Mother hissed. "Are you in trouble?"

"Not a Westin this time," I said, patting her hand. "Miss January is in trouble."

I pushed back my chair and Fab asked, "Have you forgotten that she doesn't like you?"

"She likes you less than she does me." I raised my eyebrows.

I wasn't about to announce in front of everyone that Fab had unknowingly slept with Ana's then-husband.

"Excuse me," I said, and stood. "I'll have grilled shrimp and rice. Be back in a moment."

I smoothed my black dress down, a favorite of Creole's with cap sleeves, a cowl neck, and a deep slit in the side. Ana looked flawless every time I'd seen her in one of her power suits and, of course, her shoes. I wouldn't mind a peek around in her closet, if only to look; I couldn't imagine her letting me borrow anything.

Slice and Ana made a great-looking couple. Both were fiercely attractive in their own way. He was a solid wall of muscle and had that scar that made him look menacing. She looked different from her court persona, her dark hair not severely pulled back and in a French roll. Tonight she wore it long. She had very classical features, dark eyes, and a chiseled nose. Slice looked up and flashed a toothy smile while Ana turned and glared when her eyes met mine.

I seated myself opposite them, without waiting for an invitation. "I hope you don't mind. I only need a few minutes of your time."

"You are the rudest bitch." Ana's eyes were ice cold and angry. "I have no desire to speak to you about anything. Call my office and leave your number with my assistant and if I change my mind, you'll be contacted."

"I want to talk to you about Miss January Higgins."

She blew out an exasperated sigh. "Of course you'd champion a drug-dealing grandma."

"I know she's not guilty. She doesn't do drugs, not even prescription. What do you want to make a deal that wouldn't include jail time?"

"Are you bribing me?" she asked indignantly. "You're my witness," she said, and threw her eyes in Slice's direction.

"Your boyfriend here knows Miss January. Ask him about her. I'm offering an information exchange. You need the name of the dealer? Names of anyone who even smokes pot within a ten-mile radius? What?"

"We have her red-handed," she snickered. "No deals. Now leave."

I persisted even though she'd made up her mind, hoping she'd rethink prosecution. "The person who orchestrated this is the driver, Carly Manning, who has an impressive arrest record. Miss January is a harmless drunk with no arrest record."

She pulled her cell phone out. "Do I need to call the sheriff and have you arrested?"

"You should leave," Slice said, sitting back the whole time, listening but showing no emotion.

I wanted to yank her around by the hair, but instead, stood and leaned into her face. "She's dying, she's got cancer, and she didn't do this." I felt a pair of hands rest on my shoulders, thumbs pressing into the muscles on both sides of my spine. The familiar, masculine touch was just the support I needed.

"Is there a problem here?" Creole asked with an edge to his tone.

Creole and Slice stared one another down, the tension palpable. Ana looked at Creole and seemed shocked that we were a couple.

"You could do better," Slice said to me as he motioned with his head.

"And so could you." I gave them both a dirty look. "At least my boyfriend has enough integrity that he wouldn't stand by while I sent an innocent woman to prison. Don't ever criticize my choice again."

Creole looped his arm around me when I turned away. "You called me boyfriend," he said. He gave me a goofy smile and nipped my neck.

I wanted to whisper, "Harder," but the middle of the restaurant didn't seem appropriate for foreplay. "It's official, we're a couple," I giggled.

"I bet that didn't go well," Fab said.

"What does Slice see in her? I've never even done anything to her."

"You stuck up for me, went toe to toe, and, let's face it, you got what you wanted and she didn't." Fab smiled.

Mother and Creole hugged. "I ordered you a beer when I saw you walk in."

Fab explained to everyone the events of the other night and the predicament Miss January now found herself in.

Creole put his arm around me. "I don't think you should worry so much. From the look on Slice's face, he'll probably investigate on his own. Just because he doesn't like me, doesn't mean he's not a decent guy. Then I would expect a change of heart on Miss Sigga's part."

Since my dinner came before Creole's, I pushed my plate over, selected a shrimp, and rolled it around in the butter sauce offering him the first bite from my fork. I pushed it against his lips.

"Eat."

His eyes smoldered with more than the want of food. He ran his tongue slowly across his lips and took a bite, savoring the taste.

Brows raised, he whispered, "Are you sure you want to do this?"

He had a little spice stuck to the corner of his mouth. I restrained myself from licking it off and used my napkin.

Fab nudged me under the table and gave me the evil eye, letting me know that Mother was watching.

"I hope you ordered something good, since you'll have to share." I gave him another bite.

"You seem to be in one piece," Mother said to Creole. "You ever think about getting a nine-to-five job?"

"That's never going to happen."

I let my mind wander to how to change Ana Sigga's mind about Miss January. Any plan would probably have zero chance of success since she disliked me so much. Somehow, I had to get Carly's confession. That, too, seemed unlikely to succeed, as she was a smart one and streetwise. She only did what was in her best interest and that would include not pleading guilty to a felony.

"Are you paying any attention at all?" Creole whispered.

I shook my head, *no.*

"We'll get Miss January out of jail. You're not without influential friends. I'll find the dealer and help get the evidence you need."

I leaned over and brushed his lips. "Let's leave, now."

"We can't eat and run. Not much longer, though."

"Are you sure?" I ran my fingers up his inner thigh.

"Behave yourself," he growled. "Spoon's watching, and he knows what you're doing."

"I want to go home," — I pouted — "take off all your clothes, and push you down on my soft sheets." I blew him a kiss.

"Does anyone want dessert?" Mother asked.

"I'll have key lime pie, to go," I spoke up.

Chapter Thirty

I left Fab at home cuddled up and laughing with Didier out by the pool and drove to the Trailer Court, an acre of concrete set off the road to see what Brad wanted. It surprised me to see the place leveled, debris hauled away with six trailers still left behind. Jake's was on the opposite corner and it didn't look very busy as I drove past.

An Airstream, getting ready to be moved for repairs, sat on a flatbed. I'd prefer to clear the whole property, but then what? The last thing I wanted was another place full of eccentrics. That word always made me laugh; everyone knows that's a nice word for weirdos.

Liam sat laughing next to the professor, who now tutored him regularly in math. Liam told me Crum made it more understandable.

Brad opened the driver's side door and extended his hand. "The place now has potential."

I refrained from rolling my eyes.

"You've only got a couple of options: Let it sit here empty — except for Crum over there — sell it to someone who will want to build high-rise condos, or we go with my plan. I choose option three."

"I'm in as your silent partner. You can do whatever you want with the property. Jake's stays where it's at." The whole project sounded fun to me, but I wasn't signing up to be full-time management. I wondered if Mac could clone herself.

"I'm going to need your expertise in junk when it comes to decorating the place. No one can see potential in a piece of crap more than you do."

"That building stays," I said, and pointed to the old deserted gas station. "I really like the building. We could turn it into an antique store or maybe we can turn it into an office for Fab."

"Hmm… I thought about tearing that down." Brad shook his head. "We could put Fab's office where the car wash used to be—"

"Have you met the Twinkie girls yet?" I interrupted Brad, who was busy scribbling notes. "We could give the roach wagon a fresh coat of lime-colored paint. This block has cute potential."

"I met the ex-wrestler one. Big as me and could kick my ass. She has perfected the art of answering questions with something that doesn't make sense. Any problems with those two, you can handle it. You have a gift for communicating with unusual people."

I laughed. "Anything criminal in nature comes

up, we'll make that Fab's department."

"You've read my proposal and you're good with my ideas? If so, then work can start next week."

"Does this mean you'll be fishing less?" I asked.

"Julie and I are talking about buying that old turquoise monstrosity on the water and rehabbing it. If we can survive an extensive remodel that would be a good sign." Brad looked happy.

"I've got great connects for different trades. A friend of Elizabeth's works in county code enforcement and then there's Spoonie. I've always been happy with his recommendations; they're not creepy, show up, do a good job, clean up, and leave."

We walked over to Liam and Crum who were still laughing. I never found anything amusing about math once I got to algebra. Crum had drug out a pair of chairs I hadn't seen before, both faded yellow plastic, and furnished his patio from roadside finds that were left waiting to be picked up by the trash man.

"What are you two up to?" I asked. "We need to have a discussion you and I." I scowled at Crum.

"He's teaching me to say 'ass-face' in different languages," Liam said.

"That's helpful." I glared at Crum.

"This from the woman who lets him spit out

the car window," Crum scoffed.

"I can't believe you told." I brushed back Liam's hair.

Brad started laughing, making spitting noises. "We used to do that as kids. She could always hurl her spit farther than me."

"A girl's got to have a talent." I blushed.

"You remember how mad Mother got when she figured out what we were doing?" Brad smiled.

"I remember I didn't get grounded because I blamed it all on you. And you didn't tell. I believe I've told you a hundred times since that you're the best brother ever."

"I wish I had a brother or sister to blame stuff on," Liam said.

The professor cleared his throat. "The sheriff was able to identify the owner of the foot. It belonged to a gentleman who was out riding his bike in the dark and got hit by a car."

"I didn't figure that story would have a happy ending, but I'm sad to hear he died." I'd read that story in the local throw paper, not connecting the two. He'd been hit by several cars and no one stopped.

"What has Crum done now?" Brad dragged over a picnic bench for the two of us.

"How come Mac thinks I hired you as a gardener?" I asked Crum.

He looked uncomfortable, which surprised me. "I'm doing a damned good job," he snorted.

"Jami is a friend and I thought I'd save her accounts, but most dumped her when gossip blew through town about the murder and everyone started saying that she would never get out of jail."

It sounded like something I would do and get Fab to help, until she put her foot down and hired someone else.

"Mac has the final word, you work for her. Let me be clear on this point: no stolen plants. Leave a list and next time you show up, plants will be delivered."

Crum pinched his nose together. "I don't steal; those plants were relocated. They had been improperly planted."

I put my fingers in my ears. "You're too smart for such a stupid explanation. If you don't have a receipt from the Garden Center, we're not paying. Ask that snotty Mark who works there for assistance, you two should get along quite well."

Brad shook his head. "Have you seen a copy of Crum's lifetime lease?" he asked.

"It arrived along with a bunch of other paperwork when the estate got settled. A rather crudely drawn-up document. But I recognize Gus's handwriting."

"There's always a loophole, I'm sure we can toss him to the curb anyway." Brad glared at Crum.

The professor drew himself to his full height,

looking down his nose. "You pernicious little bastard," he said, his fists clenched.

"Stop!" I stepped between them, noticing my brother's smirk. He fully enjoyed setting Crum off. "We will honor his lease because it's what Gus would've done, but this has nothing to do with your sparkly personality." I winked at Crum and said, "One more thing, you are now under the two-sheriff rule: They show up twice and you're out."

Liam stood wide-eyed, looking a bit disappointed that a brawl hadn't broken out.

The two men stood face to face. Brad said, "As long as we agree, you keep the riffraff out during construction, so that means entertain your friends somewhere else. Keep helping Liam with his math. If his mom finds out you're teaching him swear words in three different languages, you're on your own, I didn't know anything about it. So far, my favorite has been ass face."

"What about him trotting around in his underwear?" I asked.

"I'm thinking we might be able to use that to our advantage in marketing. Just stay covered in your private areas." Brad pointed and made a crude gesture.

"Just so we're clear, I would have sued you," Crum said.

"If I want you out of here, there will be no court hearings. You'll find yourself relocated before there's time to say good-bye." Brad brushed his hands together.

I fist-bumped his shoulder. "I didn't know you had those kinds of connections."

"I believe we've come to an agreement," Crum said. "I'll honor my word, you do the same."

Chapter Thirty-One

Fab flew into the kitchen, long hair flying. "Get your ass up and let's go."

I looked at her and devoured the last two bites of my turkey-avocado sandwich, and downed the last couple sips of a fruit smoothie.

"That could easily be construed as snotty," I said, "and I'm busy."

"Doing what?" she shrieked.

I rubbed the side of my head. "That hurt my ears." I hoped I could draw out this little drama for a while so that I could enjoy every moment.

She handed me my phone. "Rearrange your schedule. Tell your crazy friends you'll see them tomorrow."

"See those," I said, and pointed to the counter next to the sink where two seashell pails were stacked. "If you can wait until after I fill those, I'm free." I bit down on my lip so as not to laugh and spoil the beautiful moment of total frustration.

Fab did a double take. "I'm going to drag your skinny ass off that stool."

I jumped up and looked over my shoulder

sticking my butt out. "Do you think it's skinny? You never say anything nice." I pouted.

She sucked in her breath for a long moment. "You have bigger boobs than me. Are you happy now?"

"Somewhat, but that doesn't solve my shell dilemma. How about tomorrow?"

"I'll go to the Shell Shack and buy you enough shells to fill those things and cover the counter." Fab leaped forward and tried to grab my arm, but I wiggled free.

"Now let's go," she demanded.

"There's a slight problem." I frowned. "You've made that same offer before and not one shell has shown up. You never did say why you're demanding my presence."

She grabbed my shirt, maintaining her grip until she had a good hold on my arm. "Get in the Hummer and I'll give you all the details."

"Oh, I can't drive?" I made a sad face.

Fab glared at me. "You're driving me crazy on purpose. Having fun?"

I jerked free. "As a matter of fact I am." I laughed and grabbed my bag off the bench and scooted out the door, one step ahead of her.

Fab looked at her watch and checked it with the clock on the dash. "I have a small window to retrieve this car and you've already wasted enough time," she grouched.

"Refresh my memory. Didn't we get arrested or kidnapped at the last job I did with you? I know we weren't shot at, that hasn't happened in a while."

"Hey, we're not dead. You know I need a driver and that person is you." Fab shot down the street and was forced to scream to a stop when a man ran the stop sign.

"Where are we going, exactly? Give me the address so I can put it in the GPS."

"I programmed it into my phone and I'm getting the directions in my ear." She patted her earpiece. "You need to get the GPS checked. It hasn't worked very well since Creole fooled around with it."

"What did you do?" I knew she did something because she looked away. "You know how Creole is about our safety."

"Don't worry; I've got your back. We'll be fine."

I turned my head and stared out the window lost in thought as the traffic blew by. My stomach took a dip at her words. I had a bad feeling, and this time it had nothing to do with the job but the showdown between her and Creole that would surely come. Not to mention the tiresome lecture I'd have to listen to. This time, if I'd have to listen, so would she—and I'd tell her to invite Didier. That confrontation had me smiling.

The SUV slowed considerably. I opened my eyes, unaware that I had dozed off. Fab veered onto the off ramp. I missed the road sign, so I had no idea what exit she took or where we were. When she got to the signal at the bottom of the ramp, and I looked east to west in each direction, I wanted to scream.

"Now would be a good time for you to hook a U-turn and let's go back to the Cove." We were in a terrible part of town to put it mildly, no wonder she refused to use the GPS.

"It's a little run down but we won't be here long. I have the keys to the Porsche Spyder. I hop in and drive away. You don't even have to get out."

Fab always made it sound so easy.

"You might want to listen to me, which I know you hate to do, but I have experience with these kinds of neighborhoods and it's always best to show up at the crack of dawn when no one is awake. Wandering around here in the middle of the afternoon is asking for trouble."

Fab completely ignored me and cruised through a commercial district, past dumpy buildings. Most of the storefronts were boarded up and empty, and there were only a few people out walking. Several turns later, we were in a residential tract. What was once a middle-class neighborhood of modest homes now needed some TLC.

"There's the car," Fab said, and pointed to the Spyder.

"I guess now would be the time to tell you I left my Glock at home." I looked out the windshield and grimaced.

"When in the hell are you going to stop doing that?" Fab barked.

"A walk on the beach doesn't require a gun," I huffed. "Listen to me, turn around now. Before we get carjacked by the group of men who just stepped into the street."

Fab had no intention of stopping and the main guy came to the same conclusion and drew a large-caliber gun, pointing it straight at her. One shot from that and she'd be dead. By my count, all six of them drew guns.

"Stop, please." A shudder ran through my body. "I don't want to die in a shootout. Maybe we can negotiate something in exchange for leaving here alive. They can even have the Hummer." We weren't in the Cove, so I couldn't throw out Spoon's name and expect them to go away.

Fab rolled to a stop in front of the leader. His cohorts fanned out surrounding the SUV. He moved to the driver's side and banged on the window, magnum cocked and ready to blow us away.

She rolled it down slightly. "We turned the wrong way. We don't want any trouble."

"All the way," he roared. His dark eyes surveyed first the two of us and then the interior of the car. He'd be a lot cuter if he put his gun down.

Fab kept her hands on the steering wheel. "You can have what you want—take it and go.

At least let her go, this is my fault," she said, and nodded at me.

I moaned and bent over, putting my head between my legs. I felt like I could easily projectile but probably wouldn't get that lucky. It wouldn't hurt to let him think that; no one wanted someone getting sick on them. Or maybe he'd just shoot me and that would take care of the matter.

"What's up with her?" he asked.

"She's pregnant and struggles with morning sickness," Fab said.

That's a good one.

"What have you got to trade for your life — and I hope it's not this eyesore which sucks on gas?" He chuckled.

I couldn't believe he was dissing my SUV, but I kept my head down. Maybe he'd let us drive away.

"I've got a Walther and some cash," Fab bargained.

He jerked open the driver door, drug her from behind the wheel, and took the keys from the ignition.

The door locks clicked and my door flew open. "Get out," a man yelled at me, and hauled me out. "Start walking."

"Where?" I looked around. The men who'd surrounded the car were now seated on the front porch of a two-story bungalow. Now two against two — it would have been a fair fight if I had my

Glock. The rest of the street was quiet. It was one of those neighborhoods where everyone minded their own business.

"What the hell are you doing here, anyway?" my captor asked.

There was nothing friendly about this man. He was short, round, bald and held a .44 Magnum that probably did a lot of the talking for him. I shot one once in a handgun safety class and blew a plastic chair to pieces, missing the intended target.

"I told her to use the GPS and she never listens to me." My heart pounded, I told myself to stay calm.

"Feeling lucky? Let's play a little game. See if you can make it to the corner without dying and I'm generously offering you a head start."

I looked at Fab. "My friend?"

"Think about your own ass. Consider yourself lucky that boss man has a soft spot for women. I'd just as soon kill the both of you." He grinned at me.

"Please…she's my best friend."

Fab gave me a shove. "Don't call *anyone*," she stressed. "I can negotiate a deal." She turned and walked across the street with the other man.

The Hummer's engine revved, a dark-haired man sitting behind the wheel. He stared at me, large sunglasses covering his face, and then he took off down the street.

"Ungrateful bitch. Get moving, now."

Fab looked at me and back at her captor. He nodded his head and she ran over to me. "Don't do anything stupid. Patience. One hour around the corner, wait out of sight." She turned to walk away and then yelled back to me, "Tell Didier, 'je t'aime.' *I love you!*"

"Fabiana..." I squeezed my eyes closed. "I don't want to leave you."

She held up her index finger and joined the leader.

My guard grabbed me by the hair, bringing me to a halt. His face contorted in anger, his voice dark and foreboding. "I'll count to five and then I'm coming after you. You turn the corner out of sight before I get to you, you live; if not, I promise you, not one single piece of you will ever show up. One more thing—the cops show up and your friend gets delivered back to you one piece at a time," he gave me a shove.

He held up a finger, "One..."

I sprinted for the corner feeling like the worst friend ever, saving my own ass and leaving Fab behind. She sounded optimistic, but the message for Didier let me know she didn't seem sure. Men loved Fab. They didn't usually want to hurt her, even the skanky dirtballs, but the tables turned when guns got involved. Surely, they wouldn't let me leave and not release her. I felt hopeful. Weren't they running the risk I'd call the police?

I slowed down to catch my breath, sweat

rolling down my back. I took a quick look over my shoulder and saw that my guard had disappeared. Fab and the ringleader stood talking under a leafy elm in plain sight. From my vantage point, they looked like old friends.

The corner house had a hedge that ran along the side. I scanned the street and there was not one single person outside in their yard or on the sidewalk. Plenty of cars in driveways, but no traffic in or out of the neighborhood and no place to stay out of sight without looking like a felony waiting for the right moment. I surveyed the gap in the bushes and sighed. I glanced over my shoulder and dropped to all fours, crawling through, praying I didn't smoosh my hand in animal poop. As long as I could make eye contact with Fab, I'd wait it out. I recalled a gas station a few blocks back; they probably wouldn't let me use the phone, but I'm sure they'd call the police. I briefly tossed away the idea of knocking on a random door, asking to call for help. Frankly, if it were me, I wouldn't open the door to a stranger. What if they were like the welcoming committee down the street? Too many questions, and all of them made my stomach ache.

My thigh started to throb, a pinched muscle signaling how much my body hated being twisted into a pretzel. I shifted around in the dirt finding no comfort, reaching out to snap off a couple of branches that had struck me in the face for the last time.

A neighborhood yellow tom strutted across the street, too fat to be homeless.

"Here, kitty," I clucked, desperate enough for a diversion that I'd talk to the cat. Maybe he knew the felons down the street.

He wandered over and lifted his tail.

"Take a hike, you dreadful thing." I ran my hand through the bushes.

He jumped back, glared at me, and hissed.

What would Fab do? She wouldn't be squatting in the bushes, that's for sure. She'd shoot him. She'd have her Walther tucked safely in her waistband, not having left it at home in the bedside drawer.

To my shock, the Hummer reappeared, Fab shook the man's hand, and then she got behind the wheel. I crawled out and wiped my hands on the back of my skirt, not wanting to be caught groveling in the dirt. I stayed completely out of view and headed in the direction of the main street. When she turned the corner, I stepped out into the road and stuck out my thumb.

"Get in," she yelled out the passenger window. "Am I glad to see you?"

"You okay?" I slammed the door. "How did you get this back?"

"Esteban never wanted this car, the 'gas pig' he called it. He had his eye on the Porsche. He watched it get dumped, and he and his crew waited to see who would show up next. He spilled the contents of my purse, finding my concealed permit and investigator license. I fessed up, told the truth that I was only in his neighborhood to retrieve the car."

"Esteban? First names?" I rolled my eyes. "Will we be seeing more of him?" I sighed with relief as she entered the on-ramp to the freeway.

Fab's secretive smile gave me hives.

"He questioned me about the jobs I'd done, wanted details. Interesting man."

Says him!

"I made him an offer," Fab continued. "I tossed him the keys to the Porsche, told him how to disable the GPS, he laughed. And then I surprised him, telling him about the back-up unit and showed him where it was located."

"You're amazing," I said in awe.

Fab flew back to the Cove in record time, but this time I didn't complain. I just sat back and downed my bottle of water, wondering how she planned to explain everything to Brick— especially the part about a missing half-million-dollar car.

"I gave Esteban my number in case he needed someone for a job. He might be a future client, but I did stress it had to be in a better part of town."

"Fabiana, he's a criminal."

"I made it clear that I only worked the gray line, no felonies. Totally sold the story that you were pregnant with your first child and thanked him for not hurting you."

"I have a suggestion for your business venture—an upgrade in clients. Brad and I talked, are you interested in the old gas station?"

"I'm claiming the space where the car wash used to be," Fab said, looking over at me.

"It's empty!"

"Leave that to me." Her sneaky smile had me rubbing my forehead.

"Esteban asked me out on a date. Told him I lived with the best man ever and I wasn't screwing it up. That's when he mentioned being associates."

"We get carjacked, and you not only get the car back but you get a date request? I get threatened and have to run for my life," I sniffed. "I hated leaving you. I only did what the short one told me because you insisted."

"You did the right thing. Do you think we could keep this little escapade between the two of us?" she pleaded.

"No exchange of bullets, no calls for help. We might not get caught," I said, and laughed. "If Creole doesn't ask, I'm not bringing it up. This is pretty close to a happy ending."

Chapter Thirty-Two

"Creole's on the phone," Fab shouted from inside the house to the patio. She stood in the doorway waving my cell.

"Yeah, yeah, hang on," she said into the phone.

I grabbed her arm and jerked it down from over her head to retrieve it. "Never leave your phone out," I told Creole. "You never know what she'll say."

"Good news," he said, and laughed. "Miss January is getting released within the hour."

"She got bail?" I smiled at Fab.

Fab raised her eyebrows, pointing for me to put the call on speaker. Creole made me promise to never broadcast his calls. When I shook my head, she tried to take back the phone.

I slapped her hand away and made a face.

"No bail. Case dismissed." He sounded very proud of himself.

"Who did you bribe?"

He chuckled. "I went to the chief with a deal: I'd bring in the dealer in exchange for the charges being dropped on Miss January. Harder sold it to Ana Sigga."

"I bet she wasn't happy." Thankfully, I only saw her around the Cove on occasion; I assumed it wasn't sophisticated enough for her, a different world from Miami.

"Harder asked her why she squeezed so hard on a woman with no record or history of drug use. And that she better have a good reason to block the deal. She didn't answer but looked embarrassed and signed off."

"We need to go to Miami," I told Fab. "Rita will have to wait until later, Miss January doesn't have anyone to pick her up." I had received a message from Rita earlier that she had information for sale and to bring cash.

"I knew you were headed to Dawg's," Creole said. "I called Mac and she went to the jail, taking Score along for the ride. She just called and they're back."

"Your next day off, we're going to spend it naked and I'll show you my appreciation for you being the best boyfriend." I let out a long sigh thinking about taking off his clothes.

"I'm going to be sick," Fab squealed.

Creole laughed. "Lift up your skirt and reassure me that you have your Glock strapped on."

"Yes, it's there." I giggled, my cheeks warming.

"Be careful. You have a tendency to close your eyes to danger. I want you to be careful and not ignore any signs."

"If plans change I'll call you," I said, disconnected, and smiled at the phone.

"Can't you control yourself until you're in the bedroom with the door closed?" Fab shook her head in disgust.

"Just for that, I think I'll drive." I smirked.

She took the keys out of her pocket and grinned.

Before I could chase her down, my phone rang again.

"I want a raise," Mac informed me. Judging by the sounds of traffic in the background, she must have had her windows down.

"You think you deserve more money to drive drunks around?" I hit the speaker. Fab and I sat back down at the island. "At least one passenger's sober."

"Lucky for me, Score had a hard day drinking and passed out, snoring all the way." Mac chuckled. "Turned out Miss January doesn't care for sobriety, asked me to stop at the liquor store for vodka and cigarettes."

Having known a drunk or two, the person had to have the desire to be sober and Miss January clearly wasn't interested. I never expected her to stay sober. It wouldn't prolong her life.

"Would you have Shirl check in on her," I asked.

"I think she missed not having Miss January around," she said. "I have more good news. The charges against Joseph were dismissed."

Fab and I shook our heads.

"There's one lucky man. How did that happen?" I asked.

"The victim wouldn't cooperate with the DA and didn't show for a court hearing. Turns out, he had an outstanding warrant from Maryland and left town. He knew any cooperation on his part and his past would catch up to him," Mac said.

"What was he wanted for, do you know?"

"He'd been convicted of grand theft and was serving time on a road crew when he walked away one day. They catch up to him and he'll get extra time for escape and no cushy minimum security hospitality," Mac said.

"Lucky Joseph. I hope he realizes he needs to stay in the Cove and get drunk or, better yet, stay home with Svetlana."

"I told him I liked Svet better than him and he took it as a compliment," she hooted.

When we hung up, I realized a good bribe was in order to make sure she stayed.

I called Dawg's to confirm with Rita and found out she had gone home for the day.

Chapter Thirty-Three

The front door slammed with such force I thought it would fly off the hinges. "What in the hell were you two doing over in Sunnyside?" Creole stomped into the living room.

Fab and I had been arguing over what take-out to order. If I'd had advance warning, I would have slid to the floor and hid behind a piece of furniture until the storm cleared but it was too late, he towered in front of me.

I looked up, almost flinching from the anger on his face. "Could you use your quiet voice?" Technically, I could say, "Where?" because I didn't know the name of the area until now.

"No," he barked, rubbing the back of his neck. "Since you two have a death wish, how about I help you and strangle you both?"

I stared at his legs sticking out from his knee-length shorts and smiled. Now probably wasn't the right time to tell him how damned hot he looked, fresh out of the shower, hair damp around his shoulders. Maybe I could throw some beach towels at him and he'd get the hint and we could go roll in the sand.

He cleared his throat, glaring down.

"That would upset Mother."

"Don't blame her." Fab stepped in front of Creole, going nose to nose with him, voice controlled. "The GPS wasn't working so I used my phone. We had no idea the neighborhood was in need of revitalization."

I peeked at Didier from the corner of my eye, watching the fireworks about to begin. Fab must have told him despite her demand that we keep quiet earlier.

Creole sat back, calm, and gave me a hard look. I didn't know exactly what he found out, but I didn't want to add to the drama by lying, so I kept my mouth shut. He turned on Fab. "If the GPS isn't working, I'll bet it has your fingerprints on it. Are you so dumb that you ignored all the signs you were in a very bad neighborhood?"

Didier's eyes never left Fab. The corners of his mouth turned up, ready for the explosion, and Fab didn't disappoint.

She jumped into Creole's face, unleashing a tirade in French. I noticed her liberal use of bad words, one in particular. Liam had been teaching me the colorful words on the sly. The professor would be proud if he knew.

Creole yelled right back at her. Whatever he said, Didier laughed and they both turned on him.

I'd had enough. Pretty soon they'd be saying stuff they couldn't take back if that hadn't happened already.

"Stop it!" I squeezed in between them. "Sit back down," I ordered Fab, "and you sit over there." I pointed to the chair I just vacated.

"Enough of this." I put my hands on my hips. "You two don't know each other very well and that's about to change. You two sit down and talk this out."

"This isn't about liking one another, it's about her blatantly refusing to use common sense," Creole raged.

No one said a word. We sat and stared at one another.

Creole sighed and stood up. "Get up," he said, and motioned to Fab. "Do you mind if I borrow your girlfriend?" he asked Didier. "We need to get a few things straight."

"Just know you're a dead man if you don't bring her back alive," Didier said. "I agree with Madison, you two definitely need to get along." He folded his arms across his chest.

"Does my opinion count?" I asked.

"I'll deal with you later." Creole glared.

I gave him a big smile. That worked in my favor. His anger lines softened, his mouth briefly turned up in the corners.

Fab jumped up and smoothed out the non-existent wrinkle in her slinky dress that tied behind her neck. "I think it's a great idea," she said in a voice that said she clearly didn't. "Come on, big ass, unless you're afraid. Time to set some ground rules."

Creole fished his keys out of his pocket, saying something to her in French. Didier threw his head back and laughed.

Fab turned and glared at him. "Don't worry," she said to me, "we'll find you a new boyfriend." The door slammed behind them.

"This isn't the worst idea, but close," Didier said. "They need to be friends if we're going to make our relationship work."

I watched from the kitchen window as Creole peeled out of the driveway. "Why couldn't they stay here?" I picked up my phone. "Salad with your pizza?"

"You could at least ask what I want for a topping," Didier grouched.

I ordered the large size, grilled vegetables on one side, shrimp on the other, stressing they were not to co-mingle in anyway. "I know everyone in this family's favorite pizza topping and that includes you."

He stood and hugged me. "What happened today?"

"A simple car retrieval went a little wrong. Fab needs to be the one to give you the details, if she hasn't already."

Didier listened, his face impassive.

"She was truly amazing." I smiled.

Didier looked lost in thought. "I knew she had something on her mind; she started several times to say something and then changed the subject.

Why couldn't she just tell me she had a bad day?" he asked.

"My guess is she never wants to disappoint you or worry you. Look back from when you first met her to now and see all the good changes. You can't snap your fingers and demand trust. You, my dear, seem to have earned hers and I hope you appreciate how hard that was for her to give."

"I love her, all wild-eyed and beautiful spirit. She makes me laugh, she's wicked smart, and so very naughty." He smiled thinking about her.

"Which one comes back with a bullet wound?" Didier asked.

"Hopefully, neither one of them," I said, and laughed. "But my guess is Fab would draw first. I wouldn't want to be there for that. I hope they went some place public where it's less likely to get out of control, forces them to use their good manners. A boyfriend once broke up with me in a pricey restaurant. I never got to tell him what I thought of him. I felt cheated."

"Bâtard," Didier said.

The doorbell rang. I opened the door to the pizza boy.

I lifted the lids to the boxes and they smelled yummy. I grabbed plates and put two slices on each, handing them to Didier, who'd tossed the salad in a bowl and spooned a little on each plate.

Didier pulled on a strand of my hair. "You

and Creole are well-suited. He's a good guy, for an American."

I got out wine glasses, setting us places at the island. Didier poured from a bottle of red wine he picked up.

"I know some people think it's all about sex but I think he and I have potential," I confided. "He doesn't try to change me. Today, Fab and I should have made better choices, we need to agree on how to handle these unsafe areas for the future, guaranteed it won't be our last. I should've been more vocal."

"She says you're like a sister to her."

"The best day was when I met her and we became friends. I was a bit lonely here by myself. In truth, I didn't mind that she moved in. I had never entertained the idea of a roommate; I would have been more likely to fill the house up with cats. At one time, I thought about fixing her up with Brad and I'm glad I didn't. I figured out he needs easy-going, not dramatic. Besides, I wouldn't have met you." I winked.

"Are you really okay about my moving in? I didn't want to ask in front of Fab and embarrass her. I'll bet she never mentioned it, did she?"

"You're like the boyfriend who slept over a few nights and never went home." I laughed. "You can't go anywhere now. You're family and your leaving would ruin our foursome. That's why those two have to get along."

We stood side by side at the kitchen sink; he

rinsed and I stacked the dishwasher. Jazz wandered in and meowed at his feet. Didier retrieved tuna from the refrigerator and bent down, talking to him, while he fed him. I watched from the corner of my eye, and saw that Jazz certainly had him trained. Real tuna! Pretty soon he'd turn up his nose at meat treats from Fab. I hoped I was there the day the cat showed her his tail and left the room.

"How about a movie?" Didier sat with the remote flipping through the channels.

I didn't have the heart to tell him I'd rather read. Maybe once the movie got started, I could sneak out a book and he wouldn't notice.

"You choose." I curled up in my favorite chair, tablet in hand, already scanning my carousel of books. "Nothing scary," I said, remembering Fab's last choice for a movie.

Fab and Creole walked in through the French doors and she threw herself down next to Didier.

"Where did you go?" I asked, scanning them for injuries.

"No wonder you two get along." Fab looked at me in disgust. "A crappy hamburger stand."

"Roscoe's?" I looked up at Creole, trying to gage the temperature.

Roscoe's, a drive-thru, served the best burgers anywhere. No outside seating to the general public, the back patio had seating by invitation only, which meant only friends of Roscoe's.

Creole nodded and brandished a bag from

behind his back, dumping the contents on the counter.

I reached out. "Can I have some fries?" I asked after snagging several.

"Keep your mitts off our dinner. His idea sucked." Fab shifted around, leaning back against Didier who'd moved in from the living room. "I'll take my hamburger on a plate," she said to Creole.

Creole served Fab her food and sat down next to me at the island.

"It wasn't totally terrible, but close." Creole looped his leg over mine and gave me a quick kiss.

I tried to push his leg off, but he wasn't letting that happen. "I just want to know one thing: Did you two kiss and come to an understanding?" I looked between them.

"Not our fault, you can blame Madeline." Fab took a bite of her burger. Didier watched in fascination as she licked her lips, then her fingers, and gave him one of her seductive smiles.

"Where did you see Mother? Not at Roscoe's." I raised my eyebrows. I snatched a French fry, dragging it through ketchup, holding it out for Creole to take a bite, and then gobbled the rest.

"You're going to pay for teasing me while I'm hungry." Creole cupped my chin. "I'm going to clean my plate because I'll need my energy."

"Your mother and Spoonie"—Fab stuck her

finger in her mouth—"were there and when they saw the two of us, she insisted we sit with them. When she figured out you two weren't showing up, the questions started." She glared at Creole. "'What did this guy do?' she demanded. He answered the first one and then, you know your mother, she had one hundred more. She ignored me and zoomed in on lover boy here."

"You should have kicked me sooner," Creole grumbled.

I leaned over and ran my hand down his leg, then just to be sure, ran my fingers from his ankle to his mid-thigh, his shorts cutting me off. A low growl resonated from his throat, and he shook his finger. "You better not have left any marks," I said to Fab.

"Madeline asked if you knew that we were out together. I wanted to yell at her, 'What do you mean?' And stoop nut here said 'Yes.'" Fab rolled her eyes. "She jumped to the conclusion we'd done something. Since he didn't get the message the first time, I kicked him hard and pulled a trick out of your mother's bag and started answering a question with a question."

"Bet that frustrated her. She's the queen of that technique," I said.

"She got all huffy and told me she wanted straight answers. I thought, 'None of your business,' but I love her. We exchanged one of those girly one-up looks, both of us refusing to look away."

Creole chuckled. "It looked more to me like 'let's meet out back and fight this out.' Roscoe stopped all conversation when he showed up with our food. Gutsy here told him we'd take a bag and I told him to put it on Spoon's check."

"It's Spoonie," Fab reminded Creole. "Who never said a damn word, just made a few googly eyes at your mother. He needs to rein her in, starting with that hideous nickname."

"She's working on it." I laughed. "She agreed to only using it in their... uh... private time."

I rendered all three of them speechless at the same time. They loved her and clearly didn't like the suggestion she may be doing something horizontal. I refused to think about it.

"Thanks for getting us out of there. I'd never have been so rude, but I'm happy you did it for the both of us. I don't have to feel bad." Creole smiled at Fab. "No hard feelings. Just stay out of the slums."

Didier turned her to face him. "I'll not be happy if I hear that you do that again." His voice remained neutral but his eyes were dark and stormy.

Fab stood up, taking a step back. "Listen up, everyone. I made a few miscalculations today in my zest to make up to Brick for what he considers my slacker attitude. I promise we'll work out a better system for problems," she said to me. "If it ever comes up again that only one of us gets away, it will be you. And should anything happen, you will know that I wanted it that way. No arguing or hesitation." She leaned down and hugged me. "You never cease to amaze me."

"You're not so bad yourself." I held on to her until she squirmed.

"I'm certainly happy that I saw your potential." She smirked.

Creole pulled me off my stool and onto his lap, my head against his chest. "What about the Porsche?"

"I gifted it to Esteban." Fab flashed a big smile, extremely proud of her trade.

"Just so you know, he could've had my 'gas pig' and anything else to let us go," I said to her.

"Stay away from Esteban Castro." Creole shook his finger at her. "He has a prison cell with his name on it and I'd hate to see you arrested because of the company you keep."

Fab ignored Creole. I noticed she left out the part about his potential as a future client. "I told Esteban you were a crack shot," she said to me. "And if I hadn't rushed you out of the house without your Glock, he'd be laying in the street. Told him I was friends with Chief Harder and he laughed in my face. I amended my answer and told him you were the one with the friendship and it was in his best interest to make a deal."

"How did you find out what happened?" I asked Creole.

"I know people everywhere. Just remember

that. Thanks for the tips on how to handle a Madeline Westin interrogation in the future," he said to Fab.

Didier smiled up at her and pulled her down onto his lap, kissing her.

Chapter Thirty-Four

I shoved my phone across the table to Fab. "I don't recognize the number—you answer it." I knew the chances of the call not ending well were high, but I wanted to finish my enchilada.

Fab turned her nose up at the phone and answered in French—that would confuse a local. I fully expected the person to hang up and call back. She hit the speaker. I looked around, happy that we were the only ones on the deck at Jake's.

"Yeah, bone jourie yourself. Is this Madison Westin?"

I didn't recognize the voice, which was nasally with a twang, and shook my head.

"Yes, now what do you want? Make it fast or I'm hanging up," Fab growled into the phone.

I covered my mouth so I wouldn't laugh.

"This is Rita from Dawg's, you said to call if I had information on Eddie's murder. I called once before and you didn't call back. I know who did it, but if I tell you I need money to get out of town," she said in a rush.

"Where did you get the information?" Fab asked, a look of disbelief on her face. "How do we know you're selling reliable information?"

"A couple of locals were in last night and I overheard them talking about the murder. It's all anyone wants to talk about down on the docks. No one's saying anything; they don't want the area crawling with cops." Her voice was a whisper, though there was no noise in the background.

I knew that to be true. If the authorities even looked as if they were headed to the dock area, it instantly became a ghost yard. When possible, they disappeared aboard their boats.

"What is it you want?" Fab asked her.

"Ten thousand in cash," she blurted.

"You're crazy, too," Fab yelled. "It's not like Jami's family. Even rewards for professional snitches don't pay that high."

I got up and closed the deck doors. Afternoons were always quiet in the bar in the lull before the folks showed up who drink their dinner.

"I can't stay in the Cove. If anyone finds out, I'm dead. Eddie had connections that would shut me up. They look out for their own, even piddly delivery boys."

"*If* what you say is true, we'll help you to get out of town. Your price better be negotiable." Fab shook her head at me.

After a long pause Rita said, "I get off at six, meet me under the overpass, in the back corner of the lot."

"You better not be wasting our time." Fab ended the call. "I don't think she knows anything, she just wants money."

I looked at my empty margarita glass and sighed, taking the last sip. "There were rumors about Edsel's drug connections, but we couldn't find a link to anyone major. The general consensus of his death around town was good riddance. Creole said he never made Drug Enforcement radar."

"I don't like Rita," Fab said over the top of her water bottle. "She's greedy. And I hate that bar. I say we blow off this meeting."

"I'd like to hear what she has to say. I'll tell her upfront I'm not meeting her payment demand."

Fab stood up. "Let's go home. We've got time for a swim."

* * *

"Looks like our friend, Rita, is kicked back drinking a beer." Fab pointed to the back of the parking lot. "Promise me this is the last time we come to this dump."

I slid my phone out of my pocket and texted Creole. Fab looked at me and snickered.

"I keep remembering that Jami told me she saw the dead body—only she said, 'we.'" I recalled her jailhouse confession, the only time I'd seen her since her arrest. She sent a note to put her final paycheck in her jail account.

"Did you ever find out why the jail visit got

cut short?"

"Mac found out a chick slug-fest broke out."

"Do you think Jami knows who killed Edsel and has kept quiet?" Fab mused. "Who risks life in jail for anyone?"

"It would have to be some scurve worse than Edsel." I waved to Rita, who stood next to an old white van. "I want to be upfront before we get started."

Fab stood back as I approached Rita.

She quirked her head and stared at me. "You sure sound different on the phone."

"I've heard that before." I half-smiled. "We need to negotiate the price. Any information needs to be verified before cash exchanges hands. I'm not paying your price, but I can connect you with a bartender job in another state. I know someone who's always looking for experienced employees." I noticed her hands shook, maybe she was afraid; when I first got out of the SUV she seemed more confident, intense.

"You're probably a nice person but too smart for your own good." She withdrew a semi-automatic from the back of her jeans.

I knew guns and recognized it as a Ruger LC9. She had an impressive piece of hardware, but did she know how to use it? At this close range, I suppose it didn't matter.

"I couldn't take the chance you'd figure it all out and this place would be swarming with cops." She waved the muzzle. "Be cool and call your friend over. Warn her and she'll be dead."

"Leave her out of this." I moved my hand to the back of my thigh, making a gun with my fingers, moving it around, hoping to catch Fab's attention.

Rita stepped forward. "Fine, she goes first."

"Run, Fab," I screamed.

Rita jammed her gun in my face. "Go ahead and run, skinny bitch," she yelled to Fab. "I'll kill your friend here."

"If this is about money, you can have what you want." We'd have to make a bank run and that would buy time. I liked our odds, two against one. We both had guns and had stared down death before and won. Times like these call for a help button on my phone but it sat on the dashboard.

Fab marched over the gravel, hands in the air, shoulder height, in full arrogance, wearing her creepy smile that made the hair tingle on the back of my neck—and I knew her. Poor Rita, Fab was out of patience.

"I know she can be annoying." Fab flung her hand in my direction. "Let's make a deal, no shots fired; no one leaves in a body bag. Happy, happy all around."

Rita motioned Fab to stand next to me. If we got close enough, I could take Fab's gun from her waistband and kill Rita. Normally, I shot to disarm; but in this case, I'd make an exception.

"Nothing personal—I just want to enjoy the

time I have left." Rita looked indecisive, which worked in our favor.

I snorted and Fab glared at me as though reminding me of my manners in this situation. "Can you at least tell us why you want to kill us?" I asked.

"I didn't mean to bash Eddie's head in, but when I told him about my HIV diagnosis, he laughed. Then he admitted he had the disease and deliberately slept around with no protection, spreading the love, he called it. I lost my mind. The next thing I know, I picked up the shovel and delivered the first bash to the back of his head and heard a crunching noise." She smiled. "He went down face first. I didn't plan to hit him but his stupid moaning reminded me of my test results. I kept hitting him until my arms got tired."

Fab and I looked at each other wide-eyed. *We didn't see this coming.*

"You were willing to let an innocent person rot in jail with the high probability that she'd get the death penalty?" I struggled to control my temper.

"You don't understand. Jami and I are friends, but I saw Eddie first and we'd been together a long time then she came in, hanging all over him. We were getting married. He didn't even break up with me—just showed up with her," she whined, her hand shaking. "Besides, I planned to give a full confession right before I died."

"It's one thing to be in jail for something you did, but to know you're innocent and have no hope to get out—" I said in disgust. "Do you know how hard it is to get a conviction overturned? With no proof other than your statement, they'd never reopen the case."

A couple of cars and trucks had pulled into the parking lot while we stood there, but no one even looked our way; they headed straight into the bar. If they had, all they would see is three women talking.

"Did you lure Edsel to the shed?" Fab asked.

"I got lucky, drove by and saw his crappy car parked in front, figured he lived there. He was easy to locate, yelling, throwing stuff around. Turns out he was looking for stuff to pawn, made him mad he couldn't get anything more than yard tools. If he got lucky, he knew they'd only bring about twenty bucks."

Rita wailed, a stray tear on her cheek. "He knew. He knew he was sick and didn't say anything, he wanted revenge. Mad that he contracted it in prison, all because of a wrongful conviction, his girlfriend crying rape when it wasn't. Then he told me he never had any intention of marrying me, he used it as incentive so I'd never say no to kinky sex."

"I know you and Jami were at the shed after you killed him, how did that happen?" *I didn't know that—but it wasn't much of a leap.*

"I had already left when I saw her peddling to

The Cottages, so I doubled back. I snuck up behind her. She didn't even scream when she saw him. I bumped her hard hoping she'd fall on him but all she got was blood on the bottom of her shoe. Turns out it was enough. We agreed not to tell anyone what we found and let the police figure it out."

What did women see in him? Unattractive, creepy personality, abusive, his life going nowhere…

Fab spoke up. "You're not going to get away with double murder. Edsel was a dirtball, so a prosecutor might offer you a reduced sentence. If you've got information about illegal dealings, use it to sweeten the deal."

"You won't know a moment's peace, Rita. My boyfriend will track my killer—you—until he brings you to justice," I told her. "And when he does, he has connections to make your prison stay a frightening, living hell."

"Do you really want to spend life on the run?" Fab asked. "I've heard the lifestyle sucks, always looking over your shoulder."

"Since the first day you two showed up here with your nosey questions, I've been working on my plan. I'll get away with it," she wheezed. "Get in the van." She slid back the door, motioning with her gun. "I've got this all figured out."

"Do you know how hard it is to dispose of two bodies that won't lead a trail right back to you?"

I inched closer to Fab. Her gun would be easier to draw than my own.

Getting in the truck was a bad idea. We'd be dead before she closed the door.

"I'm going to take you two to the dump," Rita said, as though the choice was obvious and we were stupid not to know.

Great. Free cremation. Locally, all trash got dumped into a cement building before being scooped into the incinerator with a skip-loader.

"I'm not getting in," I told her. "You're going to work for this kill. Good luck dragging our bodies into your ratty van by yourself. I may be dead, but hopefully you'll live long enough to fry—zzzz." I imitated the sound of electricity.

Rita flinched, then said, "You'll get in because if you don't I'll shoot your friend right in front of you."

Fab hit my thigh, a head nod to the front of the van. Rita and I heard the crunch of gravel at the same time, but only she turned, giving us just enough time to draw our guns. Creole stepped out from the opposite side in his cop uniform— blue jeans—holding a Glock, and caught her by surprise. She hesitated in pulling the trigger. He shot her in the upper shoulder before she screamed and dropped her gun to the ground.

In full fury, blue eyes blazing, he jerked her to a standing position, ignoring her screams, and pushed her face against the van, snapping the cuffs on her wrists.

She continued to scream a litany of variations of the "F" word at the top of her lungs. It drew some lookers but no one stepped forward to help.

Creole pushed her face down on the floor in the back of her van. "If you move, you'll be sorry," he barked.

He frowned down at me. With a gentle finger under my chin, he lifted my eyes to his and said, "Good thing I was in the area. I'll see you later." He wrapped his arms around me and crushed me to his chest, hugging me until I groaned.

A Tarpon Cove sheriff car blew into the driveway and skidded to a stop. Kevin got out, and it surprised me he showed up solo, no partner in tow. He and Creole nodded to one another and Creole disappeared back the way he came.

Fab put her arm around me. "You okay?"

I leaned on her. "We should retire while we're both still alive."

Kevin nodded to us and walked over to Rita, yanked her to her feet, and read her rights. Seconds later, two more sheriff cars arrived and a paramedic van. Kevin waited for a stretcher, and the medics strapped her down. "Either of you need medical attention?"

"Take her," Fab told him, and pointed to Rita.

Kevin slammed the door and the van took off. "I need to ask you some questions for my report."

It was the first time Kevin showed any sympathy to either one of us in yet another shooting situation, and there were no unfunny comments about dead people. It was evident that Creole had set him straight that he wasn't a drug-dealing felon and was actually working on the same side as Kevin.

"You won't have to worry about how to tell Didier about our night." I nudged Fab.

Fab looked confused.

I inclined my head to the Mercedes that just flew into the driveway.

"I'm liking your boyfriend more and more," Fab said, and ran to meet Didier who jumped out of the car, whirling Fab off her feet and into his arms.

Chapter Thirty-Five

My eyes fluttered open, the morning sunshine streaming through the small windows, announcing a beautiful day. Lying in the crumpled sheets from the night before, I stretched against Creole's hard body, snuggling within his arms, my head on his chest. I lay there listening to the rise and fall of his breath, his heart beat pulsing in my ear.

Fab and I had to give several statements to law enforcement regarding the new developments in Edsel Winer's case, ending up in the district attorney's office. I blew out a big sigh of relief when I found out that Ana Sigga hadn't been assigned the case, so the questioning went fast and there was no drama. It would take a few days for Jami to be released, only after detectives verified everything we told them about the murder. Rita wasn't cooperating, saying she was the victim and that we had tried to kidnap her and she only defended herself.

The next day, it caught me off guard when Fab and Didier had their bags packed by the door and left saying, "See you soon."

It wasn't until late the next afternoon that

Creole finally burst through the door, sweeping me off my feet. Once upstairs, he tossed me onto the bed and climbed on top, giving me a hot, bruising kiss and, to my dismay, releasing me just as quickly.

"Put on that black wrap dress I like and pack an overnight bag, I have a surprise for you." He smacked my butt.

"The only surprises I like are the ones I figure out in advance," I giggled, and rolled away from his outstretched hand.

He tapped his watch. "Be ready in fifteen minutes or I'm leaving without you."

I sulked. "You wouldn't do that, would you?"

He cupped my face between his hands. "Probably not. Now hurry up." He brushed my lips with his.

It was a warm evening as we set off going south down the Overseas Highway to our unknown destination—unknown to me, anyway. Creole put the little-used convertible top down on the Hummer. I scooted next to him, my head on his shoulder, and he put his arm around me and held me tight, the salty wind blowing in our faces. It didn't take long to feel fairly certain we were headed to Key West, a very romantic place for us, and I hoped this time wouldn't be any different.

To my disappointment, he veered off the highway at Stock Island, several miles north of Key West. We wound through the streets to the crystal waters of the Atlantic side, pulling into the exclusive members-only Harbour Club. Creole rolled down the window and pulled a pass from his pocket.

"You know I could've snuck us in." I smiled at him.

The guard nodded and motioned him to a reserved parking space.

"I'm going to see to it that you enjoy every minute," he growled in my ear, and ran his teeth down the side of my neck, nipping the top of my shoulder.

Creole opened the door and handed the keys to the valet, clicking the locks for the bags. He reached in and pulled me across the seat and out the driver's side.

Our two bags left on a cart ahead of us. Creole gave me a quick kiss, took my hand in his, and led me down to the dock, stopping at the steps of a pristine three-story white yacht. A member of the crew stood waiting.

"Your luggage has been brought on board and stowed in your stateroom." The man in crisp white shorts and shirt introduced himself as LaRouche.

I tried not to openly gawk, but I'd never seen a boat this size up close. I looked at Creole in shock and caught the nervous laughter as it was gurgling up.

"I'd be happy with a roll in the sand," I whispered, before removing my shoes and climbing the stairs.

"You're so easy to please. You never complain about my erratic hours. I wasn't passing on having five days with you on a luxury yacht."

LaRouche ushered us through the salon and to the stern, where a table for four had been set for dinner. Fab and Didier were draped over one another on the couch in a serious make out session, their legs wrapped around each other.

"Fabiana Merceau," I grouched, imitating Mother. "Where are your manners?"

They both jumped, and when she realized it wasn't Mother, she squealed and ran over, hugging me. "Isn't this fabulous?"

Fab had on a skimpy white bathing suit under her sarong cover-up, Didier in swim trunks and a T-shirt that stretched across his chest, in a dark blue that matched his smiling eyes.

I hugged Didier and kissed his cheek. "I'm so happy you two are part of the surprise." I blew Creole a kiss.

LaRouche appeared, holding a tray with glasses of white wine. We each helped ourselves and sat on the couch toasting the last glimpses of sun over the ocean.

Creole ran his fingers up my back, wrapping them around my hair, and pulled me close. "We have Didier to thank for the invitation."

Didier swept his arm around. "This belongs to one of my clients and he's offered the use of it several times and this time I took him up on it.

Later, I'll give you a tour and show you to your guest suite. If you want anything, there's a button in every room." He pointed to the wall. "The steward will appear and grant your wish," he said, and laughed.

I couldn't wait to see the rest. I'd been on a boat before, but nothing like this. Even Brad's commercial fishing boat was about half the length. I eyed the hot tub, the steam rolling off the water. I wanted to sit in every room and try everything that even remotely looked like fun.

The dinner rivaled that of a five-star restaurant and Didier told us the chef had prepared a fresh salmon with dill sauce, vegetables, and a surprise for dessert. Music played in the background and we talked about everything but our jobs. After dinner, we moved to double chaises and sipped wine and laughed, enjoying the quiet, no phones ringing, no last-minute emergencies.

Didier showed us to our suites down a long marble hallway. The door opened to a king-sized bed and amazing burl-wood cabinetry. We had an en suite bathroom, every finish top quality, with a moon-shaped bathtub that could seat six comfortably; but the walk-in glass shower was the centerpiece with a dozen jets and bench that had me thinking naughty thoughts.

* * *

"Morning," Creole said, as he peered down at me under his lashes, eyelids heavy.

I rolled over in his arms, now face to face. "Did you sleep well?" I smiled and kissed his chest.

He hugged me to him, running his foot up my leg, resting on my butt. "I always sleep well with you in my arms. Five mornings of this." He smiled.

"Did I thank you properly for this amazing surprise?" I linked my hand through his and raised it to my lips kissing his palm.

"It's really Didier's surprise, but I'd never passed up a proper thank you." He pushed me on my back, rolling on top.

Our lips met and reignited the lust from the previous night. I wrapped my legs around his waist as his lips moved to nibble my earlobe. Moving lower to my neck, he was biting gently, feeling my response.

A sudden pounding on the door had us both turning and staring.

"Get the hell up," Fab yelled. "There's crappy coffee on deck."

I buried my face in his chest and giggled. I knew I was the only one who drank "crappy" coffee, so someone must have remembered to bring me a can of mix. It says French on the can, how bad can it be?

We heard Didier say, "Fabiana…"

"Can you translate?" I whispered.

"He demanded she get away from the door and stop yelling. Just when I think he's got some control over her, I find out it's an illusion. Great, they're still out there and it's all silent."

Fab pounded just as loudly a second time. "Five minutes or I'm using a lock pick," she yelled.

I twisted the sheet over us just in case and yelled back, "What are you wearing?"

"Bathing suit, now hurry up."

I ran my fingers down his chest. "I'm going to need a nap later."

"You certainly are," he grumbled. "I'll make sure she doesn't bother us a second time."

I frowned. "I didn't bring a bathing suit. You said overnight bag. I don't have any clothes," I wailed.

He covered my mouth with his fingers. "Shh. Didier packed for you."

I smiled. He'd done that before, and I looked hot. "And you too?"

"Hell no," he said, and laughed. "I can get my underwear packed without any help."

He put his hands on either side of my head and pulled my face against his, plastering his lips to mine, moving one hand around to the back of my head to pull me in closer. We attacked each other's mouths, which went on until, eventually, coming up for air.

He sighed and scooped me into his arms, setting me on the floor. "Times up, you know."

I laughed and crossed the room to open the armoire to see what Didier had packed.

* * *

Creole and I maneuvered our way to the stern of the boat, holding hands and stopping to peek into each room. There were several guest suites, a library, living room, and dining room along the way. The floor plan was larger than my house. A breakfast bar had been set up under a canopied area not far from the Jacuzzi, where the unobstructed view of the water never got old. The engines fired up after Fab's screaming episode and we were making our way slowly out to sea.

Didier packed several bathing suits and I chose my favorite, an emerald green tankini, and matching gauzy wrap tied around my waist. The sight of Creole in his black trunks and tight T-shirt made my fingers itch to run up underneath and lightly rake my nails down his chest.

I wrapped my arms around Didier. "Thank you, your surprise is amazing."

"Just think, for the next few days, the jailbirds will have to find their own way home." He laughed and ruffled my hair.

Creole and I grabbed coffee and shared a chaise facing out to sea.

What would it be like to live this lifestyle, I wondered.

Didier stood and motioned to the steward. A few minutes later, an oblong table and chairs had been set up along the railing.

"Do we have a destination?" I asked.

"We can jump over to the Bahamas," Didier said. "Or we can anchor and spend time aboard playing with all the water toys."

The guys stared at one another, their competitive sides jumping to the surface.

"Rafts?" Creole snickered at him.

"We've got jet skis and water cars. We can drag out the sea pool, hook up the waterslide, and play some basketball." Didier nodded to Creole. "A little one on one."

I stuck my finger out at Fab. "You, me, water cars?"

She rolled her eyes. "You're never going to win."

Creole laughed. "I vote we stay on board and explore. LaRouche told me about the impressive arcade, pool table, and pinball machines. I bet we don't run out of things to do." He licked the column of my neck and bit down.

"You taste like the sea," he murmured.

I looked at him and yawned. "Don't forget nap time," I whispered, "every day."

Creole's phone gave a short ring, announcing a message. He pulled back a chair at the railing for me, coming back with two plates. One was filled with breakfast temptations: omelet, potatoes, waffle, and bacon; and the second was filled with fresh sliced fruit.

"If that's work, you can swim back." I glared at him. We should all surrender our phones and not get them back until we docked. Mine sat at the bottom of my travel bag, turned off.

"It's your mother," he said, and nudged me. "Family barbeque—your house, today. Wants to know why your phone is going to voicemail?"

"You thought about Jazz and told Mac, but not Mother?" I asked.

Wait until Mother finds that out.

"One of us needs to call her," he said, and looked directly at Fab.

I almost laughed at the look of horror on her face. I held out my hand. "I'll call her."

"We should draw straws. Isn't that what you Americans do?" Didier chuckled.

Fab crossed her arms. "I choose Madison. She already said she would call."

Creole whispered in my ear, fingers tugging my hair. "Choose Fab."

I changed my answer and said, "Fab can do it."

She smirked, knowing Didier was last to vote, so it wouldn't be her making the call.

"I can't vote against you, Cherie." He kissed her cheek.

"What? No!" She jumped to her feet. "I'm not doing it." She upended her plate, most of which she'd eaten.

Creole stared at her. "Wait until I tell Madeline you don't really like her after all. Refused to give her a call to ease her worries."

The two were in a deadly stare off. What was going on? Why would Creole ruin our good time? Didier didn't look ready to intervene. I started to move away and Creole held me firmly in place, feeding me another bite of eggs.

"Give me that phone." Fab blew out an angry breath.

"Hit the speaker button so we know you're not talking to dead air," Creole said, and motioned with his finger.

She stared at the phone for the longest time, finally calling.

"Madeline," she started.

"Hi, honey, I'm so happy you called. I need you to stop and get dessert. Make sure you and Madison get here before the others."

"We...uh..." Fab stammered. She took a deep breath. "We can't make it. We're out of town," she blurted.

"What?" Mother shrieked. "I need your help, both of you," she sniffed. "You didn't say good-bye. I thought we were closer than that."

Fab squirmed. "Madeline," she sighed.

"Are you okay? You don't sound like yourself." Mother sounded sad. "You'd tell me if there was a problem?"

"Sit still," Creole whispered. "Madeline's working her."

Fab's face pained; she hated emotional drama. "Didier surprised us with a trip on a friend's yacht. We'll be back in a few days."

"I'm sure you're having fun." She perked up. "I won't keep you on the phone. Could you tell Creole I'll pay him the five dollars when I see him?"

"We'll call you as soon as we get back on land." Fab said good-bye and hung up. "Five dollars," she murmured, looking at Creole.

An instant later, she threw his phone at him. I covered my face.

"That was far less painful than getting strangled." He glared back.

Didier and Creole laughed.

"You knew," she accused Didier.

He opened his arms and she flew into them. "Thank goodness. When she sounded disappointed, I thought I'd be sick. I forgot how good she is."

I winked at her and motioned her to the deck railing.

I stood and stuck my finger in Creole's chest. "Don't go anywhere."

"Would it be rude if Creole and I were to go take a nap? We can meet you two back here in a couple of hours." I bit the corner of my lip so I wouldn't smile. "I'm tired for some reason."

"We can drag out the water toys tomorrow when we're well-rested. Didier needs a nap too," she said with a straight face. "How about we meet back for dinner and spend the rest of the day doing what we want?"

"You're the best." I hugged her. "Please do not bang on the door again or I'll hurt you."

"I have something I need to show you," she said as she whisked Didier off.

"Hurry up!" I snapped my fingers at Creole and raced across the cabin and back to our suite, Creole right behind me.

Creole closed and locked the door, picking me up. As my legs wrapped around his waist, he walked me backward to the bed. "How much time do we have?"

"Until dinner." I smirked and crawled out of his grasp.

"Oh no you don't." He tried to grab my foot.

I jumped off the bed and stood in front of him, my hand on his chest. "I'm going to tell you what to do for a change."

"I never do that." He grinned.

"Strip," I growled in perfect imitation.

"Shower."

"In the middle of the bed."

"On!" He jerked me on top of him and rolled over, offering no escape.

~*~

PARADISE SERIES NOVELS

Crazy in Paradise
Deception in Paradise
Trouble in Paradise
Murder in Paradise
Greed in Paradise
Revenge in Paradise
Kidnapped in Paradise
Swindled in Paradise
Executed in Paradise
Hurricane in Paradise
Lottery in Paradise
Ambushed in Paradise
Christmas in Paradise
Blownup in Paradise
Psycho in Paradise
Overdose in Paradise
Initiation in Paradise
Jealous in Paradise
Wronged in Paradise
Vanished in Paradise
Fraud in Paradise
Naïve in Paradise

Deborah's books are available on Amazon
amazon.com/Deborah-Brown/e/B0059MAIKQ

About the Author

Deborah Brown is an Amazon bestselling author of the Paradise series. She lives on the Gulf of Mexico, with her ungrateful animals, where Mother Nature takes out her bad attitude in the form of hurricanes.

Sign up for my newsletter and get the latest on new book releases. Contests and special promotion information. And special offers that are only available to subscribers.
www.deborahbrownbooks.com

Follow on FaceBook:
facebook.com/DeborahBrownAuthor

You can contact her at Wildcurls@hotmail.com

Deborah's books are available on Amazon

amazon.com/Deborah-Brown/e/B0059MAIKQ

Made in the USA
Las Vegas, NV
03 June 2024